VANISH WITHOUT TRACE

An absolutely addictive crime thriller with a huge twist

BILL KITSON

THIS IS A REVISED EDITION OF A BOOK FIRST PUBLISHED AS "CHOSEN"

Revised edition 2019
Joffe Books, London

First published as "CHOSEN" in Great Britain 2010

ISBN: 978-1-78931-214-0

ACKNOWLEDGEMENTS

My grateful thanks go to the following people who have contributed towards the writing of the Mike Nash series, *Vanish Without Trace* in particular, and my writing in general.

Peter Billingsley MD, who advised me on drugs, other medical matters and is the only doctor to have ever given me a specimen!

My readers and critics, Cath Brockhill and Pat Almond, whose advice and input have been invaluable.

Derek Colligan, whose jacket designs show a brilliant understanding and interpretation of the plots.

My own 'in-house' copy editor, critic and proof reader, Val Kitson.

Mark Billingham, for his continuing support and encouragement.

Bill Spence (aka Jessica Blair) and all the members of Scarborough Writers' Circle for their help, advice and friendship.

My family and friends for continuing to put up with me.

DEDICATION

For Val
Wife, lover, best friend, critic and editor.

FOREWORD

SEATTLE TIMES

Friday 11 March 1983
MISSING GIRLS: 3 BODIES FOUND

Detectives investigating the disappearance of three local teenagers were called to a brownstone house in West Seattle late yesterday. The landlord of the property entered to take possession following the disappearance of the tenant. He made the discovery of three bodies in the basement.

Stacey Carter (18) disappeared after a Halloween party two years ago. Ten months later Joanlyn Brough (19) vanished after completing her shift at the Seattle Center bar where she had worked for six months. Sue-Ann Landers (16) was last seen on the way to a Valentine's Day High School disco a year ago. Seattle Police Department investigators were frustrated by lack of evidence or eyewitness reports. There had been no clue as to the girls' fate until yesterday's grim discovery. A statement is expected later this evening from Chief of Police Chuck Andrews who will name the man police are anxious to question.

The crime scene remained sealed off today as forensic teams and medical examiners continued their investigation. An SPD spokesman said earlier, 'There is some confusion here. We've gotten immediate identification, yet the Medical Examiner tells us the girls have been dead a long time. We're not sure how this is possible.'

CHAPTER ONE

Viv Pearce usually drove fast. But not that day. The occasion didn't warrant it. Besides, Pearce's thoughts, like those of his passenger were elsewhere. They'd been travelling almost half an hour. During that time neither had spoken. Eventually the silence was broken by the ring-tone on Clara's mobile.

'Mironova,' she answered it without glancing at the screen. 'Sorry, sir, I didn't notice who was calling.'

She glanced across at Pearce and mouthed, 'Tom Pratt.' Viv nodded, his face grim.

'Pretty awful,' he heard her say. Then, 'Not many. Apart from Mike and us, only the Trelawneys and a couple of friends from university. Stella was an orphan, remember. There's an elderly aunt I believe; lives down South. But she's too frail to travel.'

Clara listened again. 'Difficult to say,' she replied, to a question Viv couldn't hear. When she spoke again the meaning became clear. 'He seemed alright most of the time, but that was when he thought people were watching. Otherwise,' Viv saw Clara shiver slightly, 'let's just say he's bottled a lot of grief up, Tom. Sooner or later that'll have to come out.' She listened again. 'Yes, I think so. In fact, I'm certain. I'd go so far as to say the guilt is tearing him apart more than the grief.' There was another pause whilst her caller spoke.

Viv thought of Superintendent Pratt, tall, broad-shouldered and paternal, everyone's image of a senior police officer. Immensely proud of his area's low crime statistics: fiercely protective of those who served under him. Hence, this phone call. Hence, his volunteering to stand in at Helmsdale Police Station whilst they attended Stella Pearson's funeral. He'd put it in simple terms. 'You knew Stella far better than I. And you're closer to Mike. You need to be there for him. If he needs someone, it'll be more likely you two than me. Jack Binns and I'll take care of the shop until you get back.'

They were a motley crew at Helmsdale. Pearce wondered if that was why they worked so well together. Mironova and Pearce had been stationed there for some time before Nash joined them after a number of years serving in the Met.

Whilst Clara continued talking to Pratt, Pearce thought about his colleagues. Although Nash was a native of Yorkshire, Mironova had left Belarus as a child, when her father had been forced into exile in Britain. Pearce himself, although Bradford born, was Antiguan by ancestry. Three totally different backgrounds, totally dissimilar characters who blended together to form a highly effective unit.

Clara spoke, and Viv realized she'd finished the call. 'Tom was asking how it went. I didn't like to tell him how dire it was.'

'Pretty bleak,' Pearce acknowledged. 'Those places are so bloody impersonal. It's like going into a supermarket. And that vicar didn't help.'

'He didn't know Stella, couldn't speak personally about her.'

'It wasn't just that. He'd obviously done half a dozen today already. He was just going through the motions.'

'How did you think Mike was?'

'Like you said to Tom, he's bottling it up.'

'It's as if a barrier went up as soon as it happened. He won't let anyone near. I wonder what'll happen when he does let go. And he'll have to. Or make himself ill. Maybe what he needs is a distraction. I mean a big distraction.'

'You're thinking about work, aren't you? Not women?'

Clara grinned briefly. 'With Mike, women are always going to be a distraction. But that's not what he needs. Not at the minute, anyway. A case like the last one would be ideal. But they don't happen too often. Not in Helmsdale anyway. Or anywhere else in North Yorkshire for that matter,' she added as an afterthought.

At about the time Clara was speaking, a man entered his study and went over and unlocked the filing cabinet in the corner. He opened the lower drawer and selected a file at random from his collection, his hands trembling with excitement, his arousal almost painful.

He took the video cassette from the file and placed it in the slot of the player. As he watched, his arousal became too much for him to contain. He unzipped his flies and began to fondle his erection. When the film had finished and he was spent, he walked back to the cabinet and began thumbing through the files in the upper drawer. His fingers moved the files slowly, lingering over each one. They paused longest at the fourth name. He pondered it for a long time before moving on. Perhaps it was a treat he was reluctant to indulge in yet. Not this time at least; but soon, very soon.

His fingers finally stopped once more. This time there was little pause for thought, little chance for doubt to creep in. The decision made, he removed the file and locked the cabinet.

His choice was made, now he would watch and wait. He read every biographical detail that he had painstakingly collected and collated, all written in his immaculately neat handwriting. The more he read, the greater his certainty became that his selection had been right. He turned to the photograph and studied it. She was beautiful, though not the most stunning in his collection. There was strong competition for that honour. After all, his standards were extremely high. Nevertheless, she would not be disgraced amongst the others.

His tone was that of a lover as he whispered gently to the photograph. 'You are lucky,' he smiled. 'You don't know yet how fortunate you are. You will soon. And when you realize I have picked you above all the others you will feel honoured. Honoured, because you are chosen.'

Detective Inspector Mike Nash walked slowly into the station at Helmsdale. The state-of-the-art building marked an innovative departure by the local authority. Faced with rising maintenance costs, and a need to conform to an ever tighter budget, they had decided to dispose of three Victorian buildings and replace them with one purpose-built unit.

Nash was oblivious to his surroundings as he walked down the corridor leading to the CID suite, oblivious to the greetings of those he passed. His mind totally absorbed. Although it was now over two months since Stella's funeral, he was still functioning on autopilot.

When he opened the door into the CID general office, DS Mironova was alone in the room. She looked up from the papers she was studying. 'I have some news that might cheer you up.'

'I doubt it. What is it?'

Clara's eyes twinkled with mischief. 'I bumped into an old friend of yours earlier today, in the market place.'

There was sufficient emphasis on the word 'friend' for Nash to look up. 'Who's that?'

'Lauren Robbins, used to be receptionist at The Golden Bear in Netherdale? I believe you got to know one another quite well?'

Despite himself, Nash smiled. 'That's one way of putting it, I suppose. What's Lauren doing back in Helmsdale? Last I knew, she was buried deep in rural Cheshire.'

'She's finished her training and she's deputizing for the manager of The Square and Compass whilst he's on holiday. She was asking how you are, and if you're seeing anyone at the moment. She said, if you get chance, why not drop in for a drink sometime.' Clara smiled thinly. 'I assume that's a euphemism for saying she's got a warm bed available if you're interested. There, I've delivered the message. Now I know what it feels like to be a pimp.'

'Clara, has anyone ever told you that you've got an extremely dirty mind?'

'I need one with you around. It's pretty quiet at the moment, so if you want to take some passionate leave, it'll hardly be critical.'

Nash winced. 'Clara, don't ever say things like that, not even as a joke. Have you never heard of Sod's Law?'

Clara shook her head.

'It's an extension of tempting providence. It states that the thing you least want to happen will happen. What's more it will happen at the very worst possible time.'

On weekdays, CID in Helmsdale operated office hours, unless there was a specific case to investigate. Only a skeleton staff of uniformed officers was on duty overnight. At weekends, one CID officer was designated the duty. When this decision was implemented as part of a cost-cutting exercise some wag had suggested contacting all the known villains in the area asking them to pursue the same policy. That Friday, Mironova had drawn the short straw. DC Viv Pearce was away on a course and would not return to Helmsdale until late that evening. Nash had been on call the previous three weekends.

Before he left, Nash said, 'Everything seems quiet enough. If trouble breaks out and it's too serious for you to handle, you can always call out the army. I'm sure the galloping major will be only too happy to help.'

'David's away on an exercise, so I can't.' As soon as she said it, Clara realized her mistake.

'The way you look after you've been out with him, I'd have thought he was getting more than enough exercise,' Nash laughed. It was odd, he thought, the way things turn out. If he and his team hadn't been involved in tackling a ruthless criminal gang, Clara wouldn't have met David, a Special Forces Officer, assigned to help them.

Clara blushed. 'Don't judge everyone by your standards.' She knew Nash was getting his own back for her tormenting him about his hyperactive love life. 'Anyway, what will you do with your time off? Will you be going to The Square and Compass for a drink with the luscious Lauren?'

'I might pop in for a quick one,' Nash admitted. 'Don't work too hard. And don't fret over the Dashing David. You'll be able to make up for lost time when he gets back. That is if he's not too fatigued by the fatigues.'

Clara glanced at the clock. 'It's past five o'clock; time you weren't here.'

She watched him close the door and looked round the empty office. Without distractions and with local crime at a record low, it promised to be a long and boring weekend. Clara sighed. She wished something would happen to alleviate the tedium. She was unaware that she'd just doubled the chance of Sod's Law striking.

Friday night brought its usual crop of minor offences. Most of these were dealt with by uniformed branch. Some, notably those involving the use or supply of controlled substances, fell within the province of CID.

Saturday morning found Mironova dealing with the paperwork. She was three-quarters of the way through the task, and beginning to wonder how she'd pass the time until what was known in the station as 'Saturday Night Fever' struck. Her speculation was disturbed when her phone rang. 'Sorry to disturb you, I've a lady in reception. Name's Mrs Kelly. She's frantic with worry because her daughter's gone missing. Daughter's name is Sarah. Apparently she went clubbing last night, and hasn't returned home.'

Clara sighed, 'Probably the usual. Ship her up to the CID suite, will you. I'll see what I can do to pacify her.'

As she waited for Mrs Kelly, Clara rummaged through her desk drawers. After some difficulty, she located the document she was looking for. She'd just placed it on her blotter when the door opened, and Mrs Kelly was ushered in. Clara thanked the officer and introduced herself to the distressed mother. 'Good morning, Mrs Kelly. I'm Detective Sergeant Mironova.' She gestured to a chair alongside her desk. 'Take a seat and tell me what's happened.'

Clara sat down and pulled the sheet of paper towards her, shielding the heading, 'MP 309 Missing Person Initial Report', from her visitor.

'It's about my daughter Sarah,' Mrs Kelly began. She fumbled with the clasp on the handbag she'd rested on her lap as she spoke. 'She went out last night, the same as she does every Friday night. She hadn't come back when I went to wake her this morning. It's so unlike her.'

'Isn't it possible she stayed the night with a friend? A boyfriend perhaps?'

Mrs Kelly shook her head. 'There isn't anyone. Sarah's never bothered much with boys. Not that she hasn't had plenty of chances; she's a lovely looking girl. I mean, she's been out on plenty of dates, but she's never had a steady boyfriend.'

'When you said she goes out every Friday, does she go on her own? Or in a group? Do you know where she goes?'

'Oh yes, Sarah always tells me. She meets up with two girls every Friday. Friends she made at school. But one of them is away on holiday. I rang the other girl, Mandy, and she told me she met Sarah at The Red Dragon, like they normally do. They were going to go on to Club Wolfgang, but Mandy wasn't feeling well. She'd an upset stomach and decided to go home. She said, when she left, Sarah hadn't made her mind up whether to go to the club on her own or not.'

'I see. I'm going to ask some more questions now. I have this report to fill in before we can take any action.'

The process took a little over twenty minutes. When Mironova finished writing, she looked up. 'Do you have a recent photo of Sarah? The description you gave me is fine, but if I have a photo, I can copy it and give it to our uniformed branch for their patrol officers. If they spot Sarah, it'll be easier to recognize her from a photo.'

Mrs Kelly opened her bag. 'I've got one I took at Christmas. Sarah was on her way to the firm's Christmas do. She looked so lovely; I just had to take it.'

She pulled the photo out of her handbag and passed it across the desk. Clara stared at the image. 'I see what you mean. She's a very pretty girl.'

She looked at the anxious mother. 'Let me explain how the system works. Unfortunately, we can't launch a full-scale enquiry just yet. There are two reasons for that. Most missing persons return home within twenty-four to forty-eight hours of going missing. In addition, we simply don't have the manpower or resources to divert to a case like this. Not at this stage,' she added hastily, seeing Mrs Kelly about to object.

'If Sarah still hasn't returned home or contacted you tomorrow morning, I want you to come back. At that point I'll discuss the matter with my boss. He'll decide what action might be justified. In the meantime, I'll copy this photo and distribute it at our Daily Management Meeting, which takes place just before the next shift change. If and when Sarah does return, I'd like you to ring me to let me know.' Clara smiled at Mrs Kelly. 'And try not to worry too much. I'm sure she's fine, and she'll turn up fit and well.'

Sarah stirred slightly then woke up. She tried to move but her wrists and ankles were restrained. She opened her eyes, but to no effect. It was dark. She was blindfolded with some sort of hood. She writhed in panic. It achieved nothing. She tried to remember what had happened, but couldn't. Questions crowded her bemused brain. Where was she? How had she got here? Who was holding her prisoner? And, much worse, why? She heard a voice. Its tone was gentle, the words soothing. Unwillingly she listened.

'Hello, Sarah. You're awake I see. You must be wondering what's happened. Don't worry, everything will be alright.

Just be patient a little longer then I'll show you why you're here. It must be difficult for you, but soon you'll be able to relax, and then you'll know how fortunate you are. Because you have been carefully selected, no, that would be an insult. No, you have been chosen.'

If the words and the timbre of the voice had been designed to dispel her fear, they failed utterly. She tried to scream, but even in her dazed state she realized how pitifully weak her voice sounded against the muffling cloth of the mask over her face.

'Now, now, Sarah dear, don't take on so. It's only because you don't realize what's happening that you're afraid. Just wait a few minutes longer then you'll calm down. I promise you. When you do, we can begin to enjoy our time together.'

Fear turned to terror, terror to blind panic and way beyond. Unable to control her emotions Sarah realized she'd wet herself. Shame and mortification combined with the horror of her situation. She began to cry.

'There, there, please don't upset yourself. You've had a little accident, that's all. It's nothing to be ashamed of. I'll take care of you. I'll clean you up and change your wet panties for some new ones. Then you'll be nice and dry again, won't you. And when I've done that I'll see if I can find a special treat for my Sarah.'

Her brain reeled. She knew the voice was a man's, but not one she recognized. And yet he was talking to her as if he knew her well, as if she was someone special in his life. In so dreadful a position, she might have expected roughness, brutality, if any words had been spoken at all. This man was talking to her like a lover, or a parent with a tiny child. It should have comforted her. It didn't. She felt the rope round her ankles being slackened then removed. A few seconds later she felt fingers undoing the waistband of her jeans; then unzipping them. She writhed in panic but her ankles were gripped by hands with the strength of a vice. 'Sarah dear,' there was a hard note of command in the voice, 'stay still so I can take your wet things off.'

It was fear that caused her to stop struggling. She felt the wet garments being removed. Then there was quiet for a few moments. What had happened? Had he gone away? Suddenly he was back, 'I'm just going to wash you, dear. We don't want you to get sore, do we?'

She felt the wet flannel, felt the gently rhythmic movement of the material against her skin. This was followed by the touch of the rougher fabric of the towel as he dried her. Sarah's horror was compounded as she realized the deeper significance behind the gently caressing motion of both flannel and towel. 'There,' she heard him murmur, 'that's better isn't it, my beautiful Chosen One?' Sarah had feared the worst when her abductor touched her so intimately, but he'd done her no harm. That might have comforted her slightly. It didn't. After drying her, he covered her with something loose, a blanket? Then he left her alone.

Hours later, as far as she was able to judge, her senses deprived by the darkness of the mask and the utter silence around her, Sarah felt the thin cotton fabric of her sleeve being gently rolled back. She tried to recoil from the touch. She heard the man speak, his voice close to her ear, whispering almost. 'Don't be frightened, Sarah, I'm just going to give you something to relax you. I don't want you frightened or upset.'

She felt his hand grip her arm above the elbow, not roughly, yet she wriggled furiously. His hand on her arm felt soft, oily, without features. She realized he was wearing gloves, rubber gloves. Her attempts to rid herself of his clutch were in vain. He was far stronger than she could cope with and the ropes at her wrist prevented movement. Something cold and wet touched her arm in a brief rubbing motion. Several more seconds passed before she felt a sudden sharp pain that ceased almost as soon as it began.

Sarah's terror was matched by bewilderment, as she realized what he'd done. What sort of abductor was this? What was he doing? He'd spoken so soothingly, yet his attempts to reassure her had increased her fear. He'd injected something into her arm, but sterilized the site first to prevent infection. What sort of kidnapper took such pains over the welfare of their victim? Sarah was no nearer solving the mystery when consciousness left her.

CHAPTER TWO

'Saturday Night Fever' kicked off early in Helmsdale, before 7 p.m., with uniformed branch reporting the arrest of a man suspected of dealing cocaine outside The Drovers Arms.

Clara had barely finished dealing with this, when she was called to attend a crime scene. The venue was the town's only electrical appliance shop. Thieves had broken into the premises via the back door and pulled a van up. They'd succeeded in loading this with several plasma screen TVs and a host of other electrical items before they were disturbed. Hearing the approaching sirens of the police summoned to the scene, the raiders had escaped by crashing the van through the wooden fence that surrounded Helmsdale United's football ground and driving across the pitch before joining the ring road.

The shop owner was distraught. Listening to him, Clara thought the football club's groundsman would also be less than ecstatic. She took preliminary details of the missing items from the shopkeeper, and extracted a promise that he'd supply a comprehensive list of serial numbers as soon as he could. She turned the scene over to the SOCO team she'd summoned from Netherdale, and left to return to the station.

As she locked her car, she hoped that would be the last she'd see of it until she went home.

No such luck. She'd barely hung her coat up in the CID suite when her phone rang. 'There's been a knifing outside The Coach and Horses,' the duty officer told her.

Mironova sighed, 'I suppose it was too much to hope that Saturday night would pass without something happening on Westlea estate?'

She heard the officer laugh. 'Sounds like a domestic, from what the lads told me. Apparently a husband found out his wife was having a bit on the side and started laying into her. She didn't like that, so she stuck him with a knife.'

'Sounds like a marriage made in heaven. Was the wife's boyfriend involved in this little piece of domestic disharmony?'

'Oh yes, held the husband back whilst the wife went for him.' The officer coughed, 'The thing is, it wasn't a boyfriend. It was a girlfriend.'

'Well, well, well, never a dull moment on the Westlea.'

After such a busy night, Clara had forgotten about Sarah Kelly until she arrived at the station, shortly before 9 a.m. on Sunday morning. As she entered the building, she noticed Mrs Kelly sitting on one of the benches in the reception area. Her knees were clamped together, handbag gripped on her lap with fingers that were white with pent-up stress. 'Oh, no,' Clara groaned inwardly, 'this isn't going to be good news.'

'I take it you haven't heard from Sarah?'

Mrs Kelly shook her head. It was obvious she wasn't far from tears. 'Okay, come through to the CID suite with me. Can I get you a cup of tea, or would you prefer coffee?'

'No, thank you, nothing.'

'Look, here's what I'm going to do. I'll phone my boss, explain the situation. I'm sure he'll want to talk to you.'

Clara went into Nash's office to use the phone. She got no response from his home number, and only succeeded in connecting with his voice mail when she tried his mobile. She thought for a few moments, then picked up the phone book.

'Square and Compass Hotel,' the voice said.

'Good morning. I need to speak to Miss Robbins urgently.'

'Who? Oh, Miss Robbins. I'm afraid she's unavailable. Would you care to leave a message?'

'No. I wouldn't care to leave a message. It's very important that I speak to Miss Robbins as a matter of urgency. Please put me through.'

'I'm afraid I can't do that. Miss Robbins left clear instructions she wasn't to be disturbed on any account. It's more than my job's worth.'

'If you don't put me through immediately you won't have a job,' Clara snarled. The Saturday nightshift had left her drained and edgy. Her mood wasn't improved when she realized she was speaking to the dialling tone. She gritted her teeth and redialled. 'This is Detective Sergeant Mironova of North Yorkshire police. Don't hang up on me again. Put me through to Miss Robbins, now. If you don't, I'll have four squad cars outside your hotel in five minutes time with lights flashing and sirens wailing. Do I make myself clear? When your guests complain, I'll make sure you get the blame. What do you think your job will be worth then?'

'Err, just one moment. I'll try Miss Robbins's extension. Did you say Detective Sergeant Mironoma?'

'Mironova!'

She waited for what seemed an age before she was connected.

Lauren's voice was heavy with sleep. 'Hello?'

'Hello, Lauren. It's Clara Mironova here. I'm trying to locate Mike. I've tried his flat and his mobile without any joy. I just wondered if you have any idea where he might be?' Like right alongside you, Clara thought with a grin.

The one thing about Lauren was she didn't bother to hide their relationship. 'Hang on, Clara. I'll wake him. Mike, Mike, you're wanted.'

'Yes, Clara. What is it?'

'Possible missing person, I've a woman here frantic with worry. Apparently, her daughter went out on Friday night and hasn't returned.'

'How old is she?'

'Nineteen. She and a couple of friends usually go clubbing every Friday, but Sarah, that's the missing girl, is usually home by 3 a.m. at the latest.'

'Probably pulled, and is shacked up with some bloke somewhere.'

You would think that, Clara thought. 'Maybe, but I can't tell the mother that, can I?'

'No I don't suppose so. You think something's up?'

'I do. She called in yesterday and I filled the form out. The thing is, from what I can gauge, this seems out of character.'

'Okay, it's your call. Let's show we're taking it seriously. I'll be straight over. Better dig Viv from his pit as well.'

His arrival coincided with that of Pearce. Mironova introduced her colleagues while Nash smiled at the agitated woman. 'Before we start, Viv, why don't you make us all a hot drink? Mrs Kelly, or may I call you Joan? What would you like?'

'Coffee, I suppose.'

Mironova went over what sparse details there were about the missing girl. Nash turned to Mrs Kelly. 'Has Sarah ever stayed out before without telling you? Maybe when she's had a few drinks?'

Joan Kelly shook her head. 'Never,' she said emphatically. 'Sarah doesn't get drunk and besides, she knows I worry. She wouldn't go one night without telling me, or ringing me from wherever she was, let alone two.'

Pearce arrived carrying a tray.

'You don't think she might have mentioned it and it's just slipped your mind?'

'I wouldn't forget a thing like that.'

He tried a reassuring smile. 'I believe you mentioned to Sergeant Mironova that Sarah usually meets up with a couple of friends on a Friday, then goes on to a nightclub?'

'That's right, Club Wolfgang they call it. Sometimes they go through to Netherdale or Bishopton, but not often.'

'Can you supply the friends' names and addresses?'

'Yes, of course, but Sarah mentioned the other day that one of them, Tammy, was going on holiday this week, so she won't be any help.'

Nash turned to Pearce. 'Nip through to the ambulance section, would you? Check what emergencies they handled over Friday and Saturday, in case Sarah's been involved in an accident. Then go through to the Duty Officer of the Fire Brigade. Tell him I want the names and addresses of all key holders for this Club Wolfgang.'

Nash switched his gaze back to Mrs Kelly. The implications behind his requests had brought a haunted expression to her face. 'Joan, do you know where they would meet up?'

'Yes, The Red Dragon, that's where most of the young people go these days.'

'Viv, get the landlord's details from the Fire Officer as well.' Pearce nodded and left. 'The next part is the hardest bit, Joan. Really, all you can do is stay at home and wait for news. I know it seems as if nothing's happening and you'll be desperate for some action, but believe me that's where you're best off. If Club Wolfgang operates a CCTV system and we can get our hands on the tape, we'll need you back here to look through it. In the meantime I want you to stay by the phone in case Sarah rings. I'll get one of my officers to stop with you.'

Mrs Kelly fidgeted nervously, clear evidence that Nash's assessment of her state of mind was accurate. She needed to feel involved, part of the action. Nash continued, 'Before that, however, I'm afraid I need to ask you some questions. I want to know everything you can tell me about Sarah, about your home life, family, that sort of thing.'

Clara Mironova listened to Nash drawing information about Sarah from her mother. She'd witnessed his questioning technique many times before. Each skilfully phrased question would be more than a prompt for facts. It would probe into Sarah's character, their home environment, the girl's mental state and much more. The art was that he would do it without Joan Kelly even realizing his purpose.

'Let's start with a few details. Tell me what sort of girl Sarah is, what her likes and dislikes are. Anything you feel might be useful. Begin with her job, where she works, what she does.'

Mrs Kelly began, a trace of pride evident in her voice. 'She's been in the same job for the last two years, straight from school. She works at Rushton Engineering. She acts as secretary for several departments.'

'Does she enjoy working there?'

'Oh, she loves it. There's always plenty to do. With all the different people and departments she reports to, I mean. She never gets chance to be bored. At night she's full of it, who's said what, things that have happened during the day.'

'Tell me about your family.'

'Sarah's my only one. Terrence, my ex-husband, left me when Sarah was four. He'd been seeing another woman for some time, an American he met when he was working over at the US base near Harrogate, you know, the one with the giant golf balls. He lives in America now.'

'It must have been hard, bringing Sarah up on your own.'

'Sometimes, particularly in the early days, but Terrence's new wife is from a wealthy family. He's always been generous with maintenance. Even now Sarah's turned eighteen, he continues to make the payments.'

'That's more than a lot do, from what I hear,' Nash sympathized. 'Tell me, does he keep in touch?'

'He telephones about four times a year, never forgets her birthday. Christmas as well, there's always a present for her. Nowadays he sends money, because he told her he doesn't know what she needs.'

'So, you've been on your own with Sarah for what, fifteen years? Have you never felt the urge to remarry? Are you in any sort of relationship, perhaps?' Joan Kelly was still quite attractive; she had retained her looks and figure. Nash estimated her as being about forty-five years old, and a tempting prospect for many a man, despite the presence of a grown-up daughter in the home.

'It never seems to have been an option,' she said a trifle obscurely. 'I've gone out with men from time to time, but it never got serious. Maybe that was because I always put Sarah first.'

'What about Sarah, does she have a regular boyfriend? Or, has she had a regular boyfriend she's finished with?'

'No, neither, she always says there's plenty of time for that later. She's more interested in enjoying life. She wants to get more experience before settling down. She went to Ibiza two years running and didn't come to any harm. Last summer she came back full of enthusiasm for Greece. She's already booked to go back. She's keeping her tan topped up by sunbathing in the garden when she can. She also wants to go to America next year, to stay with her father.'

Nash's tone was deliberately casual. 'Tell me how she gets on with the neighbours?'

The sudden shift of emphasis of his question seemed to throw Joan off balance briefly. 'Er, alright I think. 'Course she's not at home during the day, only weekends, so she doesn't see much of them, those we know, that is. We only moved there about three years ago.'

'How's Sarah been recently? Anything upset her? For example, any mood changes, or that sort of thing?'

'She's been absolutely normal.'

'No arguments, disagreements, problems at home or at work, or with her friends perhaps?'

'Nothing at all. Like I said, she's been exactly as she always is.'

'I assume Sarah uses a computer at work? Everyone seems to these days.'

Again the unexpected change of direction seemed to throw Joan momentarily. 'Yes. She has to deal with e-mails and that sort of thing.'

'Does she have a computer at home as well?'

'She has one in her bedroom.'

'Do you know if she uses chat rooms and the blog sites that are so popular?'

'Yes, she does. I know because I heard her talking to Mandy; she's into computers as well. I remember it 'cause I'd never heard the word blog before.'

'Any hobbies?'

'Tennis in summer, and she goes to Netherdale Swimming Baths occasionally.'

'So, Sarah's perfectly happy and content. Are there any issues you can think of? What about her health, any problems?'

'She's fine. I can't remember the last time she went to the doctor.'

'I think that's enough to be going on with for the moment. I'm going to start things moving to find her. Clara will take you home and stay with you in case she turns up. Do you have any family who might come and be with you?'

Suddenly, Joan Kelly felt very much alone. 'No, I'm an only child, just like Sarah. Both my parents are dead, and I have no other family.'

'In that case, it's even more important that an officer stays with you until this is all cleared up. I'm going to ask DC Pearce to call in later, and I'll be in touch as soon as I have anything to report. I'm not going to insult your intelligence by saying "don't worry", because you wouldn't be a mother if you didn't.'

'Thank you, Inspector.' Joan Kelly's simply worded plea went straight to her listeners' hearts. 'Just please, find Sarah safe and well, that's all I ask.'

Nash glanced across at Clara, but she was already on her feet, waiting to escort Joan from the building. He was still staring at the door, reflecting on what he'd been told, when Pearce re-entered the room.

'I've got all the info,' Pearce laid a sheaf of papers on Nash's desk.

'I take it you drew a blank with the ambulance service?'

'No female casualties, apart from a fifty-year-old woman who got glassed in a cat fight at The Cock and Bottle last night. Nothing unusual for that place.'

'Right, I want you to follow Clara out to Mrs Kelly's house. I want you to have a good look round, use your eyes and ears. Ask Mrs Kelly if you can take a peep into Sarah's room. Check the garage and any outbuildings, all the usual. I want you to get a feel of the atmosphere. According to Mrs Kelly, the home life was close to idyllic. I want to know that she was telling the truth. Ask Clara to get Mrs Kelly to let her check Sarah's computer. She'll know what to look for. As soon as you're finished, I want you straight back. In the meantime, I'm going to rustle up a uniform to replace Clara. You can both be of more use here.'

'What's your own feeling, Mike?'

'I'm not sure, Viv. I'm going to alert Tom before I make a start on these,' Nash indicated the paperwork Pearce had brought him. 'I know it's early days, but, if something has happened, the next twenty-four hours could be critical. One more thing, Viv, while you're at the house, find out the name of the family doctor. Daughters don't always tell their mother the truth, particularly about certain health matters.'

'Tom? Mike Nash here. Sorry to disturb you on a Sunday.'

'It's okay. What's the problem?'

'We've a potential missing person. Nineteen-year-old girl went clubbing on Friday night, failed to return home and hasn't been seen since. Mother's frantic. I've been through all the usual, family fall out, girl getting laid or getting pissed. According to the mother none of them fits.'

'You reckon there's cause for concern?'

'There seems to be no reason for the girl to stay away of her own free will.'

'Let me know if you need me to come through. Anything you need in the meantime?'

'A sensible, kindly WPC to nursemaid the mother, if it can be arranged. Clara's with her at the moment, but I need her here.'

'I'll sort that. There's a WPC at Bishopton would fit the bill perfectly, anything else?'

'No, that's fine.'

It proved to be one of those frustratingly fruitless days in an enquiry when little is achieved, and any information gathered is of a negative value. The small team of CID officers established that everything Joan Kelly had told them appeared to be true.

Sarah's friend, Mandy, added little to their stock of knowledge. She explained that she'd felt unwell early in the evening and had gone home, leaving Sarah alone at The Red Dragon. Sarah had been undecided about whether or not to continue on to Club Wolfgang. She definitely hadn't planned to go to Netherdale or Bishopton. She appeared to be her normal, bright and cheerful self. Certainly hadn't mentioned any worries or problems. Nobody had tried to chat up either girl at the pub or even engage them in conversation. As far as Mandy remembered, the clients were mostly regulars, people the girls knew.

The landlord of The Red Dragon told much the same tale, adding only that as far as he was aware, Sarah had left around 10.30 p.m., alone as he remembered. He too was unable to recall Sarah in company with anyone but Mandy.

All of which was frustratingly inconclusive. The question of what had happened to Sarah Kelly after leaving The Red Dragon was still unresolved. Information from the nightclub itself was much more revealing. Nash interviewed the manager, the DJ, the staff on duty on Friday night. The DJ, one of the barmaids, and both bouncers remembered talking to Sarah, who, along with Mandy and Tammy, was amongst their most popular regulars. Each of them had asked her where the other girls were. In addition, the DJ confirmed having seen Sarah talking to several others during the night and dancing with a couple of men. This might have had more significance but for the bouncers' resolute statement that they recalled her leaving alone at around 2 a.m.

The manager brought in CCTV tapes shot within the club. Mrs Kelly was brought back to the police station to view these, along with Mandy. The footage confirmed broadly what the nightclub staff had told the police. Mandy was able to identify two out of the three men Sarah had danced with. Both had been at Helmsdale Secondary School with the girls. The third was a stranger to Mandy, to Sarah's mother and to the nightclub staff.

The videotape also confirmed the accuracy of the bouncers' statements. Sarah had indeed left the nightclub alone, shortly after 2 a.m. The tape also showed one of the locals and the stranger leaving much later, both accompanied by girls. Mandy snorted with derision on seeing the stranger's companion. 'That's Sharon Bell from Westlea Council Estate. The sort that gives slags a bad name. She'd shag anyone for a pint of lager. No make that a half,' she corrected herself. 'Sorry, Mrs Kelly.'

The third man Sarah had danced with had remained in the club until closing time, by which point Sarah should have been at home and in bed. Crucially, the one piece of evidence that might have given them a clue as to what had happened to Sarah after leaving the nightclub was not available. The street surveillance camera (SSC) installed only a few months earlier had been out of action. The lens had been damaged by vandals during the week and the maintenance company hadn't repaired it. The news left Nash fuming with anger and frustration. 'I'm going to watch the CCTV tapes again,' he told Mironova. 'There's something I noticed first time round might be worth a closer look.'

He picked the first of the tapes. He wound it on and they started to watch. A few minutes into the footage Nash paused the film. 'This is it. This next bit, Sarah's at the bar. She gets a drink and goes to sit down.' He played a few seconds more of the tape. 'Then she stops to talk to someone. There!' He stopped the tape again. Clara peered at the screen. The man's face was in shadow, his back half turned to the camera. Deliberately? She wondered.

Nash moved it forward frame by frame, but they were unable to get any clearer image of the man Sarah had spoken to. 'The trouble with those cameras is the resolution's so poor it's difficult to get a good likeness,' he grumbled.

'If necessary, we could get it enhanced digitally,' Clara suggested.

'It's early days for anything so radical, but worth bearing in mind. In the meantime I want you and Viv to find any taxi drivers who were working the late shift and may have seen anything significant.'

Tom Pratt arrived in Nash's office to see if there had been any developments. He discussed what little evidence there was. Nash was in no doubt. 'The fact that Sarah left the club alone, sober and early, rules out the more innocent reasons for her disappearance. If there was evidence suggesting she got stoned on drink or drugs, I might be persuaded she was lying low but there's absolutely no reason to suspect that. All of which points to something more sinister.'

Pratt glanced at his watch; it was almost 6.30 p.m. 'Supposing you're right, what do you intend to do next? I'm not saying I disagree with you, mind. I can't think of a plausible explanation that doesn't involve foul play either.'

'Mironova and Pearce interviewed the taxi drivers. There weren't many of them around, so we're going to have to try at a later hour. I'm not suggesting one of them picked her up but it's a possibility. One of them might have spotted her. That's about all we can do for today. If there's no positive news by morning I think we should search the area surrounding Sarah's route from the club to her house, especially any areas of open ground. We'll need a lot of men to do that thoroughly.'

'Okay, I'll go along with all that. Don't worry about the manpower. I'm going back to Netherdale now. I'll get working on it. Every available uniformed officer will be here at first light, unless something turns up in the meantime. I'll get one of our liaison lads to do a press release tomorrow, unless, as I said, something turns up.'

Mironova and Pearce had talked as they were driving back to the station. 'One bit of good news,' Clara had said. 'I think Mike's beginning to get over the worst of his grief.'

'How do you work that out?'

'When I'd spoken to Mrs Kelly this morning, I'd to ring him. I ran him to earth in Lauren Robbins's bed.'

'She'd make any red-blooded male cheer up.'

'It's the first time he's looked at a woman since Stella died. I was beginning to think he'd been gelded.'

Nash told them of his conversation with Pratt. 'Tom's arranging for search parties to start tomorrow. I'd like you both to talk to the neighbours in the morning. Ask them specifically if they've seen any strangers loitering around, any odd callers, cars they didn't recognize, the usual sort of thing. Then meet me back here.'

CHAPTER THREE

Helmsdale police station was crowded with officers drafted in from Netherdale and surrounding areas. The short briefing they received from Tom Pratt split the assembled force into three sections. One would cover the area close to Club Wolfgang. The second would search along the route Sarah would have taken to walk home. The third group would concentrate on the open areas in and around the town – sports fields, parks and playgrounds – before switching their attention to the banks of the River Helm that meandered through the nearby countryside.

Nash had a brief conversation with the managing director of Rushton Engineering, who confirmed that Sarah was happy there and well thought of by employers and staff alike. Arrangements were made to speak to all the employees on Tuesday, if it became necessary.

The Kelly family doctor informed them that as far as he was aware, Sarah Kelly had no health issues. Her last visit to the surgery had been several years earlier, for routine injections prior to going abroad. Nash was still on the phone when Tom Pratt dashed into his office. 'Got a minute!' His whisper was an excited one.

'Excuse me a moment,' Nash lowered the receiver. 'What's up?'

'I've just heard from the team at Club Wolfgang. They think they've found something. You coming?'

'You bet. Hang on while I finish.' Nash resumed his call. 'Thanks for your help, Doctor. If I need anything more, I'll get back to you.'

'What have they got?' Nash asked as they hurried across the yard to Pratt's car.

'A woman's handbag, more like an evening purse according to the description. It was under one of those big industrial wheelie bins, at the back of that little ginnel running alongside the nightclub. It's a short cut, one that Sarah could possibly have taken. Sounds as if it might have been kicked under the bin: in a struggle maybe.'

Both entrances to the alley had been taped off. Nash assessed the position where the handbag lay. It was little bigger than a purse, black, with a satin-like finish and a serpentine pattern picked out in brightly coloured glass beads, the sort that could be bought fairly cheaply in a host of different outlets. His nose wrinkled in mild distaste as he bent to peer underneath the bin. The smell of stale urine left him in no doubt as to what many of those frequenting the alley used it for. The bin was almost at the end of the narrow pathway, as it emerged on to the relief road that served as a bypass for the High Street. He straightened up, concentrating his gaze on the main road for a few seconds, then looked round. Nash pointed upwards, indicating to Pratt. 'I found out yesterday that street camera was damaged a week ago. It might have been a random act of vandalism. However, I'm not so sure. There could be a more sinister motive.'

'You think it's been done deliberately? If so, that could mean a carefully planned abduction, rather than an opportunist attack.'

'It may be pure coincidence, but it needs checking. It's far too high up for kids throwing stones. Though it would be a fairly easy target with an airgun.'

'Surely the camera would have recorded them shooting at it?'

'Not if they fired from an oblique angle. If that is Sarah's bag and she was attacked here, it's damned suspicious that the camera just happened to be out of action.'

'You seem fairly convinced.'

'I think it's a hell of a coincidence. Look at the facts we know. Sarah left the club on Friday night, after which she wasn't seen again. She had to come this way, or walk an extra mile to get home. Now we've found a bag on that route. The place we've found it is the most vulnerable point, a deserted, dark alleyway with an SSC conveniently out of action. What would you think?'

'Put like that, I find it difficult to argue. I'll get SOCO involved. We can't afford to waste time.'

'We also need to get the report on the damage to that camera,' Nash paused and looked at his superior. 'Tom, you do realize that if an attacker planned this, if he shot the camera and laid in wait for her, we've a very harsh set of questions to ask ourselves.'

'Hang on. I've just spotted a flaw in your theory. How would an attacker have known she'd be alone? It was pure chance that one of the girls was away. Even more of a fluke that the other was taken ill. He'd have had no guarantee she'd walk down this alley at all, let alone on her own.'

'He could have been fairly sure,' Nash contradicted him. 'Both the other girls live on the far side of the High Street. They'd have no reason to walk down here. It'd have been out of their way. That in itself means something else.'

'What's that?'

'It means if there is an attacker, he's been watching and planning this for a long time.'

Pratt left to call in the specialist forensics team and Nash walked out of the alley to the relief road. He looked to the right and left, absorbing his surroundings. This side of the road merely showed the backs of the buildings along the High Street. Most were shops, sprinkled with the usual collection of banks, building societies, estate agencies, an Italian restaurant, a Chinese take-away and a café.

None of these was likely to be the scene of much activity at 2 a.m. on a Saturday morning, apart perhaps from the Chinese. But that was at the far end of the High Street, getting on for a quarter of a mile away.

Nash stood quietly. The scene in his mind's eye was totally different from what was before him. It was no longer Monday morning. It was Friday night and the road was deserted and dark, the nearest street lamp was unlit.

Nash stared straight ahead into the darkened yard belonging to the nearest shop. A car was parked, no lights showing. Inside, a man was sitting hunched and tense behind the steering wheel. Waiting; but for what?

'Is that what you did?' He asked in a murmur. 'Did you watch her, plan all this? Did you shoot out the camera? Park here in this yard with a view of the entrance? Was that it? You've anticipated this moment for a long time, wanting Sarah, your need for her growing. Now the time's come and your lust can't be denied any longer, can it? You've got to have her. The need will drive away any fear. The lust for her young, sweet body will drive out any inhibitions. The desire has become agony, hasn't it? Tonight you'll claim your reward. You're no common rapist though, are you? No, far from it, you've selected your victim with care. You'll have the car window open, waiting for the sound of her footsteps. The sound will clatter, amplified by the confines of the alley. Then you'll get out of the car. The street's deserted, safe. But you knew it would be, didn't you? You knew it because you've watched it so often, waiting for the right moment. It's all part of your planning, your careful, meticulous planning. Nothing left to chance.

'Is that her footsteps? You'll have to hurry to conceal yourself behind the big wheelie bin. You know exactly how much time you've got, because you've planned it all so well. Then you'll wait until Sarah's alongside you, or will you leave it until she's gone past, perhaps? Then you'll step forward and claim her. That's how you did it.'

One of Mike's fellow officers in the Met observed once: 'Nash seems to go into some sort of a trance at times. When I asked him what he was doing, he said he was committing the crime. I didn't understand at first, but when he came out of it he'd a string of questions no one else had thought of. I know we're all supposed to try to get inside the mind of the criminal, but he goes one further. He plans and commits the crime all over again, like watching action replay. I tell you, it spooked me.'

'Are you alright, Mike?'

Nash blinked and stared at Tom Pratt for a long moment, as if seeing the superintendent for the first time. He blinked rapidly as he dragged himself back to the present. 'Er, yes, sorry, Tom, I was just trying to think things through.' Nash saw Pratt's sideways glance and wondered what his boss was thinking. 'Tom, I wonder if you could use your influence to get hold of someone from the council. We need to know if that street lamp at the end of the ginnel was working on Friday night. If not, what was wrong with it? Ask them to send one of their cherry pickers out.'

Pratt nodded. 'Anything else?'

'I think we should have another look at the CCTV footage from the club. I'd like to get someone to enhance the image of the bloke Sarah spoke to by the bar. Then we can show it to the staff and customers, see if anyone recognizes him. In the meantime, it'll be a while before SOCO get here, even longer before they're ready to release the handbag to us. Unless you have any better ideas, I suggest a coffee and bacon butty's called for. There's a café on the High Street. The bacon's tasty and the coffee's not bad either. I reckon it'll be lunchtime before the lads are through here.'

As they ate, Nash asked Tom how he wanted to tackle the investigation.

'I'm happy for you to run with it. Standard operating procedures say mine should be the lead name, but you've more experience of this type of enquiry than I have. I'll run the admin. Just find the girl. Find out what's happened to her, and if needs be, find the bastard who's kidnapped her. Keep me up to speed with progress, that's all I ask.'

Nash began to outline his ideas. 'If it proves to be Sarah's bag, we need every possible media machine in action in the hope we can find someone, somewhere, who might be able to tell us something. I think we should also check the Sex Offenders' Register to see if there's anyone living locally who might prove likely candidates.'

'You think this might be a sex crime?'

'Can't see any other motive. We can discount jealousy, revenge, and we can certainly discount profit. Sarah Kelly hadn't been in a failed relationship. She hadn't nicked someone's husband or boyfriend, and she certainly isn't from a wealthy family. That leaves a motiveless psychopath or a sex crime. Okay, I know psychopaths have been known to plan an attack carefully, but somehow that doesn't seem to fit.'

Nash and Pratt had only been back at the station fifteen minutes when Mironova and Pearce returned from canvassing the neighbours. Nash greeted them. 'A handbag's been found near the nightclub. We'll have to show it to Mrs Kelly once SOCO have finished with it. That's down to you and me, Clara. What did you find out?'

'A few were out at work but the men we talked to all think Sarah's a thoroughly nice, decent lass,' Pearce told him, then grinned. 'I suspect most of them would prefer it if she wasn't, but daren't admit it in front of their wives. The women also thought Sarah's nice. A normal set of reactions from a normal enough bunch of people.' Pearce hesitated for a second, 'for the most part, that is.'

Nash lifted an eyebrow.

'There was one bloke seemed a bit shifty. Clara has him marked down as a weirdo. He'll warrant consideration.'

Mike turned to Mironova.

'It's the way he looked at me. I get plenty of looks from blokes; it's a bit of a compliment, normally. Occasionally, though, a man looks at you and it makes you shiver. You may not know exactly what he's thinking, but you get a damned good idea and it isn't nice, it isn't nice at all. That's how this guy made me feel.'

'Netherdale's going to handle the computer work because we're going to be too busy. Ask them to check the neighbours on the PNC. What do we know about the character who undressed Clara with his eyes?'

'This was far worse. It was a sort of promise, a threat almost. As if he was thinking of what he would do given the chance. Not only that but visualizing it.'

'As you said, not very nice.'

Pearce consulted his notes. 'His name's Roland Bailey. Forty-eight years old and single.' He looked up. 'His employers are Rushton Engineering.'

The visit to Joan Kelly had been distressing. Nothing could disguise the grim conclusion Sarah's mother reached on seeing the handbag. She identified Sarah's purse, which contained over £100 in notes. Along with the usual assortment of feminine bric-a-brac they also found a set of house keys. Clara tried one of them in the front door lock. It fitted exactly and turned easily.

Pratt was talking to DC Pearce when Nash and Clara returned. It didn't need Nash's nod to confirm the identification. The grim expression on their faces was proof enough.

'We must assume the worst,' Pratt said heavily. 'This moves the enquiry to another level. You must decide what resources you need. I've sorted a press release, but for the time being I'll concentrate on arranging a media conference. What do you reckon, Mike? Wednesday or Thursday, unless something turns up?'

Clara shivered. 'What you mean is, if anything bad was going to happen to Sarah, it already has done?'

Nash agreed, 'Exactly. She may not be dead. But she's certainly not safe and well.'

'Are you thinking of putting Mrs Kelly in front of the cameras?' Pearce asked.

Pratt and Mike exchanged glances. 'If nothing breaks within the next forty-eight hours we'll have to. Apart from focusing the public's attention on the case, the media will demand it,' Pratt said.

'And if we get her to a media conference, it might prevent them camping out on her doorstep, causing her more distress,' Nash agreed.

'I'm going back to Netherdale to organize things from there. I'll check on the PNC progress,' Pratt told them.

Later, Nash received a phone call from Pratt. 'I've a couple of bits of news. I've had the reports back on the surveillance camera and the street light. You were dead right. The lamp was out of action on Friday night. Both it and the camera were disabled by airgun pellets.'

'As we suspected.'

'I agree, so I've put more men to work on the background info. The computer reports should be ready for you by around 9 p.m. tonight.'

'Thanks. Can you send the paperwork over in a squad car? I'll give Viv and Mironova a break so we can work on it overnight.'

'You'll need a break at some stage, Mike. This could be a long haul.'

'Maybe, but I'm used to doing without sleep.'

'Now, extra resources. You set up the incident room. I've organized staff to man the phone lines.'

'I think we should extend the search areas into the countryside. There's a hell of a lot of ground to cover. I suppose that's really always been the most likely place to find her.'

'What you mean is, that's where we'll find her body,' Pratt agreed sombrely.

It was at 8 p.m. that night when he rang again. 'Would you believe it, the PNC's gone down for "routine maintenance". It's been out of action all evening. We can't get anything till tomorrow at the earliest. What do you want to do?

As soon as it's up and running, every force in the land will be logging on for info, so it'll take a while, even when we can get through.'

'In that case, we'll get a decent night's sleep and try again tomorrow.'

It had been a dreadful few days for Monique. She'd had them before of course. But this one was more severe than most. Monique knew when the first signs appeared: migraine. It knocked her out. As soon she'd felt the symptoms start, she phoned work. Her boss was understanding, as he'd seen the effects before during the ten years she'd worked there. 'Come back when you're fit.'

She dug out her medication and filled a flask with cold water. Then she went to bed. The curtains were drawn tight. The phone and doorbell disconnected. Eventually the pain eased. The flashing lights dimmed. She slipped into unconsciousness. Then the visions began. Her brain, its defences weakened, began to replay her ordeal. With it came guilt and the unanswered questions. What had happened?

Then Danielle appeared, pleading for help. Help she was unable to give. How could she when she couldn't remember?

It was another three days before she emerged from her bedroom. Her legs were weak from disuse. Her pallor and the dark circles under her eyes were clear evidence of her ordeal. She set about restoring order. She replaced the telephone cable in its socket, reconnected the doorbell and pondered whether to ring the office.

Charleston's was a busy estate agency. Monique was in charge of the Helmsdale branch. Despite this, she decided not to return yet. Even though she knew the owner was going on holiday, she couldn't face the thought of going to work. Potential clients could wait. Far better to rest, go back fully restored.

Monique couldn't think of food until late the following day. She prepared a bland meal of chicken and pasta and carried it through to the lounge. She needed a comfortable chair and the sound of a human voice, if only the newsreader on TV.

She was midway through her meal, when the bulletin turned to local news. Monique paid scant attention to the first two items. The opening words of the next report focused her mind instantly. 'Police in Helmsdale have expressed their concern over the whereabouts of nineteen-year-old Sarah Kelly who vanished....'

Monique stared at the screen, her body frozen into immobility. She listened, heedless of the sauce dripping on to her lap. The newsreader gave out some scant facts. As the incident phone numbers were being given out, the girl's photo appeared on screen. Monique stared at the image, transfixed. She began to shake uncontrollably. She put the tray down and ran to the downstairs cloakroom. She was violently sick.

Sarah tried to clear her brain. Consciousness returned slowly. Something was different. Her mouth felt dry, her tongue heavy and wooden, her throat parched. She remembered the injection. Obviously she'd been drugged. Something had changed, but what? In her drowsy state it took her a long time before she could work it out. Several times she felt she was on the point of solving the mystery when she fell asleep again.

She was now tied to a chair. The ropes were still fastened to her wrists and ankles. The hood was still over her head. Her neck hurt. She moved slightly, as much as her bonds would allow. Something rustled. She moved again and heard the same noise, faint but definite. Was that her making the sound? She wasn't wearing anything that rustled. She moved again; again the rustle. She was definitely making the sound, but how?

As Sarah puzzled it over she felt another new sensation. Something was touching the skin of her neck. It felt like a necklace. But she never wore a necklace. She moved again, this time achieving a little more movement. There was something odd about all her clothing. It felt looser, less restrictive than the stretch jeans and tight-fitting top she'd been wearing.

'So, you've woken up once more, dear Sarah.' She heard the soft voice again and shivered involuntarily. 'I think it's time for us to meet properly.'

The hood was loosened and slipped off. The bright light dazzled her. Instinctively she lowered her head to avoid the glare. She gasped in bewilderment. She had been right. She was wearing a full-length evening dress. A string of pearls had been placed round her neck. Long evening gloves and a matching evening bag lay on her lap.

She could tell she was no longer wearing her flat shoes, replaced by what she knew to be heeled shoes. Sarah squirmed slightly at the strangeness of it all and was shocked to find that even her underwear had been changed. The bra felt strange, new and unworn.

Her eyes had adjusted sufficiently, she looked up, her eyes widened, her brain reeled. Was she in the middle of some dreadful nightmare? Suddenly she knew it was only too real and the realization of what she was looking at came to her. Hot bile rose in her throat, threatening to choke her as she stared in horror at the nauseating sight before her. She had gone far beyond fear, into a realm of terror she could never have imagined. Sarah began to scream. She screamed until eventually her brain was no longer able to cope with the level of disgust and revulsion, and shut down. Sarah lapsed into merciful unconsciousness.

CHAPTER FOUR

Rushton Engineering was on the outskirts of Helmsdale, where the red-brick town merged into the countryside. Every attempt had been made by the management to soften the ugly outlines of the factory. The depot was a small, specialist unit, with a workforce of no more than sixty. A large open area in front of the building had been planted with trees and shrubs, hiding the car park. This was where Nash found Mironova waiting.

As they crossed the yard to the company's offices, Mike noticed they received one or two curious looks from passing members of the workforce. He cast a sideways glance at his companion. For the first time, he realized that Clara, with her height, good figure and striking looks, was sufficiently like Sarah to merit a second glance. Her long blonde hair emphasised the similarity.

The Managing Director was eager to help. 'Sarah's very popular. She's a good, efficient secretary, careful but quick. If you give her a job to do, you know it'll get done. She's cheerful, and gets on with staff and customers alike and she's not frightened of hard work. If there's a job to be done, Sarah stays until it's finished, even if it means working late. Our business is either famine or feast. We're either laying people off, or we're rushed off our feet, running three shifts 24/7.'

'What's it like at present?'

'We're fairly busy, about to get busier. We've a couple of contracts due for signing.'

'In that case, we'll try not to get in the way, but we need to speak to every employee.'

'No problem. There are some things more important than making money. Just don't tell my shareholders I said that. There's a small dining suite at the end of the canteen where we entertain clients. You'll be able to talk to people there. I've left instructions with the departmental managers to send their workers for the mid-shift break in relays, and for the men to report to you first. It'll start in about ten minutes, so by 11.00 you'll have had chance to talk to everyone on this shift. If you come back later this afternoon, you can do the same with the other shift. We're only running two at the moment. I'm putting it up to three in a couple of weeks, but for now that should get everyone in front of you. The office workers take their lunch break in rotation anyway, so that'll follow on nicely.'

'That sounds ideal.'

'Planning and neatness: always been essential to me. Part of my nature, if you like, although my wife says it's an obsession.'

Nash glanced round the man's office. The desk had only a telephone and blotter on it. Elsewhere everything looked neat, spartan. Not a file or piece of paper out of place. Almost like a showroom display, Nash thought.

They'd spoken to more than half the shift when Clara nudged Nash. He looked up at the approaching man. His clothing marked him out from the rest of the workforce. Whereas they all wore boiler suits, this man was in street clothes.

He walked hesitantly forward, every step reluctant. His gait, a sort of shuffle, added to the furtive air. He was wearing a fawn zip-up jacket and equally bland slacks that failed to match. His shoes, old-fashioned brown lace-ups were dull, unpolished. Nash studied him keenly. Everything about his appearance and demeanour was nondescript. He peered from behind a pair of round, black-rimmed glasses whose high degree of magnification gave him a wide-eyed, mildly manic stare. He had a salt-and-pepper thatch of hair, of a style that defied description.

Nash gestured to the chair then noticed that the man wasn't looking at him. He was staring at Mironova, who shifted uneasily in her seat. 'Sit down,' Nash's tone was sharp.

He sat down, his gaze still on Clara. 'I've seen you before. I remember you.' Each word in the statement was innocuous; the whole conveyed a slightly sinister overtone.

'That's correct, Mr Bailey,' Mironova told him coldly. 'This is Detective Inspector Nash.' She turned to Nash. 'This is Mr Roland Bailey, one of Sarah's neighbours.' Her eyes conveyed her message.

Bailey looked fleetingly at Nash and dropped his gaze to the table.

'Why are you dressed differently?'

Bailey looked puzzled by the question. 'I'm in the stores.' He spoke so softly they'd to strain to hear him.

'So, Mr Bailey, not only are you one of Sarah's neighbours, but you also work in the same place.'

The statement sounded like an accusation.

'Yes,' the monosyllable was no more than a mutter.

'Then I expect you saw more of her than any of your colleagues. You walked the same way to and from work. You ever walk with her, Mr Bailey?'

'Never.'

'Sure about that? Not once? I mean, Sarah's a very attractive girl? It would be only natural to want to walk with her, talk to her. That would be neighbourly, surely?'

'No, I didn't.'

'But you see her all you want at Ash Grove, at home, in the garden, don't you? You ever see her sunbathing? Ever watch her? She's a nice looking girl, isn't she?'

'I don't know.'

'Come off it, you can't expect us to believe that. Living near a pretty girl and you reckon you've never noticed. She got you excited, did she, and now you're ashamed to admit it? Or don't you like women, Mr Bailey? Do your preferences lie elsewhere?'

Mironova, observing quietly, noticed that Nash's insinuations were beginning to needle Bailey. A fine bead of sweat gathered above his top lip, another on his brow.

'No, they don't.' There was real emotion in his voice, this time disgust.

Nash tried again. 'When did you last see Sarah?'

'I don't remember, last week sometime.'

'Was it Friday? Did you follow her home from work? Admiring her figure? Walking behind her? Getting excited, aroused even? Is that what happened?'

No, it wasn't! I didn't see her on Friday at all, definitely not on Friday.' This time there was alarm.

'You'd see her on Friday evening as she went out. She'd have to pass your house on her way down Ash Grove, wouldn't she?'

'I suppose so. But I didn't see her.'

'Why was that? I don't think you'd miss the chance to look out for her.'

'I didn't see her, I tell you. I wasn't home on Friday night.' The admission was torn from him. For a moment Nash thought Bailey was about to add more.

'Where were you?'

The question remained unanswered so long Nash was about to repeat it, when Bailey said, 'Netherdale.'

'Whereabouts?'

'I went to the pictures.' The words were no more than a mumble.

'You're going to have to speak up. Where did you say?'

There was definite colour in his face as Bailey snapped, 'At the pictures.'

Mironova spoke for the first time. 'But the Netherdale cinema's closed for renovation, Mr Bailey.'

The glance Bailey shot Clara reminded Nash of a rabbit confronted by a fox. 'So, where did you go?' Nash asked.

'I went to a club.' All trace of colour had gone. Now he looked ashen.

'The Gaiety Club, by any chance?' Mironova asked.

Bailey returned to monosyllables. 'Yes.'

Nash pressed him. 'What was the title of the film?'

'I don't remember.' The unspoken message was clear.

'Perhaps it's one you'd prefer not to say in front of my sergeant?' The riot of colour in Bailey's cheeks spoke volumes. 'Is that the case?'

'Yes, I suppose so.'

'Could anyone vouch for you being there? Another member? Someone who works there?'

'No, I don't think so.'

'What time did you leave? In time to see Sarah on her way home? Get a bit confused by what you'd just been watching? Wonder if Sarah might do the sort of things the girls in the movie did? Try to get her to do the same with you?'

'I've told you. I never saw her. Not on Friday. I didn't, I swear it. I was in Netherdale all night.'

Bailey's tone was a mixture of nervousness bordering on alarm, but with something added. Something Nash could not pinpoint. All he could be certain of was that somewhere in Bailey's vehement denial there was a lie.

The interview had taken far longer than the others and Nash judged it time to bring it to a close, before Bailey became cause for gossip. 'That's all for now. I may want to speak to you again. Send the next man in.'

Bailey rose shakily and walked towards the door. He looked back. Nash saw him stare, not at him but at Clara. The expression on his face was fleeting, but it made Nash shudder.

Their interviews were concluded by one o'clock. During the short drive to Helmsdale police station, Clara asked Mike his opinion of Bailey. 'He's everything you said and a lot more besides. For my money, if anything's happened to Sarah, Bailey has to be the prime candidate. The Gaiety Club's a porn house, isn't it?'

'Yes. They show some of the hardest stuff on the market. They were raided by Vice a couple of years back, just before you arrived here. It was rumoured they were showing snuff movies, but they didn't find anything. The only reason they get away with it is because it's a members-only club.'

Nash grinned. 'Your choice of words could be better, but I get the point. I'm willing to place a small bet with you that Bailey's name appears on the Sex Offenders Register when we eventually get it.'

'That's a bet I'm not prepared to take.'

'If he's not, then it's only a matter of time. I reckon he's capable of almost anything evil. Unfortunately, we can't arrest someone for the look in their eyes.'

'If I never see him again, I'll not lose sleep over it.'

'There's another thing about Roland Bailey that worries me. For all he got a bit agitated, beneath it he was well in control of himself. That may be down to a clear conscience. Then again, it might be because he has no conscience.'

'What do we do next?'

'We'll see what the search parties have found, if anything. I suspect the answer's nothing, because your squawk-box hasn't gone off. Then I want to look through the evidence we have so far. I'm going to let you and Pearce come back here and interview the workers on the other shift. After that, I'd like you to call on Mrs Kelly and update her. It's going to be a long day, but we should get a bit of relief tomorrow.'

Nash swung the car into the police station car park. 'We might as well see if they've had any results at the desk.'

Mironova frowned. 'You're not expecting much, I hope. It's usually a collection of nutters, cranks and well intentioned no-hopers.'

'You never know your luck in a big city.'

Inside reception, it seemed Mironova was going to be proved right. A young, harassed-looking constable was attempting to placate an elderly man intent on telling his story to 'someone in charge'.

The visitor was in that condition referred to locally as 'market fresh'.

'Listen,' the man demanded, with only the slightest slur in his voice, 'I've got news. Summat important to tell. Might be very important.'

'Yes, Mr Turner, you've told me that already. Several times, in fact. Why not tell me what this important information is?'

He wasn't about to divulge so priceless a pearl to just anyone. 'Wouldn't you like to know,' he told the constable, wagging a finger at him. 'Bur 'am not tellin'. Not tellin' you. I'm only tellin' someone important, in charge like! Somebody who's in charge of all this.' He gestured round the room.

'That'll be me then,' Nash said from behind him. 'How can I help?'

The constable looked up, his relief obvious.

Startled by this unexpected assault from the rear, Turner wheeled round, with near calamitous results. They watched in amusement as he staggered in a Zorba-like dance down the length of the room. He steadied himself, grinned a trifle sheepishly, and walked with elaborately cautious steps back. 'Who're you?'

Nash took an involuntary half pace backwards. He liked Theakston's bitter but not second-hand. 'I'm Detective Inspector Nash; I'm leading this enquiry. Is that important enough?'

'An' who's this,' he leered at Clara. 'She yer girlfriend then?'

'This is Detective Sergeant Mironova. She's also involved in the investigation,' Mike's severe tone disguised his desire to burst out laughing.

Turner inspected Mironova. 'Well, say what y' like, I reckon yer a bit of alright, lass. Y' can lock me up any time you like, day or night.'

'Thank you. That's very kind,' Clara told him politely. 'So what is it you have to tell us?'

'What? Oh yes, 'ave summat to tell yer. How the devil did you find out? You must be a bloody good detective.'

'You told us so, Mr Turner,' Nash reminded him patiently.

'Did I? Well, after all, that's why 'am 'ere. Well now we've got that settled, I'll be off. Pleased to meet you, Sergeant Min … in … Mini … Miniver.'

'Mironova,' Clara corrected him.

'You still haven't said why you're here, Mr Turner,' Nash reminded him.

'What? Oh no, yer right, silly me. Well, it were like this, see. Last Friday, Friday night, I went fer a pint or two at T' Horse and Jockey, at end of High Street, tha' knows. Ah were there until Barry told me it were time to bugger off home to t' wife,' Turner paused and shook his head sorrowfully. 'I told him, it's nivver time to go home to her, but he insisted. So ah had to walk home.'

'What time was this?' Nash asked.

Turner's frown deepened. 'Now that's a bloody good question. Ah'm not sure. Barry might remember. I'd 'ad a few by then,' he added defensively.

'You set off to walk home,' Nash prompted him.

'Aye, you're right, ah did, but ah 'ad to stop for a Jimmy. Barry threw me out before I'd a chance. So ah walked round the relief road,' Turner giggled. 'Looking for somewhere to relieve myself. That's when I saw it,' he told them triumphantly.

'What did you see?'

'The car, of course,' Turner said impatiently. 'Ah remember thinking, that's bloody funny, that is. What's yon bloke up to? Only by then I was busting so I had to have a Jimmy and forgot about it.'

'And what do you think he was up to?' Nash's interest sharpened noticeably.

'That's the point. It was what he weren't up to. He weren't doing owt. Just sitting there wit' engine off, windows open an' no lights showing.'

'Where was the car?'

'Ah well, when ah need a Jimmy, an' I usually do, I go in that yard. Where t' car were parked I mean.'

'Which yard was it?'

'The one agin t' snicket. By t' nightclub. Where yer poster says.'

'Now, Mr Turner, I want you to think very carefully, because it might be very important. You saw a car parked next to that alleyway, no lights on, engine switched off and the windows open. You're certain there was somebody in the car?'

'Aye, that I am.'

'Could you describe them? Do you know whether it was a man or a woman?'

Turner thought about it before replying. 'Ah thought it were a man. Never entered me head it were a woman, but it might ha' been.'

'What about the car? Make, size, shape, colour, anything that might help us?'

'It were very dark. In t' yard, I mean, not car. It were a big un, not one of them Land Rovery things, but big. Aye it were big, right enough. A saloon bar,' Turner giggled again. 'I mean a saloon car. It were light coloured. Not white though, mebbes silver.'

'Were it parked, I mean, was it parked nose into the yard or facing you?'

'It were towards me. That's how I knew there were somebody inside. I could see t' shape through t' windscreen.'

'Is there anything else you can tell us? Is it a regular parking spot?'

'No, that yard's allus empty.' Turner thought for a moment. 'No, hang on. There were a car in there a couple of weeks back.' He studied a little longer. 'Come to think of it, that were a Friday night an' all.'

'In that case, I'd like you to pop back tomorrow morning and set down everything you've told us in a formal statement. Before then, I'd like you to give the constable here your full name, address and phone number, in case we need to contact you. Okay?'

Turner smiled. 'Right then. Al do that. Will Sergeant Miniver take me statement?' he asked hopefully. 'I like Sergeant Miniver,' he winked at Clara.

'I'll see what can be arranged. Thanks for coming in, Mr Turner.'

They headed for the incident room, where they saw Tom Pratt was about to leave. 'How's it going?' Nash asked him.

'No joy so far. I've got one group concentrating on the river banks. The other groups are doing a sweep through open ground on the east of town. That's all we'll get done today. It's going to be a long job. How did you get on at Rushton's?'

'Nothing startling to report, although we met a neighbour of Sarah's; guy name of Bailey. Remember Clara mentioned him? I'm not at all happy about him. He's a member of the Gaiety Club in Netherdale. Said he was there on Friday.'

'I understand your interest. Has he got an alibi?'

'Not really, at least not one we can verify.'

'He must have been pretty scared to admit being there. It isn't the sort of club where the members meet for a social drink during the interval. As for someone noticing him, it's not easy telling one dirty raincoat from another.'

'Just to be sure, we'll ask around at this Gaiety Club, but I'd be more interested to see if his name comes up on our computer search.'

'That reminds me, the info from the PNC's been e-mailed through to you.'

'Good, I'll look through it and see if anything jumps out at me. Clara and I had a very interesting chat with a drunk as we came in,' Nash explained. 'As Turner appears to be either pissed, half pissed or on his way to getting pissed all the time, I can't see his evidence standing up in court. Come to think of it, I can't imagine Turner standing up in court. However, it does seem significant there was a car lurking so close to where Sarah disappeared on two occasions.'

'You don't think he might have got the wrong night? He sounds as if he's easily confused.'

'It's possible, but somehow I don't think so. Clara, you've got half an hour to spare. Nip along to The Horse and Jockey and have a word with the landlord. With a bit of luck he'll confirm at least part of Turner's story and he might also give us an idea of the time Turner staggered off home.'

Mironova groaned. 'I get all the worst jobs.'

'If you'd prefer it, I'll send someone else and you can spend the next couple of hours crawling through the undergrowth in the woods, "Sergeant Miniver",' Nash said pointedly.

'Okay, you've convinced me. Anyway, you never know your luck. Mr Turner might be in the pub. He could buy me a drink.'

With every available officer drafted into the search parties, the station was quiet. Nash spoke to forensics about the CCTV tapes. They promised to get the enhancement done as quickly as they could. When he'd finished, Nash decided to study the files culled from the PNC.

He printed them off and began reading. The phone rang. Nash listened for a few seconds then spoke tersely, 'Right, I'm on my way.'

He disconnected, then pressed a button on the phone's base unit. 'Clara? Your afternoon's just turned into a pub crawl. Meet me in The Cock and Bottle as fast as you can get there. There's been a stabbing; it's fatal.'

CHAPTER FIVE

The Cock and Bottle might have been a smart, respectable town-centre pub once, but that must have been a long time ago. It hadn't stood the test of time well. It had a dilapidated, neglected air. The paintwork round the doors and windows was cracked and peeling. One window had been boarded over. The uniformed officer standing at the door informed Nash, 'In the yard at the back, Sir.'

The interior mirrored the rundown exterior perfectly. The ceilings, once white, were now a dark unpleasant caramel shade. Nash wondered how many thousand cigarettes it had taken to achieve that effect.

The carpet felt slightly tacky beneath his feet. The bar rail and the wood beneath his fingers was sticky to the touch. There were half a dozen customers in the bar, all men. He presumed the others had been scared away by news of a corpse in the back yard, or that police would be sniffing round. The seedy appearance of those that hadn't left suited their surroundings. A barman, who looked only just over the legal age to be serving alcohol, slouched towards him. He was tall and lean, wearing a grubby football shirt and ragged jeans. Dispensing with formalities, the youth jerked a thumb towards the rear of the building. 'She's out there.'

'Who is?'

'The stiff, the one you're here about.'

'Is she a customer?'

'Not anymore,' the humour, if such was intended, was deadpan.

'Was she, then?'

'I suppose so.'

'What was her name?'

'Dunno.'

'Perhaps you wouldn't mind showing me the way?'

'Sorry, can't leave the bar unattended.'

Nash looked round at the punters and nodded. 'I see your point. Where's the landlord?'

The barman's face twisted into a sneer. 'Upstairs, glued to the telly, watching his money coming in seventh at Kempton Park.'

'Fetch him down.'

'More than my job's worth.'

Nash leaned towards the barman and smiled humourlessly. 'When this place closes, which will be in about ten minutes time, I can make sure it never re-opens again. How much would your job be worth then?'

The barman turned away disappointed, accepting defeat.

Clara arrived. 'What's going on?'

'A woman's been stabbed, body's in the back yard apparently. I'm waiting for the barman to fetch the landlord. If he can drag him away from watching racing on television.'

'Obviously the caring sort.'

'Grieving takes many forms, Clara.'

They heard sirens wailing and an ambulance pulled up outside; two paramedics hurried in. Their entrance coinciding with the return of the barman, accompanied by another man. Nash signalled the paramedics towards the door indicated by the barman. 'Be right with you. You know the drill.'

Nash surveyed the newcomer. The man was in his mid fifties, and like the pub hadn't aged well. He was no more than five feet six inches tall and would probably once have been described as strongly built. All the muscle had long since run to fat. His T-shirt strained to cover his belly, leaving an unattractive bulging strip of flesh hanging over the waistband of his jeans.

His facial features were equally unprepossessing. A stubble of black whiskers studded with grey would have been better shaved off. His nose had been broken, obviously on more than one occasion, and had set crookedly. A jagged white scar ran down one cheek giving him a permanently sinister leer. His hair, streaked with grey like his beard, hung in lank, greasy profusion down to the grimy collar of his T-shirt.

'Mr Parkinson?'

'No,' the man smirked.

'You're not the landlord, then?'

'Course I'm the bloody landlord.'

'So what's your name?'

'Rawlings, Joe Rawlings,' the man's attitude was immediately beginning to irritate Nash.

'Are you aware, Mr Rawlings, that it's an offence under The Licensing Act for the licensee to fail to display their name over the door to the premises?'

'So what?'

'So I'd be within my rights to shut you down, and apply to the licensing magistrates to have your licence revoked.'

The regulars had been enjoying Joe's verbal sparring with authority. This was more fun than Match of the Day. At Nash's last sentence, however, they stirred uneasily.

'You wouldn't do that.'

'Don't try me.'

Nash and the landlord stood eye to eye, optical arm wrestling. 'Okay, okay; follow me.'

Nash turned to Mironova. 'Stay here. Make sure none of these characters does a runner. Get on the radio, tell Tom what's happened. We need Pearce and SOCO here, PDQ.'

The yard was piled high with beer kegs and crates of empty bottles. A second officer was standing by the back gate. The woman was lying in the middle of the concrete. The cause of death was easy enough to establish. The long-handled knife sticking out of her chest gave it away.

The paramedics had checked for signs of life, shook their heads sorrowfully and departed. 'Who is she, Rawlings?'

'Name's Lizzie Barton; off the Westlea estate.' Rawlings, it appeared, had decided to cooperate.

'Known to us, do you reckon?'

For the first time, Nash saw a glint of genuine humour in Rawlings's eyes. 'Isn't everyone from that estate?'

'It isn't compulsory, but most of them are.'

'Listen, Inspector—?'

'My name's Nash.'

'Oh yes. I heard about you on the radio yesterday, about the missing girl. Have you found her yet?'

'No, we haven't. Anyway, about this one, Lizzie Barton, you said her name is. Was she married?'

This time there was no doubt the laughter was genuine. 'Not formally, at least not that I know of. She's half a dozen kids, all by different blokes. They used to tease her in there,' he jerked his thumb in the direction of the pub. 'Said she was after her own football team and every player would have a different name on his shirt. She won't make it now.' Rawlings's humour turned mordant. 'Ah well, there's always six-a-side.'

Nash turned to look at the dead woman. Lizzie Barton looked probably just the wrong side of forty, or maybe that was a result of her lifestyle. She was attractive enough in a bold, slightly second-hand way. It looked as if she'd been around a bit and the journey hadn't been an easy one. She was dressed in jeans, sweat shirt and trainers, almost a uniform for those frequenting the pub. Her handbag lay alongside the body. It had tipped over on its side and her purse had spilled out. Even without touching it, Nash could see the purse contained a quantity of notes. That in itself was a minor miracle. 'Who found the body?'

'The barman. He had to change a keg and there's not much room in the cellar, so we bring the empties straight out here.'

Looking closer, Nash noticed the ankle bracelet. He could never remember the significance of which ankle the bracelet was worn on. 'Was she a pro?'

'On the game? If she got short of money, I reckon she wouldn't have minded charging for it. She never touted it in the pub, though.'

'Naturally, because you'd have to tell her it was against the licensing laws and you'd have to ban her, wouldn't you?'

'Of course I would, Inspector,' Rawlings replied solemnly, acknowledging Nash's sarcasm.

'Did you ever—?' Nash let the question hang in the air.

Rawlings smiled. 'If I admit that, am I a suspect?'

'You've just as good as admitted it. You're already a suspect, but by the sound of it you'll not be short of company.'

Rawlings said resignedly, 'We did slip upstairs to my flat some afternoons. Lizzie was good in bed and enjoyed it too. A genuine enthusiast.'

'Presumably only when there was no racing on telly?'

There was a touch of pride in Rawlings's voice when he replied. 'Exactly; business before pleasure. I let everyone in the pub think I lose a lot, but in fact I make more money from gambling than I do from running this place. Last year I cleared £70,000 after tax.'

'So you'd be in a position to pay Lizzie, if she charged for it?'

'Lizzie, and a few more besides. I may not be good looking but that doesn't stop me wanting it, Mr Nash, and if there are women prepared to go to bed with me, why not?' He shrugged. 'And if they need money, again, why not? We've all got to make our way in this life the best we can.'

'Was Lizzie in the pub at lunchtime?'

'If she was, I didn't see her, and I didn't go upstairs until about two o'clock. The first race was at 2.15 and I'd a fair amount riding on it.'

'How did it go?'

'I backed the favourite. It won in a canter at 6/4. I cleared three thousand pounds.'

'So Lizzie might have been on her way here and got waylaid?'

'Could be,' the landlord looked down at the dead woman. 'Lizzie didn't deserve this, I reckon.'

'Was the pub busy at lunchtime?'

'On a Tuesday, you must be joking. Just those you saw and half a dozen more. It's hardly worth opening.'

'Then you'll have no trouble remembering the names of the others then, the ones who scarpered before we arrived.'

Rawlings shifted uneasily. 'My regulars wouldn't be happy me giving their names to the … police.'

'Perhaps they'd be happier having a couple of my officers sitting at the bar every night for a week or two, until I'm sure we've interviewed everyone?' Nash suggested mildly.

Rawlings looked horrified. 'You drive a hard bargain.' He raised his hands in mock surrender.

'Did Lizzie have any enemies you knew of?'

'If she did, she never told me. She was popular in the pub. Mind you, she'd been through most of the blokes at one time or another, but it wasn't serious with Lizzie, just recreational. I don't think any of them bore her a grudge or would harm her.'

'What about their wives or girlfriends? Had she made anyone in particular jealous enough to want to hurt her?'

Rawlings hesitated. 'I couldn't say for sure.'

He was lying, Nash was sure of it. What was more, Rawlings knew he was aware of the fact. Nash detailed the officer to remain with the body and led Rawlings back inside. There, he found Pearce had joined Mironova and the two of them were taking details from the customers. 'I'll need you to come into the station and make a formal statement, but that can wait. You can go back to your racing if you want.'

Rawlings glanced at his watch. 'It's okay; the last televised race is over.'

'We're going to have to close the pub until the forensics people have finished,' Nash warned him.

Rawlings nodded resignedly. 'I expected that. Thank God it isn't Friday or Saturday.'

'You should be able to re-open tomorrow lunchtime. One thing I would advise, though. Get on the phone to a signwriter. Have that sign over the door repainted. If I noticed it, others will.'

Nash walked over to talk to the superintendent, who'd just entered. He briefed Pratt and took him into the yard to view the body. 'We need to clear this up ASAP,' Pratt said. 'We're stretched enough as it is.'

'Tell me about it. One thing does puzzle me, given the reputation this place has. Why have we never objected to the licence?'

'Because sometimes it's an advantage knowing exactly where to find certain people.'

'You mean, keep all the villains in one place?'

'Makes life simpler for us.'

'I'll finish up here as fast as I can. The landlord's giving us the names of everyone who was in here at lunchtime. I'll send Mironova and Pearce off to talk to them. There won't be that many.' A thought occurred to Nash and he waved the landlord across.

'Would the back gate have been unlocked?'

Rawlings nodded. 'Some of the regulars use it as a short cut. Besides which, we have deliveries twice a week, so I leave it open.'

'So, whoever stabbed Lizzie needn't have come into the pub at all?'

'Not if they knew the gate was open.'

Nash waited until the landlord was out of earshot. 'I'm going to have a word with the barman. I've a notion he might have something to contribute, and I think I know how to make him spill it.'

At first it seemed Nash's confidence was unjustified. In face of the barman's sullen defiance Nash merely smiled and said, 'I hope you're going to tell us all you know without me making it difficult for you?'

'I don't know anything.'

'You found the body, for one thing. You know more than anyone else. Tell me about it.'

The barman shrugged. 'I'd to change a barrel. I took the empty keg out and there she was.'

'That's a load of rubbish. I'll tell you why, shall I? The reason is, I already know what you're not telling me.'

'Don't know what you're talking about.'

'You know exactly what I'm talking about. It wasn't only an empty keg you took outside, was it?'

The young barman's face lost what little colour it had, but he managed to reply. 'Course it was.'

'I see, and did you dial 999 as soon as you came back inside?'

'Why wouldn't I?'

'You didn't by any chance make another quick phone call first, from your mobile?'

'Why should I?'

'Maybe to tell your pal not to come for the crate of lager? The one you'd put out for him? Nice little scam that. A busy pub like this, who's going to miss the odd crate now and again? You pile the empties high then put a full one on top of the stack. Rawlings can't see it because he's only a short-arse, and besides, it's not out there long. Your pal drives up, collects the crate, sells it on and you split the difference. It must have shocked the living daylights out of you, finding the body. With us about to crawl all over the spot, it would only have been a matter of time before somebody found the crate and put two and two together,' Nash's smile was wolf-like as he concluded, 'and now, your worst fears have come true.'

'You can't prove it.'

Nash laughed. 'I don't have to. All I have to do is whisper the magic words in Rawlings's ear and you'll be out on yours. So you'd better talk and talk fast.'

'I told you. I've nothing to say.'

'Fine, I don't care one way or the other.' Nash signalled to Pearce.

'Take him to the station, Viv. Charge him with the attempted theft of a crate of lager. Get the value from Rawlings before you go,' Nash turned away.

'Hang on a minute. What do you want to know?'

'I want to know what time you found the body. If you can't remember, check the time of the call on your mobile. I want to know what you saw. In other words, I want the lot.'

'It'd just happened, I mean literally that second. I went out with the keg, the yard was empty and the gate was shut. I'd already stashed the crate of lager in the Ladies after Rawlings went upstairs. There were no women in the bar, see, and I figured it'd be safe until my mate came along. I came back inside, picked up the crate, put it on top of the stack and that's when I looked round and saw her. Lizzie I mean, lying there with this bloody big knife stuck out of her chest. She wasn't moving. The gate was open, and I got a glimpse of somebody. I didn't see them proper, just a blur.'

'Then what did you do?'

'I went to the gate and looked down the alley.'

'What did you see?' Nash's tone was patience itself.

'I saw somebody legging it.'

'Man or woman? Can you describe them?'

'Could be either. Maybe a bit taller than Rawlings. Wearing jeans and a brown jacket, one of those short ones, a bomber jacket. Not fat, not skinny, dark hair, could have been black.'

'Is that everything?'

'That's everything. Honest.'

'Right, Viv, take him to the station.' The barman began to protest, but Nash raised a hand. 'Get a formal statement from him. Then I want a list of all the customers who scarpered before we arrived, plus the names of all the regulars he can think of, both male and female. I'll get Clara to do the same with the landlord, then I want the two of you to visit everyone on the two lists.'

'You think it was one of the customers?'

'I reckon so. Only the regulars would have known about the short cut through the alley.'

'Yes, but this'll scupper our interviews at Rushton's.'

'I'll attend to them.'

Nash repeated his instructions to Mironova. 'Remember to keep your eyes open for that jacket.'

Before he left, he updated Pratt, 'I need to get back to Rushton's to interview the rest of the workers.'

'Okay, Mike, I'll run the crime scene and we'll meet back at the station.'

The interview session took longer than the earlier one, principally because Nash had to take all his own notes. By the time he'd finished and returned to the station it was past six o'clock. His arrival coincided with that of Tom Pratt. He responded to Nash's question with a despondent shake of the head. 'I've stood the search teams down for tonight. They'll start again at first light. You had any thoughts about the Barton murder?'

'My guess would be Lizzie's complex social life was behind it. That reminds me, I should have asked for child welfare officers and a social worker to go to the house and look after the kids, but with everything else that was going on I clean forgot.'

'Don't worry, I've seen to it. I arranged for Mironova and Pearce to drop in and talk to the kids after they finished checking the addresses the landlord gave them.'

'Thanks, Tom.'

Their conversation was interrupted by Mironova and Pearce's return.

'Got anything?' Nash asked.

'Nothing significant. Certainly nobody with dark hair who owned up to having a brown bomber jacket,' Clara smiled.

'What's funny?'

'Viv asked one woman if she'd mind him looking through her wardrobe. She said, "You're welcome, love.

You'll not find anything your size but you can get into my knickers any time you like". He didn't ask again.'

'She was the only dark haired woman we saw,' Pearce said defensively. 'Most of them were blonde, brassy blonde at that.'

'What sort of reaction did you get when you told them why you were there? Was there any hostility towards the victim? From the women in particular?'

Mironova shook her head. 'None of them seemed against her, and most were shocked at the news. Most of them knew their partner had been with Lizzie at one time or another. One woman said, "At least when he was screwing her, he was leaving me alone".'

'How did you get on at the Barton house?'

Clara grimaced. 'Whatever else she was, there's no doubt she was a good mother. Her eldest is eighteen, the youngest only six, but they obviously all get on well and thought the world of their mum. They were all distraught, that's natural, and it occurred to me the kids and their mother had struck up some sort of bond against whatever life threw at them. The house itself was clean and tidy and so were the kids. None of them knew anything that could help us. I think perhaps Lizzie kept that side of her life from them as much as possible. To be honest, the state they were in, I wasn't prepared to push too hard.'

'We had a word with a few of the neighbours whilst we were there,' Pearce added. 'They all gang up against the police on that estate anyway, but once they knew the reason, they loosened up a bit. Nobody objected to Lizzie's lifestyle. They all commented about it, but not maliciously and none of them could think of a reason for anyone to harm her.'

'I reckon that's about it for today,' Pratt suggested. 'I think we should shut up shop for the night. God knows what tomorrow's going to throw at us.'

Nash agreed. 'I reckon we're going to have to wait for the SOCO report and the results of the post-mortem before we can do much more. I don't know about the rest of you, but I'm famished. I haven't eaten a thing since breakfast, and that feels like it was three days ago. Anyone fancy a quick meal?'

Pratt excused himself, but the others settled on the Italian restaurant in the High Street where they steered clear of the subject of work, Nash's only reference being in response to Mironova's question.

'No, I haven't had time to look at any of the PNC stuff. I've got the papers in my briefcase. I'll study them later.'

Nash's plans got waylaid. He'd barely got home when the doorbell rang. He was surprised to find Lauren Robbins standing outside. She smiled. 'I switched shifts today. I'm due back in Cheshire the day after tomorrow and this will be the last chance I have to see you before I go. So I thought I'd better bring you a leaving present.'

'What's that?'

'Me.'

She stepped inside the hall and let the door swing to behind her. She reached forward and took his hand. Nash's voice was husky with desire, 'Let's go unwrap my present.'

Sarah started to regain consciousness. She daren't open her eyes. The memory of what she'd seen was too horrible. She was lying down again, stretched out and wasn't tied up at all. What had woken her? She hadn't wanted to wake up. Consciousness brought terror and unspeakable memories. She heard a noise, a pleasant sound, a musical jingling, tuneless yet melodic.

Her clothing had been changed again. She was no longer wearing the evening dress nor had her jeans been returned. The garment she had on was loose fitting, a type of soft brushed cotton she guessed as she felt it against her thigh. She moved slightly and realized that her underwear had been removed. This disturbed her and she shifted uneasily.

She heard his voice, he was addressing her. She had no name for him. What conscious thought she was capable of just labelled him as 'he'. 'Sarah dear, would you like something to drink?'

Her mouth and throat were parched. Her tongue clung to the roof of her mouth. She managed to croak, 'Yes, please.'

As his arm went round her, she managed to repress a shiver of repugnance. He lifted her gently to a sitting position and supported her. Sarah still dared not open her eyes. She felt the cold rim of a glass touch her lips. 'Sip it slowly, Sarah, there's a dear.'

She took several sips before the glass was removed. 'That's enough, dear Sarah. We don't want any little accidents during the night, do we?'

She was lowered back down; her head came into contact with something soft. She heard footsteps then a door closing. Hoping against hope that she was alone she screwed up her courage and opened her eyes. It took a while to focus, even longer for her brain to sort out and identify the images. The first thing she saw was dolphins. Above her head they swam, dived, rose again and bumped together. It was this bumping sound that had woken her and Sarah understood what she was looking at. It was a child's cot mobile. The dolphins had created the gentle cacophony she had heard on waking.

She looked further afield, taking in the room's wallpaper. It was gaily patterned in bright pastel colours dotted here and there with figures she recognized instantly. They were some of her favourite cartoon characters. She turned and looked across the room. She saw a large set of pine drawers, on top of which was an array of stuffed toy animals. Alongside the drawers stood a much larger, far nobler-looking animal. His proud neck was arched, his head carried proudly aloft. A long mane was swept to one side of his dappled grey body; a rocking horse. Sarah realized she was in a child's nursery. But where was the child?

She looked at the single bed on which she lay, with a duvet covered by more figures she remembered from childhood. The garment she was wearing was a flannelette nightdress covered in similar characters. A fresh wave of horror overcame her as Sarah realized *she* was the child!

She was unable to cope with the implications of this. It seemed like too much trouble. It was far easier to lie there, relaxed and content. What she had seen ought to be disturbing, frightening even. But it didn't seem to matter much anymore. Her desperate situation didn't seem as alarming. After all, she wasn't being mistreated, really.

In the next room her captor carefully washed the glass, dried it methodically on a tea towel and replaced it in the cupboard. He brushed his teeth in a well-established routine, counting each stroke. He dried the toothbrush and placed it precisely on the shelf above the basin. He dried his hands and looked at his watch. Twenty-five minutes had passed, ample time for the drug to take effect. He glanced in the mirror, smiling slightly at his excited reflection.

He returned to the room and looked at the girl. 'Not asleep yet, Sarah dear? Never mind. Now let me put the duvet over you. We don't want you catching cold, do we?'

He crossed to the bed and deftly slid the duvet from beneath Sarah's body. She stared at him throughout, her expression one of puzzlement rather than fear. A sure sign the drug had worked. He touched her cheek. 'My word, you are cold, dear. Never mind, we'll soon have you warm.'

Moving the duvet to one side he stared at the curves of her body. He smiled gently, longingly. He continued to gaze at her as he began to unfasten his shirt.

CHAPTER SIX

Nash walked the short distance through Helmsdale towards the police station. His thoughts were on Lauren. Fun to be with, demanding no commitment. He'd miss her. Suddenly his mind crowded with memories of Stella: Stella laughing, Stella in his arms, Stella's beautiful smile. He shook his head to dismiss them. Guilt pricked his conscience. For the moment, however, he'd a case to solve. One he knew would test him to the limit. It was as well Lauren was going back to Cheshire. More guilt; he still hadn't got round to reading the PNC information. Fortunately, the details couldn't have prevented the crime, couldn't have avoided whatever had happened to the missing girl.

By mid morning Nash had caught up with some of his delayed reading. It yielded a surprisingly large number of offenders whose profile fitted the search parameters, although there was none who seemed likely to be the suspected abductor. He called Mironova and Pearce into his office. He was about to start when Tom Pratt wandered in. 'I've left the search parties to it. I'm not built for scrambling through undergrowth. Not interrupting anything, am I?'

'Certainly not, Tom. We're about to run through what we've got on the two cases.' Nash turned to his colleagues.

'Unless something breaks soon this looks likely to be a long haul. We can start by eliminating those possible suspects we have. I'm talking about Bailey and one or two candidates from that list.' He waved a hand towards the PNC documents, 'Plus the man Sarah spoke to in Club Wolfgang shortly before she vanished. We've also got the Lizzie Barton murder. At least we're certain that's a crime that has actually been committed.'

'I thought you were convinced Sarah Kelly had been abducted?'

'I may be, Clara, but that wouldn't stand up as evidence. All we've got at present is supposition, based on meagre facts. Yes, we found her handbag, but she could have dropped that because she was under the influence. Or she could have lost it whilst she was having a knee trembler in the alley.'

He stilled Pearce's protest with an upraised hand. 'I'm not saying either of those happened. The only fact we have is that her disappearance is completely out of character.'

'What do you suggest we do?'

'Keep asking questions; check some of these characters out.' Nash tapped the PNC reports, 'And keep on searching all the likely places she could be.'

'Do you mean where her body is likely to have been dumped?'

'Yes, Viv, I'm afraid that's exactly what I mean.'

'Which case gets priority?'

'We've got to concentrate on the murder. It goes against the grain to push the Sarah Kelly case into the background, but we have to.' Nash turned to his boss. 'Anything to add, Tom?'

'No. I think you've summed it up as well as you can. Depressing I know, but our job's like that.'

When Pratt had gone back to receive the reports from the search teams, and Viv had been sent on coffee-making duty, Clara looked at her boss. 'You okay, Mike? You look tired. Is the case getting to you? Not starting with nightmares again, are you?'

He shook his head. 'No, nothing like that. I didn't get much sleep last night,' he confessed ruefully. 'That'll change though. Lauren's going back to Cheshire tomorrow.'

'Have you ever thought of settling down? Living a more normal lifestyle, I mean?'

Nash's expression changed. 'Once maybe, not now.'

'Sorry, Mike, I wasn't thinking. Perhaps you could do with a change. That place of yours is too big, too many memories. Get a smaller flat or something.'

Nash sighed, 'You may be right.'

'Why not try Helmsdale Properties? The woman we met there, Helen Tate was it, remember her? She'll be happy to find somewhere for you to lay your head. I'm sure she'd be more than pleased to show you what she's got on offer.'

'You never miss a chance to have a go at me, do you?'

Clara smiled. 'I've got to get my fun where I can. Seriously though, as well as Helmsdale Properties, have you thought of trying Charleston's? They're a big outfit, with branches all over the place. They'll even help you move home.'

'Sorry, I'm not with you.'

'They've all sorts of additional services to offer. Not the sort Helen Tate has in mind for you,' Clara added with a wicked grin, 'but equally useful. Charleston's have a removal company, a firm of solicitors, mortgage brokers, the lot. They even own the firm that puts up the FOR SALE signs. They'd be my first port of call. But then, I don't fancy Helen Tate.'

The Home Office didn't consider their part of North Yorkshire warranted a full-time pathology department, so post-mortem examinations in the area were carried out by Pedro Ramirez, Professor of Pathology from York University. At some stage, an officer with a better than nodding acquaintance with *The Ballad of Eskimo Nell* had nicknamed him 'Mexican Pete'. Despite the fact that he hailed from Madrid!

Nash got a call regarding the post-mortem. The conversation was brief to the point of curtness: 'I viewed the body yesterday. I have lectures all day. Be at Netherdale Hospital at 6 p.m.' Before Nash could reply the line went dead. He stared at the phone for a bemused second.

Mironova was watching, a smile on her face. 'Mexican Pete?'

Nash nodded.

'Talkative was he?'

'As ever,' Nash agreed.

'He's a damned good pathologist, even though he is a pervert. He tries to feel my backside every time he sees me.'

'That's not perverted. That's good taste. I'm off to see Rawlings again. Want to come?'

Predictably, Rawlings was studying the morning's racing paper. He was sitting on a bar stool, a mug of coffee and an overflowing ashtray in front of him. He looked up as they entered. 'What is it this time?' His tone was resigned, but Nash guessed this was more habit than genuine resentment.

'Some questions, I'm afraid.'

'As long as you're quick. It's the barman's day off and I want to phone the bookies before the pub gets busy.'

'We'll keep it as short as we can.'

'Fire away then,' Rawlings lit another cigarette and looked at them directly for the first time. 'What do you want to know?'

'The lists of customers that were in the bar yesterday lunchtime. Was there anyone on, or not on them for that matter, that Lizzie might have been seeing on a regular basis over, say, the last year?'

Rawlings thought about it. 'Not to my knowledge, not the last twelve months, and I reckon I'd know.'

'How, Mr Rawlings?' Clara asked.

He gave her an amused smile. 'It's a landlord's business to notice things like that. Comes in very handy: especially in a place like this. Knowing who to keep apart, stop a fight breaking out.'

Nash persisted. 'The way you said it, sounded as if you knew something outside that time limit.'

Rawlings grunted. 'You don't miss much, do you? Lizzie and Alec Jennings were going at it hammer and tongs a while back. Alec wasn't in yesterday; that's why he's not on your lists. I teased Lizzie about toy boys, because Alec's ten years younger.'

'How'd you find out about it?'

'Usual way,' Rawlings grinned. 'Caught them at it. Had to change a barrel one night and when I took the empty outside, I found him giving her a knee trembler in the yard. His girlfriend had just walked out, so I suppose it was a case of any port in a storm. Anyway, I said, "Don't mind me, carry on", and you know what, they did. It went on for a few months, then fizzled out about a year back when Cindy, that's Alec's girlfriend, moved back in. Alec didn't waste any time, maybe he wasn't prepared to risk her taking off again. He put Cindy up the spout almost immediately. She must be five or six months gone by now.'

'There's no one else you can think of? Nobody more recent?'

Rawlings shook his head. 'No, that's it.'

'One more thing; where does Alec Jennings live?'

'Westlea estate, like most of my punters. This pub would have gone bust long ago if the Westlea hadn't been built.'

As they walked back to the car, Nash turned to Mironova. 'I've just remembered. That old soak Turner was supposed to have been in to make his statement. Give the station a bell and find out whether he's made it. If not, we'll go round via his house and drag him in.'

'Okay, but we might be better off going straight to the Horse and Jockey,' Mironova replied.

Turner hadn't made it to the station, nor was he at home or at the Horse and Jockey. Their informant was Mrs Turner.

Nash rang the bell of the small terrace cottage without response, so he knocked loudly on the door. As he was about to knock again, the door opened a few inches on its chain. One eye peered suspiciously out. 'Yes?'

'Mrs Turner?' Nash produced his warrant card. 'Is your husband at home?'

'No.' The door started to close, but Nash put his hand on it. 'Can you tell us where to find him?'

'What do you want him for? He's just a harmless old drunk.'

'If you open the door, I'll explain.'

There was a pause, then the chain rattled and the door swung half open. 'Well?'

Mrs Turner was angular with a thin, scrawny body, pointed face, hair greying into a dirty off-white. Her mouth was a thin, tightly compressed line, turned down in the corners into an expression of permanent disapproval. The brown frames of her glasses housed lenses liberally smeared with grease.

She was wearing a white, lace-edged blouse buttoned tightly up to the neck, over which was a hand-knitted cardigan of vivid blue, the buttons of which had been pushed through the wrong buttonholes. That, and the cardigan being two sizes too big, gave her a lop-sided appearance. A skirt of startling floral pattern hung below her knees. Her matchstick-thin legs were encased in thick lisle stockings and her feet in tartan carpet slippers.

As she spoke, Mironova was fascinated to see the cigarette in the corner of Mrs Turner's mouth bobbing up and down in time with the words, like a conductor's baton. 'What do the police want with Turner?'

Nash explained.

Mrs Turner sniffed derisively. 'It'll be the first time in living memory he's done owt useful. If he's not in T'Horse and Jockey pissing his pension against the wall, he'll be up at his allotment pretending to be gardening. Gardening,' the repeat was a snort. 'That means knocking back cans of ale.'

She was about to close the door, when Nash asked, 'Where is his allotment?'

'Is it up by Westlea estate?' Mironova asked.

'Yes, you'll find him up there with all his boozing cronies. Much good it'll do you.' The door slammed shut.

'I'll tell you what, Mike, I'm no advocate of people drinking, but you can understand why Turner does.'

Nash nodded, his face straight. 'That's true. It also goes a long way to explaining why he fancies you.'

The allotment came as something of a surprise. Nash parked at the end of the broad track leading through the middle of the gardens. An old man was sitting by a shed at the front of the second plot smoking a pipe and reading the morning paper.

'Excuse me,' Nash called out. 'Do you know which allotment Mr Turner has?'

The old man lowered the tabloid and considered the matter. He took his pipe from his mouth and replied, 'Aye, I do.'

Nash smiled at the old man's little jest. 'Would you mind sharing that information with us?'

The ancient relented. He'd had his bit of fun. 'Last one on this side, you can't miss it. It's the biggest. Jonas might be in his shed, potting on tomato plants. Be careful though, I'd call out for him before you go rushing in if I was you,' he ended cryptically.

They walked down the row of neatly tended gardens. As the old man had predicted, there was no sign of Turner. They stared at the allotment in silence. They'd expected a wilderness with Turner sitting by the shed surrounded by empty cans.

Instead, there were neat rows of potato plants, carefully earthed up. Symmetrical square patches containing onion sets, young cabbage and cauliflower plants, rows of carrots and parsnips as straight as a line of guardsmen, and canes supporting scarlet and white runner beans.

Mironova read the sign on the gate, 'Beware of the goose' and frowned. 'What do you think that is, Turner's idea of a joke?'

She opened it and stepped through. There was a sudden flurry of movement, a hissing, a flapping sound, and a yelp of pain from Clara. She leapt back through the gate and slammed it behind her.

A bright beady eye regarded her balefully through the mesh fence. The goose had emerged from the protective cover of a rhubarb patch alongside the gate. 'Now you know,' Nash said, trying unsuccessfully to keep a straight face.

'It's not funny, it damned well hurt.' She examined the wound. 'Look, the sodding thing's drawn blood.' She cast a venomous glance at the goose and hissed, 'Christmas dinner.' The noise had alerted Turner, who emerged from his shed and was walking down the path. 'Did you know there's a law against keeping dangerous animals?' Clara snarled spitefully.

'Aye, and did you know there's a law against trespassing,' Turner smiled dourly. He pointed to the gate and added sarcastically, 'You must tell me which part of the notice you didn't understand.'

Nash was intrigued. It was clear from both Turner's speech and demeanour that he was stone cold sober. Everything about him was at odds with Mrs Turner's portrayal. Nash gestured to the allotment. 'This is a bit different from what we expected, especially after what your wife told us.'

All trace of humour vanished from Turner's face. 'Oh, you've met the old b … you've met her, have you?'

'She seemed to think you'd be sprawled out legless by this time.'

'Aye, well that's what I want her to think. This place is a good little earner. I don't want her getting her hands on the money to waste it playing bingo with all the other old biddies. I've a mate has a mobile greengrocery van. He goes round the villages; I supply a lot of his stuff. As well as the money I get from it, the allotment keeps me out of her way.'

'You don't enjoy being at home, then?'

'You've met the old bitch, haven't you? I reckon if I'd to spend all day at home, you'd have another murder to solve.' Turner's eyes sparkled dangerously at the pleasurable thought.

'You weren't as sober as this yesterday,' Mironova stated bluntly.

'Aye, well, it was market day and my day off. Would you like to have a look round? Then you can give me a lift to the station and I'll do that statement for you. That's why you're here, isn't it?' He saw the doubtful look on Clara's face and added, 'Don't worry, Sergeant Miniver, Esmerelda won't harm you if you're with me.'

'Esmerelda?' Mironova had never heard the name before.

'Pantomime,' Nash told her. 'Esmerelda's the goose that lays the golden egg.'

'That's right, and there's the reason Esmerelda attacked you,' he pointed to the line of eight goslings clustered round Mother Goose. 'They'll fetch between forty-five and fifty pounds each come Christmas.'

Before Turner signed his statement, he told Nash, 'You asked me what time it was when I saw the car on Friday night.' Nash nodded. 'Well, as I was walking to the allotment this morning, I was passing the church, and the clock was striking. That's what reminded me. As I came out of the pub I was talking to Barry, when I heard the chimes of the church clock. I thought "Ayup that's two o'clock". I reckon by the time I got to the alleyway it'd be about ten past,' Turner grinned, 'given that I wasn't exactly walking in a straight line.'

'Thank you for coming forward, Mr Turner. You've been very helpful.'

When Mironova had seen Turner out of the station, resisting his offer to join him for a pint at The Horse and Jockey, she returned to find Nash, who told her, 'I'd best get off. I'm taking an hour off. I'm going to look at a flat.'

'Which estate agent?'

'Helmsdale Properties.'

'I'm sure Helen Tate will be delighted to show you all she's got.'

The search parties had just changed shift, returning after another fruitless day. Nash fought his way through the mass of bodies in the reception area. The CID suite was also crowded with a contingent from Netherdale. Tom Pratt was receiving reports from the search leaders and Sergeant Jack Binns was fielding phone calls. Nash pointed to his office and Clara followed him in. 'How did the flat hunting go? Did Helen Tate have what you wanted?' Clara's face was a mask of innocence.

'They've nothing suitable on their books. I'll try some of the other agents when I get chance.'

Binns poked his head round the door. 'Sorry to disturb you, Mike, but I've got our WPC from Mrs Kelly's house on the phone. Apparently there's a horde of reporters camped outside the house and they keep shouting questions through the letter box. Mrs Kelly's quite distressed, and they're ignoring our officer.'

'That's the last thing she needs. They're like bloody vultures at times like this. Clara, nip round and clear them out. Take Jack with you. Give them the hard word. Let them know our officer on site will be reporting back.'

Pratt and Nash discussed plans for the following day, which would follow broadly the same pattern as the past two, with the addition of a media conference regarding Sarah's disappearance. 'I'll hang on for Clara, then I've got to attend the Lizzie Barton post-mortem,' Nash told him.

When Clara and Jack returned from the Kelly house they both looked subdued. 'How is she, Clara?'

'Bad doesn't begin to describe it, Mike. The longer it goes on without news, the worse the torment gets.'

Binns agreed, 'That's the hardest part of our job, dealing with the relatives at a time like this. But I don't think we'll be having any more problems from the press.'

'Thanks for your help, Jack. I'm sure Clara will reward you with a cuppa. I'm off to see Mexican Pete, but I'll call in when I get back into town, see if there's been any developments before we call it a day.'

The autopsy on Lizzie Barton yielded little new information. Ramirez proved much more forthcoming than he had been on the phone. 'She seems to be in generally good health,' adding with a flash of macabre humour, 'except that she's dead. She died, as I've no doubt you've guessed, from a stab wound to the chest. You'll no doubt have also deduced that the murder weapon was the same one forensics removed from her body.'

'Can you tell me anything I don't already know?' Nash asked a trifle sarcastically.

'I can tell you from the stomach contents and preliminary tests on her internal organs, that on the morning of her death she ate toast and butter and drank coffee. The previous evening she ate something that was composed largely of minced meat and cheese, probably lasagne. No doubt the fact that she last ate breakfast tallies with the time of death. Somewhere between noon and 2 p.m. yesterday.' A brief smile flitted over Ramirez's face. 'But then you probably knew that as well. The deceased was slightly over the age of forty. She was sexually active and, from the condition of the vagina, I would suggest very sexually active. She had given birth not once but several times. Not recently and she was not pregnant.'

'Anything else I should know?'

Ramirez paused, looking at the corpse. Nash waited uncomfortably. He detested mortuaries and the memories they brought back. If he never entered another one, he'd be less than unhappy. It wasn't that he was particularly squeamish, but the heavy chemical smells seemed to linger for days after each visit. Even they weren't as bad as other odours associated with the post-mortem process.

When Mexican Pete eventually replied, his tone was guarded and he chose his words with great care. 'There are one or two indications that may point to a certain medical condition. If that's the case, it may have relevance to your enquiry, but I'm afraid you'll have to wait on the results of further tests.'

'How long will those take?'

'That's out of my hands; a few days at least. The laboratories have a tendency to prioritize their work in favour of the living.'

'I thought there was a Home Office laboratory?'

Ramirez sighed, 'Keeping a laboratory staffed for this area wasn't considered viable.' Ramirez laid a heavy sarcastic accent on the last word. 'I'm afraid that medicine, like police work, is now controlled by accountants.'

'Tell me about it,' Nash said with feeling. 'You'll let me know the minute you have those results?'

'Naturally.'

'If that's everything, I'll be off back to the station. Good night, Professor.' Nash didn't offer to shake hands. It's an unwritten rule amongst police officers that you never shake hands with a pathologist. Especially one who's just completed a post-mortem and is still wearing surgical gloves.

CHAPTER SEVEN

Lee Machin wasn't the most popular character on the Westlea estate. In his late teens he'd formed the habit of loitering close to the vicinity of the school and children's playground. When his presence became a source of disquiet to local mothers, a few of their menfolk had what is euphemistically called 'a quiet word'.

He had other unacceptable traits; his use of controlled substances was one. The other a tendency to carelessness in the manner of his dress, to the extent that certain parts of his anatomy became visible. Curiously, this only seemed to occur when young girls were in Lee's immediate vicinity. On more than one occasion, Lee had appeared bearing the marks of a little rough justice, meted out by an irate elder brother or parent.

When Lee left Helmsdale Secondary School, not entirely of his own volition, a number of former pupils were more than a little surprised to learn that Lee had taken up with a woman on the estate. Karen Thomas may have been several years Lee's senior, but she looked younger. She was slim, wafer-thin almost. This, together with her baby face and short-cropped hair, made her appear barely to have reached the age of consent. Certainly far too young to have a nine-year-old daughter.

Karen hadn't been below the age of consent when she conceived Emily, the product of a rash romantic impulse. An impulse instantly regretted. Never to be forgotten. The father had long been forgotten. Her memory was not helped by the partiality she shared with Lee for a variety of the drugs readily available in the area.

The couple lived in a fair degree of squalor, in a tiny flat on the extreme northern edge of the estate, their existence, for the most part, dependant on 'the social'.

Lee's contribution was by no means dependable. It relied on him obtaining money by whatever means he could, usually illicit. Both he and Karen were known to the police. Both had a string of convictions. Their offences included possession of drugs, shoplifting and, in Lee's case, an instance of petty theft that had tried the patience of the local magistrates too far. As a consequence, Lee had spent six months in prison. If the magistrates hoped this would teach him a hard lesson, they were right. It taught him to be more careful.

Karen, who was more the specialist shoplifter than Lee, narrowly escaped a similar fate on the occasion of her last court appearance. Following Lee's release, the couple decided they needed a more reliable income. The responsibility fell on Lee. The search for a suitable job proved no easy task, but in time he landed one he was actually rather good at. The pay wasn't lavish, but provided the opportunity for a lucrative sideline.

The couple's fortunes definitely seemed to be on the up. Emily began to wear clothes that had actually been bought. She'd had to wait until Lee and Karen had bought their new clothing and certain essential electrical items first.

It was around dusk, as Mike Nash was en route from the post-mortem to Helmsdale. One of Lee and Karen's neighbours, who was returning from an after-work session in the local, crossed the waste land at the back of the estate. Designated as playing fields, it had never been utilized as such. The perimeter was fringed with shrubs and bushes. Left unchecked, they'd grown into a thick, unruly mass. Only the hardy souls determined to cut half a mile off their walk home kept a couple of gaps open.

The returning reveller stared at the base of a bush close to one of these openings as he was about to step through. He blinked in surprise. There was something protruding from the base of the bush. It was a pair of feet.

Staggering slightly, as much from the uneven ground as the effects of the alcohol, he reached down and parted the leaves. Lee Machin was lying face upwards, unconscious. His face badly battered and covered in blood, his left arm at an unnatural angle. The man stared. He tried attracting Lee's attention by kicking him gently. Getting no response the man did an uncharacteristic thing, possibly as a result of the amount of drink he'd consumed. He went home and rang for an ambulance and the police.

When Nash arrived back at Helmsdale, the station was almost deserted. All the officers assisting in the search for Sarah had departed. Mironova too was absent, and when Nash entered the CID office only Pearce was there, poring over paperwork.

'Where is everybody?' Nash was marginally surprised until he glanced at the wall clock. 'I didn't realize it was as late as that.'

'I've a couple of messages. Superintendent Pratt said to let you know he'll be here first thing tomorrow. Mrs Kelly rang too. She's prepared to go in front of the cameras. Poor woman sounded desperate, but I suppose that's to be expected. Finally, I've a message from Clara. Some bloke off the Westlea's been badly beaten up. Found unconscious on some waste ground.'

'We'll have to wait until she rings in to find out what the score is on that one. How have you got on?'

'I'm just finishing sorting the rest of the files from the PNC. It's taken most of the day to sift through everything. I'm surprised how many villains we have on our patch. Some of them are quite heavy too. We've a couple of convicted murderers, three rapists and several paedophiles. There are any number of drug dealers and a whole raft of minor criminals too.'

'Good work, Viv.' A thought struck him as he turned away. 'Tell me, did Roland Bailey feature in any of the files?'

Pearce shook his head. 'Clara reminded me to keep a lookout for him. It looks as if you'd have lost your bet.'

'You surprise me. I'll phone Clara. See if I can find out what's going on at Westlea, then I'll get us some coffee.'

Nash was unable to raise Clara and assumed she'd be at the hospital. As they drank their coffee he told Viv the results, or lack of them, from the post-mortem. 'I think we should pull this character Alec Jennings in for questioning. He's the most recent intimate connection.'

'Yes, and he lives on Westlea not far from where the bloke was attacked tonight.'

'I wonder if there's a connection? Tell you what, we'll schedule Jennings for a chat tomorrow. Do you know where he works?'

'Yep,' Pearce paused. 'How strongly do you believe in coincidence?'

'Go on, surprise me again.'

'Alec Jennings works on the late shift at Rushton Engineering.'

'Now that is a coincidence.' Nash frowned, 'I don't remember a Jennings when I interviewed them yesterday.'

'That's because he wasn't at work. I spoke to the MD. Jennings rang in sick late morning yesterday, about an hour before he was due at work. I asked if he went absent often. The MD said it was most unusual. Jennings is one of their more reliable workers.'

'That sounds dodgy. I don't suppose Jennings was the bloke who was attacked tonight, by any chance?'

'I've no idea. From the description I heard, he'd been beaten almost beyond recognition. We'll have to wait for Clara.'

It was after 10 p.m. when Mironova telephoned. 'I'm at Netherdale Hospital,' she told Nash.

'What do you know?'

'His name's Lee Machin, early twenties, lives on the estate. He's been well done over, but the injuries aren't life threatening. Looks like a punishment beating. His face is a mess, virtually unrecognizable. His partner Karen only knew him by the shirt he was wearing. She's with him here, but she's well nigh hysterical. His arm's broken and he's got several cracked ribs. It looks as if someone worked him over with an iron bar or something similar.'

'Do we know him?'

'Oh yes. He's a regular in front of the magistrates. Not recently, though. Last time he got six months for theft and possession. He's been out eighteen months or so, kept out of trouble since then.'

'Those injuries don't sound like he was keeping out of trouble.'

'True. We know his partner as well. Karen Thomas. She's got form. Her speciality's shoplifting. Nothing custodial, but it was close on her last outing. She's also steered clear of us recently. One other thing; they're users, but no one's ever suggested either of them was a dealer.'

'Do you reckon drugs might be behind the attack? Or might it be linked to the Barton murder?'

'No idea. There's not much more I can do tonight. I'll set off back.'

'No, get yourself off home. I'll see you in the morning,' he replaced the phone. 'Come on, Viv, home.'

Nash ate a quick meal of pasta. He loved cooking, but tonight it was far too late to think about it and he still had work to do.

It was only later, when he was reading the paperwork Pearce had given him, that Nash gave any thought to a remark he'd heard earlier. He tried to figure out whether it had been merely a platitude, or whether there was some significance behind the statement. He resolved to find out the following morning. He downed the remainder of the tin of beer he'd allowed himself and headed off to bed, so weary that he almost forgot to take his medication.

'Morning Jack. Before you get started on anything, could I have a word?'

'What's the problem, Mike?'

'It was something you said yesterday; I didn't pick up on it at the time. When you were talking about the effect on relatives, it sounded almost as if you were speaking from experience?'

Binns's cheerful expression clouded over. 'Yes, I'm afraid so.'

'Care to tell me about it?'

Fifteen minutes later, Nash called Pearce and explained what he wanted. 'I want you to make this your number one priority. Get all the help you need. I want the information on my desk by this evening.'

Nash passed the DC a piece of paper. 'Start with this name and work backward and forward from there. I've written some parameters, so hopefully you won't pick up too many false leads.'

'Do you want me to restrict the search geographically? I mean, within North Yorkshire?'

Nash thought about it for a moment or two. He was never sure what prompted his decision. 'No, Viv. Don't put so tight a limit on it; try the whole of northern England.'

Clara entered as Viv was leaving. 'Here's my report on Machin. I'll make coffee whilst you're reading it. Superintendent Pratt's outside, he's planning the media conference, with Mrs Kelly on display. He wants us there to hold her hand, so to speak.'

'Yes, I got the message last night. I'll read your report now, but make the coffee strong please, Clara, and none of that decaffeinated muck either. I need as much caffeine as you can pack into a mug. It might keep me awake until lunchtime.'

'What's tiring you? Work, or your hyperactive social life?'

Nash smiled ruefully. 'I wish it was the social life. Last night I was up until the early hours reading Viv's reports. There's plenty for us to look into, but I'll be surprised if any of the villains on that list are in the frame for the Sarah Kelly abduction.'

'You're still convinced it's an abduction?'

'I am. I've no solid evidence, but I can't see any other explanation.'

'If it's intuition, Mike, I'd back you to be right. It may be more difficult persuading others, but you've been right too often to bet against you.'

Nash glanced at his watch; it was 8.15 a.m. 'Did Viv tell you I want Jennings pulled in for questioning? After you've had your coffee, go get him. Take a uniform with you.'

Nash was reading the final sentence of Mironova's report when Pratt walked in. 'Morning, Mike, how're you? Been on the nest? You look terrible.'

'No such luck. Just a late night,' he said tersely. 'Nothing to worry about, as long as Viv doesn't keep giving me bedtime reading.'

'That's why you're in early then. What about Mironova and Pearce? Is insomnia catching round here?'

'Things have moved on. We've got a suspect in the Lizzie Barton murder. Clara's off to pull him in. I'm hoping to get to speak to him before the press conference. He works at Rushton Engineering.' Pratt raised his eyebrows, acknowledging the connection. 'I've got Pearce following up something else in connection with the Sarah Kelly disappearance. In addition, we had a serious assault on the Westlea last night.' Nash detailed the attack on Lee Machin.

'I remember when you were transferred here. I told you Helmsdale's normally a sleepy little market town.'

'I remember,' Nash said with a grim smile. 'Every time we have a serious crime your words come back to haunt me.'

'I want you to run the media conference today. It's scheduled for two o'clock this afternoon. That way, we get it on tonight's local news bulletins, and in tomorrow morning's papers.'

Nash's first impression of the suspect was his air of mild protestation. It was an understated expression of innocence and injustice, but it was there nevertheless. 'What's this got to do with me?' Jennings appeared to be saying.

Jack Binns switched on the tape machine. 'I expect you're wondering why you're here? It's in connection with the murder of Lizzie Barton. I understand you knew her?'

Jennings looked mildly surprised. He cleared his throat. 'A bit, she used to drink in The Cock and Bottle.'

'She did, and that's where her body was found. But I understand your friendship was a little more than just a bar-room acquaintanceship.'

'Everyone in the pub knew her,' Jennings stated vaguely.

'Come on, Jennings, you knew her rather better than most.'

'Maybe.'

'Let me put it another way. You were poking Lizzie left, right and centre. Is that blunt enough for you?'

Jennings shifted uncomfortably in his chair. 'Yes, well, but that was a long time ago. Just a bit of harmless fun. No great romance.'

'When did this "bit of harmless fun" come to an end?'

'About a year ago.'

'Was it your idea to end it, or hers?'

'Mine, I suppose.'

'Why was that?'

'I got bored.'

'Don't give me that. A bloody attractive woman, in an affair you've admitted you were both enjoying so much you couldn't keep your hands off her. You were even seen against the wall in the back yard of the pub. Despite that, you expect me to believe you "got bored". Try again.'

'Well, maybe it was Lizzie, I don't remember.'

'Why would she? She liked sex, she obviously liked you, had no other commitments. Sorry, Jennings, that's just rubbish. Perhaps the real reason is your girlfriend came back and insisted. Isn't that it?'

'I suppose so,' Jennings muttered.

'Then why didn't you tell me that earlier?'

Jennings became more assertive. 'Look, this has nothing to do with Cindy, nothing at all, right?'

'I didn't suggest it had. Can't have been easy. It must have been tempting, seeing Lizzie in the pub regularly, maybe sharing a drink, a joke. Were you never tempted to rekindle things, you know, just a little fling for old times' sake?'

Jennings's face was redder than at any time during the interview. Nash noticed the ring of sweat under each armpit. 'No, I didn't.'

'Come off it, Jennings. I bet you and she got up to some real antics together. I bet you wanted to do it again. In fact, you did. What if I was to tell you I've a witness who saw you together within the last twelve months?'

The bluff worked.

'Well, maybe I did see her once or twice. That was months ago. Not a crime, is it?'

'Your girlfriend might argue that point. Did Cindy find out?'

'No, she didn't know anything about it.'

'But she knew you'd been with Lizzie whilst she was away?'

'Yes, she knew that.'

'Did Lizzie threaten you? Threaten to tell Cindy everything?'

'No, she didn't.' Jennings sounded almost outraged. 'Lizzie wouldn't do anything so mean.'

'When did you hear she'd been murdered?'

'I heard it on the radio yesterday.'

Nash switched tack suddenly. 'Why weren't you at work on Tuesday?'

'I wasn't well.'

'That's quite a coincidence. On Tuesday you just happen to be feeling unwell when the police are at Rushton's making enquiries about Sarah Kelly. On the day Lizzie Barton was murdered. Don't you think that's a strange coincidence?'

Jennings shrugged his shoulders.

'You see, I don't believe in coincidences. What I do believe is that you deliberately failed to turn up for work, because you knew we'd be there. My problem is trying to decide the reason for you keeping out of our way.' Nash leant forwards, directing his gaze straight at Jennings. 'Was it to avoid questions about Sarah Kelly's disappearance? Or was it Lizzie Barton's murder? Which was it?'

Jennings was now becoming very fidgety. 'I told you, I wasn't well.'

'Okay, so you weren't at work and you weren't at the pub. Where exactly were you, when Lizzie Barton was murdered?'

'I was at home.'

'Really; how do you know?'

'I don't understand.'

'Let me explain. I vetted the media statements and made sure no time was mentioned, either for the murder or the discovery of the body. So how come you know the time?'

Jennings kept his eyes fixed on the table in front of him. 'I didn't know … I assumed … I was at home all day,' he stammered unconvincingly.

'Anyone confirm that?'

'Cindy was there.'

'All the time?'

'Except for an hour or so, she went shopping.'

'What time was that?'

'I don't know, round lunchtime, about half past twelve.'

'Now that's bad news. The only time you've no alibi for is the time when the murder was committed. Where were you last Friday night?'

Jennings was completely baffled by the switch in the line of questioning. Eventually he answered. 'I was at work. Then I went to the pub for the last hour before I went home.'

'You weren't tempted to go on to a nightclub? Club Wolfgang, for example?'

Jennings looked up in confusion. 'No, why should I?'

The answer was lame, unconvincing. 'Well, you're obviously a ladies man. We already know you're capable of running a girlfriend and a mistress. It's only natural to want another scalp on your belt. A very attractive, bright young girl would be something to brag to your mates about. A girl like Sarah Kelly for instance?'

Jennings stuttered, the words coming out in a rush. 'Look, I knew Sarah at work. She's a damned nice girl. That's all. I never met her outside work. I'm sorry she's disappeared. I hope she turns up safe and well.'

Again Nash fixed Jennings with a penetrating stare. 'How well do you know Club Wolfgang?'

'I've been in a couple of times, that's all.'

'I realized you didn't know it well,' Nash's tone was conversational. 'If you had, you'd have known about the CCTV cameras.' Nash was trying another bluff.

Jennings looked up in alarm. The stammer worsened, 'CCTV, what cameras? I didn't—'

'The CCTV camera that shows you quite clearly, close to the bar last Friday night, talking to Sarah Kelly. And the one that shows you leaving the club only minutes before Sarah. And that image of Sarah leaving is the last before she disappeared.'

Nash didn't need to check Jennings's armpits. Sweat had broken out on the man's forehead. 'I spoke to Sarah, that's all. Only a few words. I didn't see her again after I bumped into her by the bar. I didn't see her leave, didn't know anything about her disappearance until I saw it on telly.'

'What did you talk about?'

'She asked me about Cindy. How she was, if I was looking forward to being a father. That's all, I swear it.'

'Okay, that'll do. I must warn you I'm not satisfied with some of your answers. I'll probably want to talk to you again. Interview terminated at 09.55 hours.'

When they were alone, Binns asked, 'Do you think Jennings had something to do with Sarah Kelly's disappearance?'

'Not sure, Jack, I'm not ruling it out. In fact, I'm not ruling anything out. One thing I am sure of, Alec Jennings knows a hell of a lot more about Lizzie Barton's murder than he's told us.'

CHAPTER EIGHT

When Nash escorted Joan Kelly into the Station to face the media, he was shocked by her appearance. During the days her daughter had been missing Joan seemed to have aged twenty years. She looked gaunt and ill, would have had difficulty passing for under sixty. Her face was devoid of colour, her eyes like empty sockets, red-rimmed from constant crying. Her posture and body language spoke volumes for her state of mind.

Nash felt a powerless rage at his inability to bring her any comfort. How much worse would it be if his theory was proved correct? He felt weary and knew it had nothing to do with either lack of sleep or his work load. This was down to the crime he had to solve and the possible outcome.

The conference was a low-key affair. No barrage of questions, no constant camera flashing. In the Helmsdale reception area, Mike, DS Mironova and Pearce faced three local reporters, a couple of correspondents from local radio stations and two TV crews. Their only exhibits were a photograph of the missing girl and the handbag.

Invited to speculate on Sarah's fate, Mike merely expressed the police's mounting concern and appealed for anyone with information to come forward. Incident phone numbers were displayed for the cameras and read out for the benefit of radio listeners; then it was Joan Kelly's turn. Her appeal to anyone who had information about Sarah was spoken in a low, disjointed voice. Her short statement was moving, her obvious distress and her haggard expression guaranteed to tug at the heartstrings of any viewers. There were one or two questions, but from the reporters' muted tones Nash could tell they too were affected by the trauma of the woman's situation. Soon, it was all over.

Afterwards, he escorted Mrs Kelly to the car that was to take her home. His final view of Joan Kelly through the car window was of her face, ravaged by grief and with tears coursing copiously down her cheeks. It was a vision that would haunt him for a long time to come.

He entered the CID room, to see Pearce waving from the computer desk. 'Problem, boss.'

'What is it?'

'The intranet link that gives us access to PNC information you asked for is down. I've called the IT boys. Their engineers are all tied up with a major installation elsewhere. They didn't sound hopeful for today.'

'That's a bloody nuisance, to put it mildly. I'll ask Tom to lean on somebody. Just because we're a rural outfit doesn't mean we don't have urgent need of a computer link. While we're waiting, go to the hospital and see Machin.'

When Viv returned, he stated flatly, 'Machin's recovered consciousness. That's about the only positive news I can give you. He's dosed up with painkillers, which doesn't exactly help, but he's extremely cagy about talking to us. Not unusual for someone from the Westlea, but in this case I reckon there's more to it than natural aversion to the police.'

'Any idea what?'

'I got the impression he knows who attacked him. He seems scared. I'm fairly sure if we press him hard enough, he'll tell us what's behind it.'

Nash thought for a few moments. 'Thanks, Viv. Tomorrow morning Clara and I will visit his partner. She might give us a lever to prise something out of him.'

The phone rang. 'Mike, I've been on to the IT people and I'm afraid we've got a major problem. They were under the impression it was just a local fault, because nobody else had reported trouble with the system. Now it seems it's nationwide, they've got to trace the problem. The earliest expectation is two to three days before they get it up and running. The guy I was talking to said they've had a fair amount of verbal from other forces.'

'We could do without this,' Nash muttered.

'What exactly were you looking for? I thought you'd pulled the relevant information already?'

'Maybe, maybe not. It was more to do with a hunch. There may be nothing in it but I don't believe we should take that chance.' Nash explained his theory.

'If you're right, and I'm not saying I'm buying into it at this stage, then you can't afford to wait a minute longer than necessary. I'll chase the IT people again. If needs be, I'll get the Chief involved. She'll put a bomb under their backsides.'

'Thanks, Tom. Tomorrow morning, Clara and I are going to visit the woman whose partner was beaten up. Then we must concentrate on the Barton murder. I'm still waiting for some test results from Mexican Pete. I don't know why, but I got the impression from what he said that they might be important.'

'Anything else?'

'Not for today, Tom. I'm going to finish early tonight.'

'Anything special on? Hot date perhaps?'

Nash thought of Helen Tate's reaction at being referred to as a hot date. 'Don't you start. I've enough with Clara making sarcastic comments.'

Nash's night's rest was undisturbed. No bad dreams such as he'd experienced in the past came to haunt him. He'd been worried they would, as pressure from the cases mounted. He wondered if his medication had kept the nightmares at bay. He grinned to himself. More likely, it had been Helen Tate's demands that had exhausted him.

He and Mironova walked up the cracked concrete strip leading to Lee Machin's flat. However Karen Thomas spent her days, it was obvious that little of her time was devoted to housework. The lounge she reluctantly ushered them into was worse than untidy. The battered furniture was set at an angle to give the optimum view of the television. On a low circular coffee table with a long irregular crack in the glass top, two large ashtrays stood, the contents overflowing. A trio of empty lager bottles matched those on the mantel. A further pair peeped shyly from behind the curtains.

In sharp contrast, there was a large flat-screen digital TV with Sky box, Blu Ray, Wii, games consoles and an expensive-looking music system. A rich variety of odours assailed the visitors' nostrils. One glance at Karen was enough to tell Nash that however concerned she might be about her partner's condition, she'd not allowed her anxiety to interfere with one of her principal pleasures. Her eyes, when they were open at all, were glazed, unfocused, the pupils like pinpricks. Her walk was slightly unsteady, her speech marginally slurred, and she showed her visitors a rich variety of mood swings in the short time they were there. That was about twenty-five minutes, longer than any of the parties to the interview wanted. By the time they left, Nash had a very good idea why Machin had been attacked. Mironova had her suspicions, and Karen was still wondering what the point of the visit had been.

Nash's line of questioning kept Mironova guessing as to his objective until the very last minute. She felt the obscure nature of the questions would certainly be lost on Karen. 'You've been taking a bit on board, I see, Karen?' he began.

'Don't know what you mean.'

'You know very well what I mean. We're not concerned about your drugs habit, but if you want, we could turn the place over whilst we're here. You've been done for possession often enough for us to get a warrant easily.'

'Oh, isn't that just fucking brilliant. My Lee gets beaten up and are you lot worried about it? All you lot are interested in is doing me for drugs. Well, you can fuck off.'

Nash smiled. 'That isn't true, Karen. We do care about what's happened. That's why we're here. I'm just a bit puzzled. You see, I was told that Lee's on the dole and you're on the Social, so I wondered how you managed to afford the habit. It's not like buying twenty Benson & Hedges, is it? Good gear doesn't come cheap. So tell me how you do it. You're not exactly raking it in. I look round and I think, how do they manage? They've got all this expensive entertainment equipment, much better than mine.' Nash glanced at Mironova who suppressed an impulse to laugh, knowing Nash used TV purely to combat insomnia. 'And on top of that, here's Karen spaced out. So come on, let me into your secret. Is Lee dealing? Is that why he got worked over, a turf war?'

'No he fucking well isn't.' There was no doubt Karen's indignation was genuine. 'Trust you lot to think the worst. If you must know, Lee's got a part-time job.' Karen realized she'd said too much and burst into tears.

Nash reassured her. 'That's all right, Karen, don't worry about it. We won't pass the information along to the Social or the Job Centre. What's his part-time job? It must be well paid?' Karen remained mulishly silent, glaring at each of them in turn. 'Of course, I could always change my mind,' Nash said quietly when she showed no sign of cooperation. 'I'm sure they'd be very interested in a little matter of benefit fraud. Or is it something that you'd rather we didn't know about? Something worse than fiddling the benefit, perhaps?'

'It's all above board,' Karen snivelled. 'There's nothing illegal in it.'

'In that case, where's the harm in telling us?' Again she remained silent. 'Okay, if that's the way you want to play it. I tried to help,' Nash turned as if to walk out.

'Wait, wait,' Karen wailed.

'Yes?'

'I'll tell you. He's got a job as a projectionist. God, I swear he'll kill me when he finds out I've told you.'

'Why on earth should he? It all sounds perfectly legal and above board, just like you said, nothing to be ashamed of. One thing though, Netherdale cinema's closed for renovation.'

'He doesn't work at the cinema.' Karen's reluctant, sulky tone told them she was already regretting having said so much.

Nash smiled benignly. 'Of course not, the cinema would insist on him going on the payroll, paying tax, declaring the income. That would blow his benefit payments. So let me guess. Somewhere he gets paid cash in hand, no questions asked. Would that be the Gaiety Club by any chance?'

'What of it?' Karen's defiance returned. 'It's harmless enough. Just a load of dirty old men in brown raincoats, watching mucky films and wanking themselves silly.'

'As you say, harmless enough. Now you take care of yourself and your little girl. If whoever did that to Lee has a grudge, they might be tempted to take it out on you.'

'You wouldn't give a toss what happened to me,' Karen muttered. 'Just fuck off and leave us alone.'

As they negotiated the broken concrete, Nash smiled. 'So now we know why Lee was beaten up.'

'Sorry, you've lost me,' Clara confessed.

'Haven't you worked it out? You saw that living room. There must have been £5,000 worth of electrical equipment in that room, and she was wearing a pair of trainers that would have set them back over £100. You're not telling me Machin got that amount of cash working as a projectionist? There's no way they'd get credit, and in addition, he's able to fund their drugs habit. If that's all come by honestly, we should retrain as projectionists.'

'Okay, but I still don't see where the money's come from.'

'Look at it this way. Machin starts work at the Gaiety Club. He's up in the projection box night after night, watching the same trash. He gets bored, so what is there for him to do? He starts watching the customers. Whether he sees someone he recognizes or the idea just comes to him, it doesn't matter, but he dreams up a great idea for earning extra cash. I mean a lot of extra cash. The Gaiety Club's punters would be prepared to pay handsomely to have their dirty little habit kept secret. There could be councillors, vicars, local businessmen, even police officers among the members. So Lee shakes them down, a little here, a little there. The trouble is, people like Lee get greedy. Eventually, one of his victims gets tired of handing over increasingly large sums of money and sends someone along to teach him the error of his ways. Let's go visiting the sick.'

En route to the hospital, Nash got a call from Pearce. 'Mexican Pete's been trying to reach you. You're to phone him. And the tech lads have said they can't do any better with the video enhancement.'

'Thanks, Viv. We don't need it anyway; we know it was Jennings.' Nash dialled the pathologist's mobile.

'I've no time, I'm between lectures. I have the results of the haematology test. The deceased, Lizzie Barton, was HIV positive, probably contracted within the last eighteen months. Not yet noticeable physically, and she probably wasn't aware of the condition.'

The line went dead. Nash sat motionless for a long while, the dial tone droning unnoticed in his ear. He repeated what the pathologist had told him to Clara.

'Do you think that's relevant?'

'It might be more than relevant, it could be vital or it might mean nothing. I need time to think about it.'

Nash stared at the young man in the hospital bed. Machin's face was a mess. The only expression came from his eyes. Nash saw a curious mixture of fear and defiance. It was more the look of someone who'd committed a crime than a victim. Nash opted for a confrontational approach.

'You're in here because your dirty little scam backfired,' he told Machin bluntly. 'I'm not sure whether you tried to shake a punter down once too often, whether you demanded too much, or simply picked the wrong man. Nor do I care. As far as I'm concerned, you got what was coming. You can tell me the name of the man who was responsible for the attack or not. That's up to you. To be frank, I don't care either way.'

'I don't know what you're talking about.'

Nash looked at him wearily. 'In that case I'll spell it out. I'm talking about the dirty little scheme you dreamed up to blackmail customers of the Gaiety Club. You realized that by threatening them, you could get them to fork out sizeable sums in exchange for your silence. Some of them were no doubt in positions where membership of a club peddling hard porn would generate considerable interest.'

'I didn't do that.' His denial wasn't even remotely convincing.

'Oh give it up. You're not even a good liar. It didn't take much working out. We've just come from your place. I was particularly interested in all that flash electrical gear. There's no way you could have afforded that on what you're pulling in. And don't try feeding me any bullshit about a win on the horses or the lottery. I've heard it all before. I might take some interest if you tell me the name of the man responsible. Otherwise, I see no reason to waste any more time on a blackmailing little toerag like you. So, if you're going to talk, talk now; if not, I'm out of here.'

Nash signalled to Mironova, with a nod of his head towards the ward entrance. He was about to move away from the bedside, when he turned back. His tone changed. 'Do you know all the club's members?'

Machin looked wary, obviously suspecting another trap, but eventually answered, 'Most of them.'

'I mean by their real names. Not "John Smith", "Fred Brown", "Tom Jones" or whatever they sign in as.'

'I know most of them,' Machin admitted, his wariness compounded by perplexity.

'Were you working last Friday?'

'Yes?' Machin was now totally mystified.

'Do you know Roland Bailey?'

Machin tried to laugh, his bewilderment replaced by scorn. 'Friend of yours, is he? It figures.'

'I take it from that, you do know him?'

'Yes, I know him. He's a complete wanker.'

'Was Bailey in the club last Friday night?'

'No, not him. The stuff they were showing was far too soft for Bailey. He likes the real hard stuff. If it's got plenty of S & M in it, so much the better. Sits there in the dark and wanks away, imagines nobody can see him.'

'I want you to think this over very carefully. I need to be absolutely certain beyond any doubt that Roland Bailey wasn't in the Club at any time last Friday night.'

'I just said so, didn't I? There were only about a dozen punters all night, and Bailey wasn't one of them. Why, what's he done?'

'Never mind. If you change your mind and want to tell me who beat you up, call Helmsdale station.'

'Don't hold your fucking breath,' Machin called after them.

Mironova shook her head in disgust. 'So Bailey was lying about being at the Gaiety.'

'Yes, and if he was prepared to use a visit to the Gaiety Club as an alibi, what was he doing?'

'You mean, what's worse than watching blue movies in a porn house?'

'Exactly. We're going to have to pull Bailey in and talk to him again. In the meantime, I want to know if we've any news on that PNC link. I'll phone Tom, remind him we're going to the pub and the night club tonight, see if anyone remembers anything, although I reckon it's a long shot.'

Nash's call to Netherdale took only a few minutes. He put his mobile away and shook his head.

Clara watched him. 'Not bad news, Mike. I don't need it. Not only that, but I haven't eaten yet.'

'Sorry. Tom reckons the link won't be repaired until tomorrow. Then we can get Viv back working on it.'

'What exactly is he going to be looking for? You've never mentioned it. If I didn't know better, I'd think you were being secretive.'

Nash explained the theory behind the search. Clara's eyes widened with shock and astonishment. 'What made you think of that?'

'It was something Jack Binns said. When I mentioned the state Mrs Kelly was in. He said it was difficult dealing with bereaved relatives. Something in his voice, the way he said it, suggested he was speaking from experience. It stuck in my mind, and later I tackled him about it. Turns out he'd to deal with another missing girl case a year or two back. A girl called Megan Forrest, I think the name was. So I asked him for details, and right in the middle of what he was saying, he told me how much like Sarah Kelly the other girl was in appearance. That set me thinking. What if there was someone out there, a predator with a taste for a particular type of victim. A killer who selects his targets because of their looks.'

She sat in silence for several moments when he'd finished. When she eventually spoke, her voice was little more than a whisper, 'Dear God, Mike, I hope you're wrong.'

It was almost 7 p.m. when they reached The Red Dragon. The bar was no more than a quarter full. He ordered a round of drinks and joined the others at a table.

'We're a bit early to start with the photo parade, aren't we?' Pearce glanced around the sparsely populated bar. Nash followed his gaze. The Red Dragon was like many others he'd seen. From the red and blue patterned carpet, the dark wood balustrades separating the dining area from the bar, to the water-colour prints of Dales' scenery churned out in their thousands by unknown artists with indecipherable signatures. It was all depressingly familiar. Even the beer tasted more chemical than organic.

'It is a bit. We might as well grab something to eat. We'll not get chance later.' Over the meal they discussed strategy for the evening's work.

'Right, you two make a start. I'll sit here and watch the customers' reactions. If anyone starts getting fidgety or acting suspiciously we'll pull them over and have a chat.'

They worked methodically, starting with the drinkers before moving on to the diners in the alcoves and finally speaking to any newcomers who drifted in. By the end of the operation it was almost closing time. Although a few of the pub's clientele recognized Sarah's photo and a couple of them even remembered seeing her the previous week, the task yielded no fresh information.

They moved on to Club Wolfgang which was in the first storey of a building whose ground floor consisted of three shop units. Entrance to the club was via a door at the end of the building. As they climbed the stairs Nash paused. 'Have either of you checked the employees out on the PNC?'

'Yes, they're clear. We checked the pub staff and landlord as well,' Clara told him.

In a small reception area, the manager was acting as receptionist. The regular girl had flown to Majorca at teatime. Alongside the reception was one of the club's two bouncers. Nash explained the purpose of their visit and the manager promised to cooperate in whatever way he could.

Club Wolfgang would never class as a venue for a big night out. The club comprised one room, scarcely bigger than the bar they had just left. Into that space was crammed a DJ console, seating area with nine tables, tiny dance floor, and a bar about ten feet in length. The cramped, mildly claustrophobic effect was compounded by the low ceiling. Across this was strung a wide-meshed net interwoven with tiny, white, fairy lights that flashed on and off in a chaser pattern. Helmsdale itself was small scale, no reason to expect its solitary 'nightspot' to be any different. Nash stationed himself at one end of the bar whilst the other two prepared to adopt the same procedure as in the pub. The plan was amended, however, when the club's DJ suggested a halt in proceedings to explain to the punters what they needed. This ensured they didn't miss anyone and stopped them getting twitchy.

They were no more successful than they'd been at the pub. Pearce was left in the reception area to intercept any latecomers. 'Get away as soon as you can, Viv. Come in a bit later in the morning. Hopefully we'll be back on-line by then.'

Nash and Clara spent most of Saturday morning reviewing paperwork. Pearce came in to report progress, or lack of it. 'We've hit a few snags. To be honest, it's a right bloody mess. It'll be much later before we're through. What do you want me to do when I've finished?'

Nash looked at Clara. 'We've got to do it, Mike. What's more, we've got to work on that information the minute it's available. Whatever time of day or night that is. You know that, as well as I do.'

'What time do you think you'll be done, Viv?'

'Seven?' he shrugged. 'Eight o'clock maybe. The problem is—'

'Go on.'

'Well, I've promised to go out tonight, and I don't want to call off at the last minute.'

'Who is she?' Clara asked.

Pearce tapped the end of his nose.

'Okay, so I was being nosey. But who wouldn't be, with all my colleagues acting like tom cats on the prowl.'

'So, it'll be up to us, Clara,' Nash interjected hastily. 'I've an idea. If I nip off home early and cook us a meal, you can bring the computer printouts over when Viv's compiled them. That way we get something to eat before we start on them, and he can go meet his queen. That is, if you're alright with that arrangement.'

'Why not? Did you think it'd damage my reputation, being seen going into your place at night?'

'Sort of,' Nash admitted.

'I don't think people worry much about that sort of thing any more. Tell Romeo here to get a move on though. I don't fancy eating after midnight.' She noticed Nash masking a grin. 'What is it?'

'I was only thinking it might not damage your reputation but it would do mine the world of good.'

'Mike, the best advertising agency in the world couldn't do anything for your reputation.'

It was a few minutes after 9 p.m. when Nash's doorbell rang. She walked past him without a word and placed a document box on the chair. 'There are fourteen cases,' she stated flatly. 'I haven't looked at them. I thought that could wait. I'm starving. What have you got for me?'

'Chicken risotto.' He held up a bottle. 'Glass of wine?'

'Just one, I'm driving.' They ate in silence, aware of the task that lay ahead. When she'd finished, Clara pushed her plate away. 'If you ever get kicked out of the police force you could make a living as a chef.'

CHAPTER NINE

'Shall we start?' Nash cleared the dining table whilst Clara fetched the box.

'What are we looking for exactly?' She dug out the stack of Missing Persons documents, printed off and placed neatly in individual files by Viv.

'Anybody with no possible reason for going missing. Any similarities to the Sarah Kelly case, no matter how small.' Before he sat down, Nash refilled their glasses. Clara was already engrossed in the first file and didn't notice.

Pearce had arranged the folders chronologically. The first file Nash opened was dated 1991, eighteen years previously. He read the two-page report on Julie Cummings. The information was sparse, but contained some similarities. Julie was about the same age when she vanished. The home circumstances were similar, with a divorced father living a long distance away. There was no apparent reason for either girl to abscond. He turned to the photograph and, although the quality of the print wasn't brilliant, he saw she was blonde.

Thoughtfully, Mike turned to Clara. He gave brief details of the file he'd read. 'That was in Lincolnshire, though. What have you got?'

'This one's dated 1994 and it's from Northumberland. The name on the folder is Sue Blatchford. There's not a lot of hard information in here. The disappearance isn't explained.'

Nash opened another file, that regarding the disappearance of Danielle Canvey in 1998. This was an original file, much bulkier, and contained a far more detailed report. 'This one's local. Viv's obviously thought to dig it out from the records,' he told her. 'Listen to this, Clara. Danielle Canvey was walking home from the tennis club after a game of doubles with her twin sister Monique. The following morning a man exercising his dog discovered the unconscious body of Monique Canvey lying on the path near the cricket field. Monique had suffered severe head injuries, the result of a savage assault with some form of blunt instrument, most probably a lump hammer. Although she survived the attack, she spent several weeks in a coma. There's a note added much later that says she suffered complete amnesia covering the forty-eight hours prior to the assault and, following her recovery, her physical health was frail and her nerves equally fragile.'

Nash looked across the table. 'This is what the officer leading the enquiry wrote. "The sisters quarrelled bitterly in the weeks leading up to the incident. The cause was Danielle's accusation that Monique had stolen her boyfriend".' Nash slammed his palm on to the table. 'From that, the bloke deduced, without the slightest amount of circumstantial evidence, that Danielle attacked her twin sister. That she ran away through guilt and fear of the consequences of her act.'

Nash shook his head in anger and disbelief at such shoddy police work, at the sheer bungling incompetence surrounding the enquiry. 'Where did he think she went? There's a note to the effect that French police had been asked to check with Danielle's grandparents to see if the girl had turned up at her maternal family home. How the hell did he think she was going to get there?' Nash muttered. 'Dressed in tennis gear and without a passport? Not only that, but who takes a lump hammer to a tennis match?'

'Hang on a minute. Didn't Mrs Kelly say Sarah played tennis?'

'Yes, another link?' He put the file aside in disgust. 'I wish I'd been in Helmsdale then.'

'But these files are from long before you came. And in any case, most of them aren't even from around here. I'm still not certain why we're looking at them. There seems to be little to connect them.'

It was slow going but by now they each had a pile of files they felt had some slight connection. 'Tell me what you've got,' he pointed to the folder in front of Clara.

Clara turned to her file. 'This one's dated 2001.' As she picked the file up the page containing the photograph slid on to the table top.

Nash picked it up and glanced at it. 'That's come out of the Sue Blatchford file, I think.'

'No, it hasn't. The name's printed below it. It's Louise Harland, she lived in The Lake District. It's the one I'm about to read.'

Nash and Clara looked at one another. 'Get all the photos out of the files we think have similarities,' Nash instructed her, 'then put them alongside one another.'

Clara assembled all the photos, including one of the attack victim, Monique Canvey. Nash brought a picture of Sarah Kelly from his briefcase and laid it alongside. They studied the collection: eight photographs. Nash was breathing heavily as if he'd been running. Clara was almost hiccupping with distress.

'Oh no!' Nash could hardly speak.

'Mike, they're all....' Clara's sentence tailed off into incredulous silence. Viewed together, the likeness between them was startling. They stared at the photos for a long time, trying to control their agitated emotions. When Nash was somewhat calmer, he pulled an A4 pad from his briefcase. Slowly, methodically, he began dictating a precis of the information in each of the files, which Clara wrote on the pad. Then he included the details of Sarah Kelly. It was a slow, laborious process, but at the end of it they knew they hadn't been mistaken.

As he stared at the photographs and their analysis, Nash felt he was once again seated in that car, in the alleyway, waiting. Then outside a pub, a nightclub, a railway station, a tennis club. Waiting for a girl to appear. Not just any girl, but the girl. The girl he'd selected.

Nash was in no doubt. 'I'm sorry to say it, but it looks as if I'm right. There is a predator on the loose, Clara. A ruthless predator with an insatiable lust for a particular type of young woman. A killer with the capacity to plan, and execute, each abduction with meticulous care. A killer who leaves no evidence behind, not even a clue that the girls have been taken.'

'But they're all from such different locations, Mike. I don't see how it could have happened. How would he pick them? If these are all abductions, they surely can't have been opportunist crimes.'

'No, they were obviously all carefully planned, by someone who knew the victims' movements, knew their habits intimately. But as to how he knew that, I've no idea. I think we're only beginning to scratch the surface of this case.'

'Another thing I don't understand. What you're saying, what we've got to deduce from these files, is that the man we're after is a sex killer. A pervert with an uncontrollable lust. If that's the case, why is there such a gap between each of these cases? I don't believe he'd be able to contain his desire for so long.'

'No, I admit that has me baffled too.'

'And what you're saying, Mike,' Clara paused, 'what we've found out from these files means Sarah Kelly's his latest victim? You're saying Sarah Kelly's dead?'

'I'm afraid that's exactly what it means.'

Nash felt suddenly weary. This revelation confirmed their worst fears. 'That's enough for tonight. You'd better get off home.'

Clara pointed to her empty glass. 'How much wine have I had?'

Nash looked across into the kitchen at the worktop. Their first bottle was empty; the second was only half full. 'Oh hell! Three glasses I reckon.'

'That means I'm well over the limit.'

'I'll ring the station and get someone over to drive you home.'

'Thanks, Mike, but no thanks. The gossips would really love that.'

'What about a taxi?'

Clara gestured to the stack of files. 'After what I've been reading in there, I don't fancy getting into a car at this time of night with a stranger. Not even with a taxi sign on the roof. I think I'll camp out on your lounge sofa, if you don't mind.'

'Take the bed in the spare room.'

'I'd forgotten how big this place is. Are you sure?'

Mike showed her to the bedroom, pausing at the door. 'There's a robe on the back of the door if you need it. Good night, Clara.'

'Good night, Mike.'

He undressed swiftly and climbed into bed. It was only then he remembered he'd not taken his tablets. They were in the kitchen. He put his dressing gown on and went to retrieve them. It was a long time before sleep came. Their discoveries that evening had been disturbing.

'Hello Mike.'

He stared at her in admiration. 'God, you look lovely,' he told her before he could check the words.

She smiled. 'What, even lovelier than the rather tasty Sergeant with the strange name, asleep next door; probably dreaming of you.'

'How the hell do you know about Clara?'

She laughed aloud. 'I know everything about you, Mike.'

She was sitting on the chair in his room. Her lovely tanned legs crossed; one tennis shoe moving gently as she swung that leg. Her long, soft, blonde hair was held back by a headband, the strip of black material contrasting pleasantly with her hair. He stared at her in speechless admiration. 'I can even read your mind, Mike,' she told him.

'Thank you for the compliment. But I don't think photographs ever do one justice, do you?'

He was dumbfounded. She'd voiced his precise thoughts.

'Besides which, Mike,' she told him, her voice low, warm, slightly husky. 'I wanted to look my best for you.'

She gestured to the white top and tennis skirt. 'I put these on especially for you. I knew it was how you'd expect me to dress. I did it to please you, Mike, as a reward for not believing the lies about me. I had no one to tell until you came along. That other policeman wasn't interested in what had happened to me. But I knew you'd be different. You'd believe me. You do believe me, don't you?'

'I don't know what to believe.'

'Poor Mike. I must have come as such a shock to you, and you've so much worry, too. Perhaps this will help convince you,' she leapt to her feet and crossed the room with swift athletic grace. She bent over him and kissed him lightly on the lips.

Nash woke up suddenly and sat bolt upright in bed. He was panting as if he'd run a marathon. Sweat was streaming down his face and he felt ill. The bedside lamp was on. Had he switched it off after he got into bed or not? He couldn't be sure. He looked across the room to the chair. It was empty. He laid back down, waiting for his breathing to return to normal. The pillow was soaked in sweat.

A dream, a nightmare? 'Danielle?' he whispered half hopefully, half fearfully. 'Danielle.'

Was his imagination playing tricks? Was his mind becoming unhinged? For a fleeting second he thought he heard a sound, a faint sound. The sound of gently mocking laughter.

Nash wasn't certain whether he'd slept at all after the nightmare. By 7 a.m. he was wide awake. He rolled over and stared at the ceiling. He felt drained and exhausted, knew he'd be edgy all day. He threw the covers back. His limbs felt stiff and his joints ached. He paused alongside the chair and stared at it for a long time. He reached the door and stopped, remembering Clara. He looked around and located his dressing gown on the floor. He felt sure he'd dropped it on the chair last night. How had it got on the floor? Had it slipped off? What other explanation could there be? Nash's subconscious suggested one, but his brain rejected it. He put the robe on and headed for the kitchen.

'If you're making coffee, can I have one, please?' Clara sounded husky with the drowsiness of sleep as she followed him in.

'Of course.'

'Give me two minutes to dress and I'll join you.'

'Did you sleep alright?'

'Pretty well, until about 3 a.m. Then I heard you call out and that woke me up. After that I kept dozing off and waking up.'

'I'm sorry for disturbing you. I had a bad dream.'

'Was it about this case?' Clara saw the movement in his face and knew she was right.

'When did you start having dreams again?'

'Last night was the first.'

'Want to tell me?'

He described the vision he'd had of Danielle Canvey and what the girl had said.

Clara looked askance.

Nash smiled. 'You mean you don't dream about me?'

'No, Mike. It's you has the nightmares.'

'Are you going home before we head for the office?'

'I'll have to, although it'll make me late. I need a shower and a clean blouse.'

'I can manage both, if you want.' Nash saw Clara's eyebrows lift questioningly. 'I've still got some of Stella's clothes in my wardrobe. She was about the same size as you. Help yourself.'

'Oh! I don't know. I didn't realize you still had any. I thought you might have, you know, sent them to a charity shop or something?' She paused, uncertain. 'I could do it for you if you want, if it would make it easier?'

Nash ignored the offer. 'There are towels in the airing cupboard. The clothes are in the wardrobe next to the window. Will you want some breakfast?'

'Toast will do me.'

'Just as well, that's all there is. It'll be ready when you've showered.'

Over breakfast they discussed how to handle the new information. 'First we've to convince Tom we're not starting a wild goose chase. We'll set up a display in the Incident Room with all the girls' photos on it. Then we'll have to start digging for background on each case and, wherever possible, re-interviewing the relatives. Right, I'm off into the shower.'

He spent much longer than usual under the hot water, trying to ease some of his aches.

They left the flat a few minutes before 8 a.m. and arrived at Helmsdale police station ten minutes later. The CID suite was empty. Nash headed for the whiteboard that covered the end wall and took down the notices from it. Clara rummaged through the desk drawers until she found the items she was looking for and they set to work.

They'd just finished when Pearce walked in, followed by Pratt and Binns. The newcomers stopped inside the door, their eyes drawn inexorably to the display.

The chatter died away as they stared at Nash and Clara's handiwork. Pratt was first to recover. 'What's this, Mike?'

The tone of Pratt's voice and the grim cast of his features told Nash the question was all but rhetorical. 'This is the result of our research into the files Viv dug out,' he pointed to the photographs. 'All but one of these young women vanished without trace, from locations throughout northern England. The disappearances cover the last eighteen years. All the girls are, or rather were, blondes, with blue eyes and extremely attractive. They were all between eighteen and twenty-one years of age when they vanished.'

Nash walked over to the wall and pointed to the photograph at the far end of the line. 'This is the only survivor. Her name's Monique Canvey. She was beaten and left for dead when her twin sister was abducted. There's been neither sight nor sound of any of the other girls since they vanished. We must assume all of them were abducted and that Sarah Kelly is the seventh victim. I believe we're faced with a ruthless and highly efficient serial killer with a penchant for young blondes.' Nash paused and added the most unacceptable part of the equation. 'What's worse is we haven't a scrap of evidence as to his identity. Apart from the attack on Monique Canvey and the vague, unconfirmed evidence of one elderly man, there's nothing to show that a crime's been committed.'

The long silence that followed was broken by Binns. 'I remember Megan Forrest. That's the girl I told you about.'

'That's right,' Nash said. 'You compiled the initial report on her. If you hadn't mentioned dealing with distraught relatives, I wouldn't have linked the case with Sarah Kelly. Tell them what you told me.'

'She lived with her parents somewhere near Bishopton. She vanished on New Year's Eve, as I recall, just failed to arrive home. It was the next day when her parents came into the station at Netherdale. They'd taken it for granted she'd had too much to drink and stopped with one of her girlfriends. It was only when one of her mates rang they twigged something was wrong.'

'Can you remember what the parents were like?'

'They were a decent enough couple. In their mid forties I guess. They had a couple of younger children, I think. The father was a lorry driver or something similar. They'd only recently moved to Bishopton when it happened. Mrs Forrest was a mite on the hysterical side, but given the circumstances I didn't blame her.'

'What was CID's view?'

Binns snorted with derision. 'That was in Hardman's day. His only view on anything was through the bottom of an empty glass,' he paused before adding, 'and that would only be a fleeting glance before the barman refilled it. Hardman dismissed the whole thing as a young girl meeting a bloke her parents wouldn't approve of and running off with him. That, according to him, explained why she didn't get in touch. Simple solution: no work for CID to do. No paperwork to fill in, case closed, what's next? Nothing? Oh well, let's go for a pint,' Binns ended sarcastically.

'Thanks for the vote of confidence, Jack. Give us your thoughts on the Forrest case.'

'I passed it straight to CID when the girl failed to turn up. After that, I had very little to do with it. Apart from when Mrs Forrest came into the station to see what we were doing. They went to the pub, asked a few questions, routine stuff, but no more. It was pretty upsetting, because she always asked for me. I couldn't tell her CID were sitting on their fat arses and couldn't give a toss. I tried to get them to do something, but they weren't interested. I thought it extremely odd that the daughter hadn't got in touch. There was nothing dysfunctional about them. I'd say they were a normal, caring unit. But if someone wants to stay hidden badly enough, they can do it.' Binns pointed to the whiteboard. 'At the time we'd nothing like that to make us suspect a crime had been committed.'

'We still don't know for certain,' Pratt interjected. 'All Mike's done is given us a possible link, nothing stronger,' he held up a hand to still Nash's protest. 'I'm not saying I'm dismissing the idea. The point I'm making is we've no hard evidence.'

'That's true,' Nash conceded. 'I'm well aware of how tenuous the connection is. In a normal murder case, at least you have a body and possible witnesses. We have neither.'

'Where do we go from here?' Pearce's question was addressed to Nash rather than Tom Pratt.

'I was about to say I haven't a clue. Which was the case until Tom spoke just now,' Nash confessed. 'But something he's said has given me the germ of an idea.'

'Would you like to share it with us?' Pratt asked.

'It's what you said about a possible link,' Nash spoke slowly, gathering his thoughts as he went along, 'and that's the point. There has to be a connection. Assuming I'm right, the abductions were too well planned and executed for it to be chance. That means the killer identified his target beforehand. Would you agree on that?'

'It seems reasonable,' Pratt conceded.

'Then how?'

'Sorry, I'm not with you,' Pratt was baffled.

'How did the killer select his victims? Given that they lived in such different places. Some of them hundreds of miles apart. If we find that out, we find the killer, or at least something that will lead to him.'

'You mean there's something these girls had in common, apart from their looks?' Pearce queried.

'Exactly, and it could be the least important thing. It could be connected with their school, sports club, work, hobbies, anything. At some point, for whatever reason, their lives crossed that of the killer. It's that crossing point we need to establish. The reports we have are sketchy at best. We have to go back and examine their lives in minute detail.'

'What about computers?' Viv asked, 'You know, like chat rooms.'

'Don't think that's likely eighteen years ago,' Clara said. 'More like, oh, I don't know, dating agencies?'

There was a long silence as the others thought over what Nash had said. Then Pratt asked, voicing the doubts they all shared, 'What do you suggest we do? In this case, for example,' he pointed to Julie Cummings's photograph. 'She vanished eighteen years ago. What are we going to find out about her now that couldn't have been found out at the time?'

'Good point, but we have one advantage. Two in fact, because we know we're investigating a possible crime. Because of that, we're not looking at Julie's life in isolation; we'll be comparing it with the others. We have seven lives to investigate. Something should provide us with the link.'

After a long while Tom spoke. 'Okay, I agree. Strictly between these four walls, I'm officially designating this as a murder enquiry. The investigation will be headed by Mike. Anyone have any questions?'

There was another long silence before Pratt continued, 'Right, Mike, it's all yours. Where do you want to start?'

'Would you mind supervising the search parties again, Tom?'

'Do you think it worth continuing, given the new facts?'

'That's your call, Tom. If we're right, the search will be a waste of time. The bodies of the other six haven't turned up, and we've no reason to suppose Sarah's will. A search will divert valuable manpower. On the other hand, we'd have some awkward questions to answer if we abandon the search and Sarah's body is discovered. If the media think we're not doing enough, they'll crucify us. Finally, Mrs Kelly has a right to believe we're doing everything possible to find her daughter.'

Pratt sighed heavily, 'At times like these I regret being a superintendent. Okay, we'll continue the search, if only as window dressing. We've been at it nearly a week now, so I can legitimately scale it down. We'll make better use of the resources interviewing those on the Sex Offenders' Register.'

'We're due a further press release, aren't we?'

'I'll attend to it.'

'How about saying we're following a new line of enquiry, and our concern for Sarah's safety is higher than ever? You never know, our killer might be an avid watcher or reader of his own publicity. Most of them are.'

'What about the rest of us, Mike?' Mironova asked.

'I'd like Viv to go through the results from the PNC and the SOR again, see if anyone's missed any likely candidates, someone who's moved area perhaps. Clara, I'd like you to help me contact the forces where the girls lived. We'll need their go-ahead before we speak to the next of kin of the girls. Once we've got that, we need to fix appointments to see them. Which in turn means we've a lot of travelling to do. Where possible, we should arrange to meet up with someone from the local force and go through their file. It might well be that they've more detail than appears on the PNC database. In fact, it might be easier if we can get copies of the original files, rather than relying on the computer info.'

'In Danielle Canvey's case, there's a note on file that both parents have died, so you'll need to speak to Monique, the twin who survived. The note makes it clear Danielle's mother committed suicide, so be doubly careful.'

'I still can't believe that nobody's linked these cases before,' Pearce said suddenly. 'I mean, given that they do prove to be connected, that the girls are all the victims of a serial killer. Why wasn't the similarity spotted?'

'I know it seems strange to you,' Nash told him. 'But you have to remember you're looking at these cases today, for the first time. Back when those first girls disappeared, there weren't the sophisticated computer software programmes you're able to use nowadays. The Police National Computer was originally established in 1974, but only as a database for stolen vehicles. Add to that the problem that occurred in 1994, when the Buncefield Oil Terminal blaze destroyed the nearby PNC building. It housed the only server covering the whole of England and Wales. It took ages to retrieve the information. Five years afterwards I attended a seminar. One of the speakers admitted they still weren't certain they'd got all the data back. The PNC had serious shortcomings anyway. Until relatively recently, and I'm talking about within the last five years, it was little more than a data warehouse for recorded crime.'

Nash pointed behind him to the photos on the wall. 'And these girls weren't considered to be the victims of crime. They were simply "missing persons". Over 200,000 people are reported missing in Britain every year. It's hardly surprising a few get missed. To complicate matters further, almost all the girls lived in areas covered by different police forces. We all know of notorious examples where the failure to pass vital information from region to region has led to tragic results. That's usually between two forces. How much harder would it be to correlate information spread between five police authorities?'

CHAPTER TEN

'How are you getting on contacting the local police and the parents?'

Nash hadn't noticed Pratt enter his office. 'Sorry, Tom, I was miles away. I've just spoken to Mrs Kelly. She's in a right mess. I suggested she appear again in the next TV appeal. She needs to feel she's doing something. I said I'd get back to her later. The WPC who's staying there is very worried, so I suggested getting the family doctor to give Mrs Kelly a sedative. Clara and I've contacted all the regional forces. They're more than happy for us to handle things for the time being. They'll cooperate fully and get involved if, and when, there's something meaningful to do. Clara's tried contacting the other next of kin. So far, she's only managed to arrange two for tomorrow. We got through to a couple of voicemails but we thought it best not to leave a message.'

Pratt nodded his approval. 'People could be anywhere on Sundays. It may be more productive to ring in the evening.'

After Pratt left, Mironova came back in to be told, 'Tom's just handed us another late finish, I'm afraid. We'll have to use this evening to try and get hold of those other parents.'

'Whatever you say.'

There was a knock at the door and Pearce walked in. 'I've finished that computer search. I got six more hits from the SOR but I've discounted two because of their sexual preference. I'm about to start rechecking the PNC results, but I need to know how specific you want to be. Do you want every offender interviewed, no matter how trivial the crime?'

'I don't want anyone leaving out, no matter how irrelevant the offence might seem. We can't afford to miss our man because we've made the criteria too restricted. Include everyone. From rapists, to a bloke who's displayed his todger in public, or played doctors and nurses behind the school bike sheds. There's no reason to suppose our man hasn't offended before, and moved on to worse crimes. I want them all interviewed. I'll prepare a list of questions. I'd like you to start as soon as you can on the locals. If needs be, we'll have to convince the other forces this is a worthwhile exercise. For the moment, you concentrate on the Sarah Kelly case. Take a break first then try later.'

'Will I get any help?'

'Tom's sending some men over to lighten the load. Unfortunately, Clara and I will be tied up on the phones. We'll all need a break if we're going to be working late. I want to try some more estate agents as well, so I'm going to take a walk before they close. They're only open for a couple of hours.'

Nash arrived back at the station as Clara was brewing coffee. He was carrying a sheaf of papers. 'I take it you've had some success?'

'Two of them had nothing, but Charleston's, that you recommended, have a couple of places worth looking at. Unfortunately, the woman who deals with tenancies was out. I left my number with the receptionist. I had to use my charm. She said I might be able to have a look at them tomorrow, but I explained that might be difficult as I was only available today.'

'Cheeky devil,' Clara said as she passed him a mug.

'The thing is,' Nash paused, 'the receptionist told me she doesn't do unaccompanied viewings, so I said I'd bring a female colleague along with me. I hope you don't mind. It would give you a break from this place?'

'No problem. I don't suppose you could ask Helen Tate to go with you, in view of the nature of the appointment.'

'I don't think I'd want Helen along anyway. If I suggested we go looking at flats she'd get the wrong idea.'

Nash had barely finished his lunch when Ramirez phoned, wanting to check some facts regarding the Lizzie Barton murder scene, and complaining he was having to work weekends to catch up on his paperwork. Halfway through giving him the information he needed, the building's fire alarm sounded. 'Sorry, Professor, I'll have to call you back.'

As the occupants assembled at their drill stations, Nash was approached by the officer who'd been on the reception desk. 'I took a message for you just before the alarm went off,' the man told him. It was the receptionist from Charleston's, the estate agents.' He handed Nash a piece of paper. 'You can visit the High Street property at 2 p.m. Then you can see Rutland Way after that. She stressed that you had to have a female with you.'

He studied the paper. 'Does this woman have a name, by any chance?'

The officer smiled ruefully. 'I was about to ask for it when the alarm went off. I'd to ditch the call.'

'No matter,' Nash said.

'You can go back in now.' Doug Curran, Chief Fire Officer, was standing only a few yards away. He smiled at Nash. 'That was a very successful test.'

'You mean that was all it was? Why didn't we know there was going to be a fire drill?'

'Because if you'd known you wouldn't have treated it with the urgency you should have done.' Nash frowned but there was no arguing the logic.

'We can see the first of those properties at two o'clock,' he told Clara.

She looked round. 'How did you find that out? I didn't see a pigeon land.'

Monique felt nervous as she unlocked the door of the High Street flat. It angered her, this fear she'd lived with since the assault. Why should that one incident ruin her life? Why had she to live with this permanent reminder of the past?

She wandered around the flat, trying to calm herself. When the doorbell rang her heart missed a few beats, then raced to catch up. She stepped reluctantly into the hall and opened the door.

There was something oddly familiar about the couple standing on the doorstep. It was the woman Monique noticed first, a tall, blonde, strikingly pretty girl in her late twenties. She resembled someone, but Monique couldn't think who. The girl's companion spoke and Monique transferred her attention to him. 'Good afternoon, I'm Mike Nash. This is Clara. I spoke with your receptionist. I'm sorry, I didn't get your name.'

As he spoke, Nash was racking his brain. He was convinced he knew this woman, had been from the second the door opened. Either that or he'd seen her recently.

'I'm Monique Canvey, manager of Charleston's Estate Agents. Please come in.'

Monique stepped to one side. She raised her hand for them to shake it, then allowed it to drop back by her side as they stood stock still, their faces registering complete astonishment. 'Is something wrong?'

Nash recovered his wits. 'I'm sorry,' he said, 'did you say Monique Canvey?'

'Yes, of course, why?' Monique felt puzzled, vaguely alarmed.

Mike gave an almost imperceptible shake of his head as he glanced at Clara. 'No, no, absolutely nothing. Shall we have a look at the flat?'

Monique led the way. The flat didn't meet Nash's requirements in several ways, mainly because there was nowhere to keep his motorbike. Ten minutes later Monique was locking the flat door. Her client had already left and would wait for her outside the Rutland Way property.

'Why didn't you mention we've been trying to contact her?' Mironova asked as they drove across town.

'Didn't you notice the state she was in? She was trembling. I reckon it must be quite an ordeal for her meeting strangers, after what she went through. If we'd told her up front we were police officers she'd have been a gibbering wreck. I'll wait until she's got used to us before I spring that on her.'

It didn't take Nash long to discover the next property was exactly what he was looking for. Little longer in fact than it had taken to decide the other flat was unsuitable. Rutland Way was a smart, modern, ground-floor flat. It was tastefully decorated with a kitchen large enough for dining. The accommodation was light and spacious, complete with an integral garage where he could house the Road Rocket in perfect safety.

'This is exactly what I'm after. I'll take it, if that's okay.'

Monique blinked in surprise. The level of rent had proved a stumbling block to several potential tenants. Monique had anticipated a tough haggling session, even if the flat was suitable. 'Perfectly,' she responded, 'I've got the forms here if you want to fill them in now. Alternatively, if you want to discuss it with your wife, we can leave it until another day. I promise nobody else will jump in ahead of you.'

Nash smiled, sadly she thought. 'There is no wife.'

Monique cast a glance at Clara.

Clara smiled. 'No, Miss Canvey, we just work together, that's all.'

'I'm sorry, I automatically assumed—'

'That's alright,' Nash assured her. 'Anyway, I don't need time to think it over. I've decided this is the property I want, so let's get on with it.'

Monique took the tenancy agreement out of her briefcase. After completing the financial information, she turned to the section reserved for personal details. After he'd given his full name and date of birth she asked, 'What's your occupation?' The pause after she asked was long enough for her to glance up.

'Police officer, rank: Detective Inspector.' Every vestige of colour drained from her face. It took a few seconds before she recovered. 'A policeman?'

'I am indeed. But I also want to rent this property. There's no sinister motive behind this meeting,' Nash glanced at Clara. 'But by the weirdest coincidence, Clara has been trying to contact you. Shall we get this document finished then I suggest we go for a coffee somewhere and I'll explain.'

Monique looked aghast at the idea.

'I'm sorry. Of course Clara will come with us. Is that okay?'

He led the way across the Market Place to the Helm Tea Room, a superior café where customers were served by a waitress wearing traditional black and white livery. The tea and coffee pots were of heavy silver plate, the crockery was bone china and the tablecloths and napkins were linen; Nash's favourite café. They secured a quiet corner table. The trolley which was wheeled to their table contained an appetizing array of cakes and gateaux, bulging with calories.

When the waitress had retired, Nash cleared his throat. 'Let me explain. I've been in a property in Helmsdale since I was transferred from London. I took it because I needed somewhere in a hurry. Now I want somewhere more suitable.

'Sergeant Mironova was trying to get hold of you on a completely separate matter. You may have seen it on TV, or read about it in the papers. About a girl who disappeared a week ago. I'm in charge of the case and, to be frank, I'm not happy that there's an innocent explanation.'

Nash paused and looked searchingly at Monique, his eyes holding hers as he continued, his tone gentle, soothing. 'I'm looking at the disappearance of several other young women, your sister Danielle being one of them. I've read the reports and I'm far from happy about how that investigation was conducted. I'm being blunt because I feel you should know the truth. I want to talk with the relatives of the girls who've disappeared and see if I can establish a link between them.'

'I thought you looked familiar. I saw you on TV with that poor woman, appealing for information.'

Nash nodded. He leaned forward, his voice urgent. 'By the time I gave that interview we were very concerned about Sarah's safety and the motive behind her disappearance. That concern hasn't abated. In fact, it's intensified.'

Monique's face was troubled, her body language defensive. 'What do you want from me? What can I tell you now that I was unable to tell the police when it happened?'

'I'm not sure. Half the problem is I don't know what I'm looking for. Apart from the assault on you, there isn't one scrap of concrete evidence to point to any crime. Nevertheless, I'm convinced the cases are linked. To make any progress I have to find that connection.'

'How many are you talking about?'

'This is highly confidential information. Including your sister, I'm looking into seven disappearances.'

'Seven?' Monique looked horrified.

'Yes, but that's over a number of years and from different regions.'

'What convinces you they're connected? I mean, if there's no evidence?'

'The first thing was the complete lack of evidence in itself. No sightings, no attempts at contact. As if they'd been abducted by aliens. Then I looked at the girls' photos. Any of them could have been mistaken for Danielle,' Nash paused before adding, 'or you, for that matter. That convinced me.'

'You know the police had a theory at the time about the assault on me?'

'You mean that nonsense about Danielle attacking you because of some row over a boyfriend? I thought it was a load of rubbish.'

Monique's eyes were hot with anger. 'Danielle would never have harmed me. Just as I would never have hurt her. They didn't understand that, didn't understand what it means being a twin. Harming me would be like injuring herself.'

'You were identical? So by looking at you we can guess what Danielle would have looked like now if she'd survived.'

'More or less.'

'Okay, here's what I suggest. I'd like you to write down as much as you can recall about every aspect of your life and Danielle's prior to the time she went missing. Don't leave anything out, no matter how trivial or irrelevant it seems. Give me a call when you've finished and we'll get together. I'm certain somewhere in your past there's a clue as to what happened to Danielle, a link to all the other girls. Could you do that?'

There was a long pause, Clara fiddled anxiously with her coffee spoon, then folded her napkin neatly and laid it on the table. She stared at Nash, signalling him to be careful.

When Monique eventually replied, her voice was low, sharp with annoyance. Her tightly clenched hands were resting on the edge of the table. 'Ever since I was attacked, I've suffered the most horrendous migraines. I was off work last week. Thinking about the past, about the attack on me, wondering what had happened to Danielle can trigger one of those migraines. I've trained myself over the years to steer clear of the subject. Now you're asking me to spend time and effort on the one thing that's virtually guaranteed to cause me illness and pain. I'll have to think it over. I'm afraid of what will happen if I go over it all again.'

'I understand how much of an ordeal it may be, and I wouldn't blame you if you refuse. But I'm not asking for myself. I'm asking for Sarah Kelly, for her mother and for the families of all the missing girls. We may be too late to rescue Sarah, and we're certainly far too late for the others,' Nash's tone softened to little more than a gentle whisper, 'and I'm afraid that includes Danielle. But if that is the case, surely you and all those other relatives should be allowed at least the opportunity to grieve? Closure, instead of more years of uncertainty. Above all, we must try to prevent it happening again.'

Monique stared at him. 'That's emotional blackmail.' She sighed heavily, 'However, I understand. I'll think about it. But I won't make any promises.' She got up to leave and smiled at Clara, an acknowledgment of her kindness. Then she paused. Resting one hand on the table, she stood looking down at Nash. 'What happened to Danielle and to me has robbed me of so much. It's taken away any normal life I had, stolen every happy memory from my childhood. I can no longer revisit the past, for fear of the damage it might do. Surely a person should be allowed at least some happy memories?'

On their return, Pearce was waiting for them. 'Superintendent Pratt has allocated three men to help me with the visits. I've managed to establish most of them are still at the addresses on file. Things have been moving quite fast whilst you've been out.'

'We've been interviewing Danielle Canvey's twin sister. Clara, why don't you bring Viv up to speed? I'll see you in my office when you're through. We'll try contacting the relatives again. Let me know if you find out anything useful tonight, Viv. Clara and I won't be in tomorrow morning. Not until afternoon at the earliest; we're off to Lincolnshire.'

Nash was on the phone when Clara entered. He put the receiver down and looked at her as she began, 'I've just been talking to the officer who was on duty when Sarah Kelly vanished. He had to attend a domestic on the Westlea during the early hours of Saturday morning.' Clara looked down at the sheet of paper in her hand. 'The row was at Jennings's house. Apparently Cindy was having a go at him with an assortment of kitchen utensils. The point is the time of the incident. The neighbour who called it in rang 999 fifteen minutes after Sarah Kelly left Club Wolfgang.'

'So Jennings is out of the frame for Sarah's abduction,' Nash nodded. 'That hardly surprises me. I was never convinced about him anyway, at least not for that crime. The Lizzie Barton murder's a different matter.

'That phone call was from SOCO. Their examination of Sarah Kelly's handbag and the surrounding area has yielded nothing. The only piece of positive news was that they'd found some DNA traces on the handle of the knife that killed Lizzie Barton and have sent these for genetic matching. That might tell us more about whether Jennings is involved.'

Nash thought for a moment. 'Tell Viv to bring Roland Bailey in for questioning in the morning. His alibi for Friday night's a lie. Check with Rushton's first; he may be at work. Then he can start putting the squeeze on him. I'll have a go at him when we get in.

'As for the interview, I'll take the Cummings details home with me tonight, bring myself up to speed. Pick me up at my place about eight o'clock in the morning.'

While they were arranging visits Nash had another phone call; from Monique Canvey. 'I realize it might make me ill, but I'll risk doing what you asked. I don't suppose I'll feel any better if I don't try to help. I owe it to Danielle, and if I don't do it I'd be tormented if the same thing happened to another girl. I also believe if anyone can solve this, you can.'

'I appreciate that, Ms Canvey and I'll do my best to make it as stress free as possible,' Nash reassured her. 'Just let me know any way I can help.'

Monique hesitated before replying. 'I thought it would be a good idea to write down bullet points rather than the whole thing. Then we could meet and go through them in depth?'

'That's fine. Let me know when you're ready.'

'We'll have to meet up at some point anyway, for me to hand over the keys to Rutland Way.' She paused before adding a little more cheerfully, 'If you're proved creditworthy.'

She put the phone down with a sigh of relief and a feeling that was not quite content, but half way towards it. Although she'd been tempted to refuse his request, she knew that was never an option. Her fear of another migraine attack was outweighed by other considerations. Her duty to Danielle and her desire for closure were the ones she'd mentioned to Nash. The desire to see him again was one she didn't admit, even to herself.

Sarah woke feeling great. She'd never felt so alive, so terrific. Whatever he'd done to her, whatever he'd been giving her, the result was sublime. Why had no one else ever had this effect on her before? She felt like doing all sorts of wild, uninhibited things. Things she wouldn't normally have even dreamed of. She felt like running through fields naked, of making love all night and all day, then coming back for more. She wanted to sing and dance and make love again and again. But she'd just said that, or thought it, hadn't she? She couldn't quite remember, but it didn't matter. Nothing mattered really. She felt strong. That was what mattered. Strong and powerful in the strength of her sexuality. Powerful in a depth she'd never reached before and with the urgent desire to express herself.

Why was she here in this nursery, on this bed? She couldn't remember. It didn't matter, it was nice here. Nothing really mattered, did it? She was sort of confused and excited at the same time. She smiled now when he came into the room because he was nice to her, and spoke to her, and called her a name that wasn't quite her own, but it didn't matter, did it? Nothing mattered, and anyway, maybe she'd got it all wrong anyway, so what?

Her mind was in turmoil, everything jumbled from the effects of the drugs. When she tried to remember something she kept forgetting the original thought. She lay giggling and content, waiting for the next time he would come for her. And what's more, she didn't care.

CHAPTER ELEVEN

Clara arrived early at Nash's flat. She parked outside, expecting him to come straight out, but after a few minutes waiting, she sighed and went to ring the doorbell. Nash answered the door. She looked at him and started laughing. He was naked from the waist up, one half of his face covered in shaving soap. 'Come in and wipe that grin off your face,' he grumbled.

When they drove away, Clara asked, 'Where are we heading for, exactly?'

Nash opened the file. 'We've a fair drive ahead of us. Barkston Frome, that's the name of the village. It's between Lincoln and Grantham. Unfortunately, the DS who was to have met us left a message on my voicemail. He's giving evidence this morning, but he's given the file to their DI and we're welcome to pop in and look at it.'

They made good time on the journey, called at the local police station, and arrived a few minutes before the scheduled time for their appointment. The road was a cul-de-sac; number 11, a small, neat semi. The garden looked as tidy as the house. Nash was reminded of Joan Kelly's house. He was looking for similarities in the lifestyle of the missing girls. Here was one, albeit a tiny one.

'Quick refresher before we go in. Julie Cummings disappeared in November 1991, when she was eighteen. She was a student at Grantham Technical College. In good health, wasn't in a relationship, nor had she been. Last seen leaving college after an evening class; intending to catch a train back to Barkston Frome. She wasn't sighted at either station, or on the train. She was never seen again.'

Nash laid the file on his lap as he pondered what he'd just read.

'Probably the most significant fact is that she wasn't seen on the train.'

'How do you mean?'

'Julie was strikingly attractive. Not someone people would miss. The train was at 20.25 and was a local service. It was a wet night, mid November. If the train was a quarter full, I'd be surprised. Passengers would probably have remembered her if the train had been packed, certain to have done so if it was almost empty.'

'What do you deduce from that?'

'I very much doubt if Julie got on that train. In fact, I don't think she even reached Grantham station.'

As Nash was thinking, he saw the bright sunlight of the afternoon fade. He visualized a rainy November night as he waited in the car. The meagre light from a street lamp glistened on the rainsoaked tarmac. Ahead of him a modern, two storey-brick building, functional in design like a hospital, a school, or a college. He let out a sigh. He was sure now, certain of exactly what had happened to Julie Cummings.

'Mike?' The single word was sharp with concern. Nash blinked and looked at Mironova. She was staring at him. 'You alright?'

'He was waiting for her,' Nash whispered, 'waiting in his car, outside the college. He was waiting because he knew she'd be there. He sat there in the street. It was no matter of chance. He knew Julie was inside the building, knew she'd be coming out. He knew she was attending a lecture, knew what time it would end, probably even knew the subject.'

'Mike!' Clara protested.

'When Julie came out of the college, he still waited,' Nash continued as if he hadn't heard Mironova. 'Waited to make sure she was alone. He had to be sure she wouldn't be being met or picked up. He had to be sure he'd have her all to himself. Then he started his engine and crept after her. He crept along, keeping far enough back so Julie didn't suspect she was being followed. When he judged the time was right, sure she was alone, when he was sure he could claim her, he pulled the car alongside and wound the window down.' Nash spoke in a whisper. The menace was louder than a shout. 'Hello, Julie. I thought it was you. Can I offer you a lift? It's on my way. It'll be better than getting colder and wetter. Have you been at college? Jump in then, and when you get home, you'd better take those wet things off straight away. We don't want you catching your death of cold.'

'Mike, stop it please.' Mironova had witnessed this before but was still appalled yet fascinated by Nash's scenario.

'Sorry, Clara.' Nash smiled ruefully.

'How do you do that? It sounds so realistic. Almost as if you were there. I know that's impossible, but anyone else would have been convinced.'

'I have the advantage of knowing the killer must have been acquainted with his victims. Well enough for them to be at ease with him. From there it's just a small step to imagining how he achieved the abduction.'

'It might seem a small step to you, but it sounded like a giant leap to me. Do you mean you actually visualized that taking place just now?'

'Something of the sort.'

'If it happened as you imagined, like you said, it had to be someone who knew Julie. She wouldn't have jumped into a stranger's car?'

'That's right.'

'And you think that was the case with all of them?'

'Yes, I think so. All we have to do is find the one person all the girls knew, and we've the identity of their killer. Couldn't be simpler.'

'Of course not: dead easy.' Mironova's tone matched the sarcasm in Nash's. She had another thought. 'Have you had any other "visualizations" about this case?'

'I had one last Sunday, near the alley where Sarah was abducted. That's how I felt certain the CCTV camera and the street light had been damaged. And I told you about the dream.'

Clara nodded. 'About Danielle? I don't suppose that nightmare had anything to do with the case?'

'I don't know whether it meant anything. More likely the result of something I'd eaten.'

'Or drunk, more like,' Clara remembered the amount of wine they'd had. She smiled at him. 'I'm glad you told me anyway.'

*

Nash's first impression of Margaret Cummings was of a doll. She was petite with tiny hands and feet. Her hair, once golden he guessed, was now snowy white. Her eyes were china blue, her cheeks porcelain pink. Then he saw the expression in her eyes and the doll-like impression vanished. They were like the eyes of a woman for whom life had already ended.

'Mrs Cummings? I'm Mike Nash. This is my colleague, Clara Mironova; she's the one who spoke to you on the phone.'

Mrs Cummings didn't acknowledge either of them, nor did she offer to shake hands. She merely gestured towards the sitting room. 'Come in.'

The interior of the house reflected the neatness outside. Everything was orderly, precise, almost unlived in. 'Please, sit down.'

'I'd better explain why we're here,' Nash began.

He was about to continue when Mrs Cummings interrupted. 'I imagine you're here about Julie. I can't think of any other reason. If you're not, you can leave right now. Nothing else interests me.'

If Nash was taken aback by the hostility in Mrs Cummings' tone, it didn't show. 'That's quite understandable, Mrs Cummings,' he reassured her. 'Of course you're right. It is about Julie. And I should explain, we're not with the local force. We're from North Yorkshire. We're currently investigating a case that may be linked to your daughter's disappearance.'

Nash considered the woman carefully before continuing. 'This may seem strange after such a long time, but we've a special reason to look at Julie's disappearance again, and we need to go over a lot of old ground, I'm afraid.'

He took a deep breath. 'The "special reason" is that as the result of another girl disappearing in North Yorkshire, we've had occasion to re-examine cases of other girls who vanished over the years without explanation and we've found some disturbing similarities.'

Mironova added, 'What Inspector Nash means is that he checked old files and made the connection we believe exists between the disappearance of your daughter and the other girls. It's through his intuition that we're at last coming to understand what might have happened to them.'

'Sarah Kelly,' Margaret Cummings whispered the name. 'I saw her photo in the paper. That's the girl you're talking about. I remember looking at the photo and thinking how much like my Julie she was.'

'That was the first thing I noticed. That all the girls looked alike. Like one another, or like someone else. That was the first link I spotted.'

'All the girls? How many are there?' Her expression turned to alarm.

Nash hesitated, dubious about revealing the information. 'Seven, we think.'

'Oh, dear God!' Margaret Cummings looked from Nash to Mironova and back again. 'You realize what you've told me, don't you? You must realize what conclusion I have to draw from it?' Nash nodded, unable to phrase a reply gently enough. Mrs Cummings said it for him. 'You're telling me they're all dead. That my Julie is dead. That they were all taken and killed by some monster.'

'We don't know for sure. I'm only confirming what you already suspected, a suspicion you've had to live with for eighteen years.'

'Since the day she didn't come home,' the mask of defiance slipped, revealing the desolation behind. 'That's what I've suspected.'

She spoke slowly, each word a burden. 'There's always doubt and a little seed of hope: a prayer for a miracle. It refuses to go away. You don't fool anyone, not even yourself. Logic butts in and says "don't be stupid". But you can't shake off that doubt. Now you've removed it. So what do you want from me?'

'I'm convinced that somewhere in the lives of the girls and their families there's a common factor. These weren't random, spur-of-the-moment abductions. They were carefully planned, which means prior knowledge. I aim to talk to all the relatives, and hope we can spot the connection. Short of actually catching the killer attempting an abduction, I can't see any other way to trap him.'

It was over an hour later when they left. 'We now have another connection between Julie Cummings and Sarah Kelly,' Nash said as they got into the car. 'They both lived with their mother and the fathers lived a long distance away.'

'Yes, but all the rest had both parents at home,' Clara pointed out.

'True,' Nash conceded. 'I suppose it was never going to be that easy.'

When they reached the office, it seemed fortune was working against them. Pearce met Nash with a message, 'I took a phone call from a Mrs Forrest. Her husband's going to be away. He's a lorry driver on European routes and he's been sent to Italy. Won't be back until the end of the week. I've provisionally rearranged the meeting for Saturday.'

'Damn, I just hope nothing else happens before then. Clara, come into my office, will you.'

Mironova followed him. As she did, he turned back.

'I asked Pearce to pick Roland Bailey up this morning. Find out what's happening there, will you?'

Five minutes later she returned. Nash was replacing the phone handset, frowning slightly. He glanced up at Clara; she looked nervous.

'Well?' he asked.

'Viv hasn't been for Bailey yet. He said he's been finishing off those SOR interviews.'

'Then I'd better have a word with him.'

'We have dumped a lot of work on him,' Clara said in his defence.

'Just ask him to come in, will you,' Nash said flatly.

Pearce strolled into Nash's office a few minutes later and moved one of the chairs by the desk preparatory to sitting down. Nash looked at his DC. 'Don't bother,' he said sharply. 'You don't have time to stay. I gave an instruction for you to pick Bailey up. You haven't done that. Why?'

'I was still finishing off interviewing people on the sex offenders register,' Pearce's tone was defensive.

'You've been allocated officers to assist with that. So now it looks to me as if you've deliberately ignored my orders. That means the prime suspect in the Sarah Kelly case is still at large when he should be in an interview room. Now you're going to tell me why. I'll be fascinated to know the reason.' There was a long painful silence. Pearce looked down, unwilling to meet Nash's gaze.

'Apparently you haven't a reason to offer. In that case, get your arse into gear and bring Bailey in now. You've got half an hour to report back with Bailey in tow. If you're not back by then, I suggest you go home and get your uniform out of the wardrobe and check it still fits because you'll be wearing it tomorrow. Now get out of here.'

Viv turned and left. Clara was heading across the CID room for Nash's office carrying two mugs of coffee. Viv drew a deep breath. 'What's eating him? He's just bitten my head off.'

Clara chewed her bottom lip. 'We did expect something like this. Forget it, Viv, you know he doesn't mean it.'

Clara brought Nash's coffee in. 'What did you say to Viv? He had a face like a slapped backside when he came out of your office.'

'That's between him and me. The problem is, we've wasted half a day when we should have had Bailey here. He remains favourite for involvement in Sarah's disappearance. Now we'll have to wait until later before we get chance to speak to him. We've another meeting soon, haven't we?'

'Yes, Caroline Barnes's parents.'

'We'll have this coffee and give Pearce time to get back before we leave. Meanwhile, take another look at the Lizzie Barton file; see if anything strikes you.'

Clara began leafing through. 'I can see the relevance in what Mexican Pete told you. I mean, I can see how Lizzie being infected with the HIV virus might provide a motive for someone to kill her, especially if she'd passed on the infection. What I can't work out is how someone could have found out she was HIV positive. It's not the sort of thing you go bragging about over a pint. If it had been common knowledge, I'm certain someone from The Cock and Bottle would have mentioned it. If Lizzie didn't say anything and there was no evidence of the disease in her face, how did anybody find out? What exactly did Mexican Pete say?'

'He was positive about it. Said Lizzie hadn't had the virus long and probably wasn't aware she was carrying it.'

'Precisely my point. If Lizzie didn't know, how could anyone else find out?'

Mironova waited, expecting a response. When one didn't come she glanced at him and noticed he was wearing that same distant, abstracted expression she'd seen earlier. This time Clara refrained from speaking. For a few minutes there was silence. 'Of course,' Nash muttered, more to himself than to Mironova.

'What is it?'

'How do you find out if someone's HIV positive? How did Mexican Pete discover Lizzie Barton was infected, for instance?'

'Well I assume he took a blood sample for testing.'

'Exactly, he did a haematology test. But that was because he suspected she might be infected, presumably because the virus must have started to infect one or other of her internal organs. But you don't carry out a post-mortem on a living person; you have to rely on a blood test.'

'I still don't see what you're driving at.'

'Think of it this way. Why do you do a blood test? Who do you test?'

'Normally I suppose if someone goes to their doctor and they can't identify the illness.'

'What if they're perfectly healthy? You wouldn't take a blood test from a healthy person as a rule, would you?'

'Not that I know of, but with the state of the NHS I wouldn't bet against it.'

Nash agreed, 'Cynical but true. Think about it, Clara.'

'Are you saying the only way someone could have found out that Lizzie had infected them is if they were ill themselves? Are we looking for someone who's ill?'

Nash smiled. 'Not necessarily ill. Remember, I said there are circumstances when healthy people are tested as a matter of routine.'

'I suppose they could be given a medical for insurance, or joining the forces, or if they were....' Clara's voice tailed off.

'Pregnant?'

Mironova nodded.

'And of course we know someone who'd been intimate with Lizzie Barton during the period in question. Whose girlfriend is now pregnant and could well have been tested.'

'You think Alec Jennings killed Lizzie Barton because she infected him with the virus?'

'That's one possibility, but there's another. That it wasn't Jennings, but his girlfriend Cindy who stabbed Lizzie.'

'You mean because Lizzie also passed the infection on to her?'

'That's also a possibility. Depending on exactly when the infection was passed on, there's a third motive, an even more powerful one.' Nash pondered for a moment. 'If the gynaecologist told Cindy that her baby would likely be born HIV positive, how much worse would that be? Remember, Jennings had no alibi? He was supposedly at home all day and the only one who could vouch for that was Cindy. Who just happened to be out shopping at the time Lizzie was stabbed. Or had she gone out to take her revenge on the woman who'd ruined her life. Ruined Alec's and worst of all condemned her baby to a dreadful fate. The barman at The Cock and Bottle said he saw someone running down the alley behind the pub. Someone dark-haired, wearing a brown bomber jacket. I'd be willing to bet Cindy has dark hair and owns a brown bomber jacket.'

'Should we pull her in?'

'Not yet. I want another word with our larcenous barman. Unless I'm mistaken, I think he's moved up from petty theft to blackmail.'

'You think he recognized Cindy?'

'I'm bloody sure he did.'

They were distracted by a knock on the office door. Viv stepped gingerly inside. 'Sorry to disturb you both. I've got Bailey in an interview room as you requested, sir.'

'Good, you can get back to your paperwork now. Don't forget, I want him sweating by the time we get back.'

'Yes, sir.' Pearce turned and walked back through the CID room.

Nash continued. 'Have you got the photos of Lee Machin's injuries?'

'Yes, in his file. Why?' Mironova was baffled by the sudden switch in Nash's thought pattern.

'I want them handy when we interview the barman. We'd better get off now. The one thing I don't want to do is create a bad impression with any of the relatives by turning up late.'

'Caroline Barnes: known as Carrie to her friends and family.' Nash read the file contents aloud as Mironova drove them towards the West Riding. 'A nineteen-year-old student at Leeds University. The family lives at Colingford, near Skipton. Father works for a bank, transferred to Skipton branch as manager. Carrie disappeared after catching the train from Leeds at the end of the university term. Mother, a primary school teacher,' Nash thought for a second. 'Hang on, what did Margaret Cummings do for a living, can you remember?'

'She's retired, isn't she?'

'She is now, but I thought she said something about "when I was teaching" or something like that.'

'It'd be worth checking.'

Nash sat bolt upright, the sudden movement causing the seat belt to grip tightly across his chest. 'Yes, by God, it would. I've just remembered something I read in Danielle Canvey's file. Both her parents were teachers. Danielle and Monique's mother was French. They met when their father took a school party to France on one of those exchange visits. Let's think about what we've got here. We know Caroline's mother was a teacher. We think Julie's mother was a teacher before she retired. And both Danielle's parents were teachers. I'm going to ring Pearce and get him to check the files on the rest.'

'He's babysitting Roland Bailey at the moment,' Clara reminded him.

'He can get a uniform to stand in. It's only going to take him ten minutes or so to look the information up.'

They were on the outskirts of Skipton when Pearce rang back. Nash listened for a while then said, 'Okay, thanks for looking.' By the disappointed tone in his voice Mironova could tell the news wasn't encouraging. But Nash continued,

'Just to be on the safe side, I'd like you to ring all the parents and check out the exact details. It may take a while but at the moment it's the only theory we've got. I'm not going to discount it without making doubly sure.'

'Bad news?'

'Not good,' Nash admitted. 'Louise Harland's mother fits the profile, she's a teaching assistant, but Megan Forrest's mother is a cook, Anne Blatchford a cleaner and Joan Kelly a secretary.'

It was much later, as they were returning from Colingford following another depressing interview, when Pearce rang back. It didn't need Nash's change of expression or his repeated 'what?' to tell Mironova the news was momentous. The incomprehensible but excited squawk of Viv's voice on the mobile was enough.

Nash turned sideways. 'Do you want the good news or the bad news first?'

She glanced at him; he was smiling. The bad news couldn't be so terrible. 'Give me the good news first then.'

'The good news is Joan Kelly is a secretary. She's secretary of Helmsdale Secondary School. As for the others, Anne Blatchford doesn't work any longer but she used to have a part-time cleaning job at their local grammar school and Tracey Forrest works as a cook for North Riding Caterers. They supply chefs to all the schools in the area. That's it, Clara. That's our connection. One or both of the parents of all seven girls worked in or around schools.'

'That's brilliant, Mike, but what was the bad news?'

'Oh that,' Nash grimaced. 'It took Viv a long time to weed out all that information. Whilst he was busy, Roland Bailey decided he'd had enough of either the interview room or our constable and slung his hook.'

'Surely he can't do that?' Mironova protested.

'He's within his rights. He wasn't in custody, hadn't been charged or cautioned. How many times have you told people they're free to leave whenever they want? The only difference is Bailey didn't wait to be told.'

CHAPTER TWELVE

They got back to the station to be greeted by Pearce. 'I've got three messages for you, Mike.' Pearce's expression was guarded, as if he expected a rocket for Bailey having walked out. He started to apologize but Nash cut him short.

'There's nothing you could have done about it, as Bailey wasn't under caution. Now, what are these messages?' In addition to the anticipated one from Tom Pratt there had been a call from SOCO and another from Monique Canvey.

He rang SOCO first. The chief forensics officer told him, 'The DNA traces from the knife used in the Barton stabbing, we've checked them out on the PNC database but there's no match.'

'I don't think that's going to be a problem, the good news is that you have a sample. I hope to be able to provide you with a couple more. One of which should give us a result.'

'Okay, but don't forget it'll take three days for an infallible match,' the officer seemed aware he was talking to a rural outpost. 'The first set of layers takes twenty-four hours minimum, by which time the match is no more than a possibility. Even at forty-eight hours the layer count yields no more than a probability. To be absolutely positive you need the full seventy-two hour profile.'

'Thank you. I'll do my level best to bear that in mind,' Nash told him. The sarcastic inflexion was totally lost on the forensics officer.

Armed with this additional information Nash phoned Pratt. The Superintendent was more than pleased with developments. 'It sounds as if you'll have the Barton murder wrapped up soon. That's excellent news. At least it'll stop the press hounding us on one issue. I agree about the Lee Machin case. If this kid was blackmailing mailing someone, he had it coming and I wouldn't waste too much time on him.'

'Yes, although he did us one favour. He shot Bailey's alibi for last Friday night down in flames.'

'You think Bailey's our man, then?'

'If there's an innocent explanation, I'd love to hear it.'

'I take your point. No further progress on the Sarah Kelly enquiry, I suppose?'

'We've established a possible link and we're looking into it.' He gave Pratt the details. 'I talked to three of the earlier victims' relatives. That was fairly harrowing. I've a load more to interview yet. I'm bracing myself for that.

'In light of what you've told me, I'll call a halt to the searches. Sounds like a waste of resources. Keep me informed.'

Nash glanced at his watch; he'd just enough time to phone Monique Canvey before the estate agent's office closed.

'I've finished writing my report, Inspector Nash, sir,' Monique told him, the mock submission in her voice making her sound like a probationary DC. 'It's just a question of handing it in, sir.'

'I'm just about finished here,' Nash told her, struggling not to laugh. 'I could make it this evening if you're free? Where would you like to meet?'

There was a moment's hesitation. 'This evening would be okay as long as you don't mind coming to my house. I don't go out at night.' She added by way of explanation, 'Since the attack, I can't.'

'I understand, what would be the best time?'

Again there was a slight pause before she replied. 'If you were to come about 6.30 I could fix us something to eat. Then we could go through the list while we're eating. The distraction might prevent me getting upset. I'm not a bad cook, and it will take time to discuss everything.'

'That's very kind, but I don't know if—'

'You need the list, don't you?'

Nash decided not to knock her confidence. 'If you're sure, then I'll see you later.'

Monique Canvey's house was a large Victorian villa, standing on a small side road, a house of distinctive character.

Nash sat at the table in the farmhouse-style kitchen talking to Monique as she put the finishing touches to their meal. 'This house must take some following for someone who's out at work all day. Do you have any help?'

Monique shook her head. 'None at all, but what I do have is plenty of free time.'

'Even for the gardens?'

She nodded. 'Even the gardening.'

Over dinner, conversation turned to the subject of his visit. Nash gained the impression of a solid family unit, with loving parents and devoted daughters, much like Sarah Kelly, Julie Cummings and Caroline Barnes. Here was another possible connection. Had the girls been picked because of their background as well as their looks?

'It sounds the perfect family life,' he commented as they were finishing their meal.

She smiled, but absently, her thoughts far away. 'I suppose it was perfect, although you never think of it as such. Later, when everything went wrong, it was too late. I stopped thinking about the past. Do you know how difficult it is to erase every childhood memory?'

Nash shook his head as she gestured to the paper containing her notes. 'Well, that's what I tried to do, but obviously I didn't succeed. I may have buried them in my subconscious but they haven't gone away. I tried to live for the present, until you bullied me into this.'

'Was that because of the attack?'

'And because of what happened later. Don't tell me you haven't got the sordid details recorded on file for every constable to read?'

Nash sensed her anger. 'Sorry, I'm not with you.'

'I'm talking about what happened to Mother. Three years after Danny's disappearance Father died of a heart attack. He told me shortly before that he knew Danny was dead. Six weeks after his funeral, Mother waited until I'd gone to work, climbed into the bath and slit her wrists. I found her body. It was only later I realized she'd killed herself on their wedding anniversary.'

'No, that isn't on file,' he was only stretching the truth slightly. The file had recorded only that Yvette Canvey had committed suicide. 'So you've had to cope alone since then?'

'Most of the time.' Her eyes were bright with some emotion Nash was unable to fathom until she delivered her bombshell. 'Of course, Danny visits me regularly.'

She saw the shock in his face and misinterpreted the expression. 'Don't you believe in such things?'

Nash recovered slightly. 'It was the way you said it that surprised me.'

Monique smiled grimly. 'Well, I didn't believe, so you can imagine what a shock it was. That's partly how I know she's dead. Everyone assumed it, apart from that berk of a so-called policeman in charge of the investigation. But I'm the only one who knows for sure.'

'How do you mean?'

'Ghosts don't appear unless the person's dead.'

'That's true, I suppose. Tell me, how alike were you and Danielle?'

'Absolutely identical.' She smiled at some distant memory. 'We used to have fun pretending to be each other. It made our teachers cross. They'd ask Danny a question and look at me or vice versa and the answer would come from the other side of the room.'

'Did either of you have any distinguishing marks, anything to tell you apart?'

'Yes, Danny had a birthmark just below her throat. It was a tiny, star-shaped mark. Mum and Dad used it to check which of us they were talking to. Why? You didn't suspect I was Danny and that they'd got things mixed up, did you?'

Nash smiled. 'When you say you get visits from Danielle's ghost, how does that happen?'

'Whenever I have a migraine attack Danny always appears during the lowest time. At times it made me wonder if I was losing my sanity.'

'Hardly surprising when you think what you've been through.'

Monique sighed, 'I hope you're able to find out the truth. Perhaps then I can contemplate a more normal life.'

'The effect on you must have been really traumatic.'

'Since the attack I've never been outside this house after dark. I even struck a deal at the office to work shorter hours during winter. Fortunately, business is quieter then. I've never been on a date, never been to the cinema or theatre, to a dance even. You're the first visitor to this house in almost six years. I mean to actually come over the threshold. You're the first man to set foot inside since Mother died.'

'One thing you learn in our job is that violent crime doesn't just affect the victims. It affects everyone around them. What's more, it continues to affect them for years afterwards.' Nash thought for a few moments before he continued. 'I wonder if the effect is worse because Danielle was your twin?'

'You're very perceptive. Danny and I did have a strong affinity. We experienced each other's emotions, pain, or happiness. That's not all, though. We knew we were one half of a whole, even when apart. Like the time I was in France and Danny was here, when she was in London and I was at home; we didn't feel we were alone. Can you understand that?' Nash nodded. 'It's not easy to explain. The subconscious feeling that you were not only doing one thing but also something completely different.'

Monique paused and took a drink of water. Her eyes darkened with sadness. 'That's the other reason I know Danny's dead. I was in a coma for six weeks. When I eventually came round, I felt completely alone. For the first time in my life I'd lost that companionship. It was from that moment I felt certain Danny had gone.'

'Were you alike in personality?'

'Pretty much, although Danny was bolder, more outgoing than I. She loved going to parties, clubbing, things like that. I preferred to curl up with a good book or listen to music. She loved sport as well, used to complain if I didn't have time for a game of tennis. She had several lovers too, whereas I'd only had one affair. One proper one, that is, if you know what I mean. That isn't likely to change. Not unless my lifestyle alters dramatically. Well, they say what you've never had you never miss.'

Nash was unable to resist asking, 'Did she tell you about it, or did you know?'

'When she'd made love, you mean? Oh yes, I tackled her about it. She just grinned and said "show me a book as exciting as that and I'll read it", something like that.'

'Suppose we manage to get this sorted out. Do you think you might be able to lead a less monastic existence?'

'I don't know. I certainly hope so, but perhaps it's too late. The damage might be irreversible. What I'd really like to do is to sell this house.' She saw his shocked expression. 'It's a lovely house and it would make a super family home, but it's wasted on me. It's become my prison, holds nothing but bad memories. I wish my parents hadn't bought it, wish we'd never moved here. At the time we were all in favour of the move but in hindsight it was a disaster.'

'I assumed you'd lived here all your life.'

'No, we used to live in Netherdale. We moved here when Danny and I were fifteen.'

'Where would you go? If you were able to sell this house, I mean. Would you stay in the area?'

Monique shook her head. 'I'd go to my other home,' she smiled at his look of surprise. 'Did you know my mother was French?' Nash nodded. 'My grand-mère left the family home to me. She died four years ago, since then my aunt and her husband have taken care of it. It's easy for them, as they live next door. They're often on at me to go live there.'

'Why don't you, if you want it so badly?'

'Partly because I'm scared, but mostly because I'd feel I was deserting Danny.'

Nash called in at Helmsdale police station on his way back home and left Monique's list on his desk. Pearce was still there, with some mildly disturbing news. 'I went round to Bailey's house after he did a runner,' he told Nash. 'It was all locked up, no sign of life. Could be he went straight home from here then scarpered. What do you want me to do?'

'Not much we can do. It's not as if he's committed any crime that we know of. As far as the law's concerned, he's innocent until we can prove otherwise. All he's done is lie about his movements last Friday. If we start hounding him, we lay ourselves open to accusations of harassment. We'll have to wait until he surfaces. Check with Rushton's tomorrow morning, see if he turns up for work.'

'Why would he do a runner, if he's nothing to hide?'

'You're thinking like a copper, Viv. Plenty of innocent people are scared of the police, for all sorts of reasons. It doesn't necessarily mean they've committed a crime. When I was a DC, I went to interview a witness to a street fight. He hid from me, and I'd to go back three times before I found him. It turned out he thought I'd come about an unpaid parking fine.'

Nash got to bed in reasonable time, swallowed his tablets and was hopeful for a good night's sleep. He thought about the evening he'd spent with Monique, and what she'd told him about herself and Danielle. He was still picturing the two girls when he fell asleep.

Something had changed again. Sarah was aware of it as soon as consciousness began to return. Something about her felt different. She felt vaguely nauseous. She opened her eyes. She was dressed again. She noticed this without it seeming in any way remarkable. Nor was she lying on the bed in the nursery. She looked round. The sudden head movement made the room swim for a moment. She waited and her eyes refocused. She felt relaxed, her limbs limp. As far as she could see, the room appeared to be a small breakfast kitchen and she was seated at the table. There was a place setting on the table directly in front of her. She realized she was hungry. She looked down. The clothing she had been put into was another strange set. A long-sleeved paisley-patterned blouse that was buttoned right up to the neck, and a fawn miniskirt. She swung her legs out in front of her and saw she was wearing white ankle socks and sandals. She frowned at the garments in bewilderment. She'd never worn anything like this.

'Sassy dearest, you've woken up at long last. I've been waiting such a weary time for you to waken.' The same gently caressing voice disturbed her thoughts. She looked up and saw him smiling at her but something he'd said was wrong. What was it? Her name, surely that was wrong? What was it he'd called her? She frowned in a furious effort of concentration. Sassy, that was it, he'd called her Sassy. But Sassy wasn't her name, was it? She felt so confused. It was all too much, too tiring. She gave up the effort.

'You must be hungry after all that time asleep. Look, I've made you your favourite breakfast, Sassy. Toast soldiers with boiled eggs, the yolks all golden and runny. Just as you like them. Come along, let me help you.'

He offered her a slender finger of toast coated in egg and she began to eat. He'd done it again. He'd called her Sassy again. If only she could remember her proper name, she could tell him. That wasn't all, the eggs and toast soldiers tasted really nice and she was very hungry, but they weren't her favourite? She wasn't really sure but she thought she could remember having corn flakes for breakfast.

She gave up trying to work out these puzzles and concentrated on eating. Even that was enough of an effort; it was making her feel oh so tired. One good thing at least, the nausea was wearing off. She felt light and airy. She was beginning to float on a magic carpet of toast covered by golden runny egg yolks. She closed her eyes and heard his voice. It sounded distant although she knew he was still close by. 'Open wide, Sassy dearest. One last mouthful, just to please me.'

He watched her, patiently waiting for the drug to work. It would be quicker this time; it always was. It was only topping up from the previous dose. He slipped his hand beneath her skirt and began gently stroking the inside of her thigh. 'Hello, cheeky boy,' she murmured without opening her eyes.

His smile widened. He stood up and slid one arm beneath her knees, the other round her back and lifted her from the chair. He carried her across the room and through the connecting door into the nursery and laid her on the bed. He stared at her for a few moments then began unbuttoning her blouse, his fingers trembling with renewed excitement.

CHAPTER THIRTEEN

It was another early start when Mironova greeted Nash and Pearce. 'What's the plan for this morning, Mike?' Nash looked tired. Was that due to pressure of work, or something else?

'We need to resolve the Lizzie Barton killing. But before we speak to Jennings and his girlfriend, I want another word with the barman from the pub. Send someone to bring him in, and we'll see if we can persuade him to change his story for something closer to the truth.'

'Do you think he recognized the killer?' Pearce asked.

'I think so, and I think I know who. But first, when you ring Rushton's about Bailey, see if Jennings is working today's shift. While you're on, speak to their MD. Ask if we can have a copy of Bailey's personnel file. We could get a warrant, but I'd rather do it the simple way as Rushton's have been so cooperative. Either Jennings killed Lizzie, or Cindy did and Jennings is covering up for her. I also want research done on our friend Bailey. That's down to you, Viv. See what you can find out. Go back as far as you can, to his childhood if possible. This afternoon we've got to see more parents so we'd better get on. Clara, you go and find Cindy Green, then put her in an interview room with a cup of tea.'

After they left, Nash spoke to Joan Kelly, who sounded close to collapse. All he could do was repeat that they were maintaining their efforts. Whilst he was talking he was idly fingering Monique's list. When he'd finished he sat for a moment, thinking. Then he rang Monique Canvey, 'How are you this morning?'

'Better than I expected. I believe it's done me good to talk about things. I've tended to keep everything bottled up, partly because I've never felt close enough to anyone to be confident of baring my soul without them thinking I was a crazy woman. Last night was different. Somehow I knew you'd understand.'

Nash laughed. 'Nutters of the world unite. You have nothing to lose but your minds.'

'That's about it. Anyway, how are you? You sound tired.'

'I'm feeling a bit jaded.'

'Is that a result of our conversation, or is it the case?'

'There are three cases I've got on my plate, all causing problems.'

'You mustn't let it get to you. I believe you're the one person who can solve this.'

'I've been looking at the list you gave me and thinking about something you said before, when we were in Helm Tea Room. I'd like to ask you a few more questions if that's okay?'

'I'll be at the office all day.'

'And unfortunately I'm likely to be tied up here.'

'If you're angling after another dinner invitation, why not just come straight out with it?' she told him with mock severity.

Nash blinked in surprise. 'I wasn't,' he protested, then added, 'however, if you're offering, I certainly wouldn't refuse.'

'I wasn't offering, but I don't suppose it'd do any harm. After all you are an "officer of the law". It was fun cooking for someone and seeing them enjoy the food. I'd forgotten how pleasant that is.'

'That's very kind, but I still need to speak to you.'

'I'm always here. Let me know when you want to call round.'

'Do you know what this is?' Nash held up a sheet of paper.

The barman squinted at it. 'No idea. You've got it wrong way round.'

'No I haven't. The blank side tells me more than the written side. Officially it's called a witness statement. To be specific, it's the statement you signed. Unofficially, I call it a load of bullshit.' Nash leaned over the table dividing them. 'I'm not surprised you haven't bothered to deny it. That's because you know I'm right.'

'You may know what you're talking about, but I've no idea.'

'Lying to a police officer isn't a criminal offence. Lying on one of these forms is. Now, I've got a couple of options. Either I send this to the CPS and get you done for perjury, or you tell me the truth. Because I'm of a forgiving nature, I'm willing to tear this up. Before you decide, I've something else to show you.'

Nash produced a photo of Lee Machin and placed it on the table between them. The barman glanced at it, winced and turned his head away. 'Not a pretty sight, is it? Go on, take a good look.'

The barman shook his head, unwilling to look at Nash. Even more unwilling to look at the photo. 'I'll tell you anyway. That lump of tenderized meat isn't off a butcher's counter. It's a man's face; a man not much older than you. I'll bet he doesn't pull many birds, looking that way. Want to know how he got like that? Someone beat seven bells out of him. Want to know why?'

Nash leaned further across the table. His face was only inches from the barman's. 'The reason someone did that to him is he's a dirty little blackmailing toerag. Like you. The problem is, one of his victims found out who he was.'

Nash sat back whilst the message got through. 'How will you stop Alec Jennings guessing who you are? I don't reckon he's the type to submit to blackmail. You could finish up like this character, or worse. He was lucky. I know you're a thief, if I wanted I could do you for that, but I haven't got time. I could mention your activities to Joe Rawlings. I bet he knows how to deal with people who steal from him. Or, I could say nothing and let matters take their course.' Nash gestured to the photo. 'I said this guy was lucky, and I meant it. Lots of blackmailers end up buried in woodland, or at the bottom of deep lakes. Some become part of the foundations of new buildings. You may be braver than me. I wouldn't take that risk. Especially as it wouldn't be any use. You see; we know who killed Lizzie Barton. What's more, we can prove it, with or without your evidence. So what's it to be?'

Half an hour later, the new statement had been typed and signed. Nash watched him leave the building, all the swagger and bluster gone. He turned to Clara. 'You know what we have to do.'

'Yes, and I don't like it.'

A constable appeared with Bailey's personnel file and handed it to Nash. The managing director had been keen to help.

'Do me a favour, Viv, have a look through it while we're in the interview room. Let me know later if you find anything relevant.'

Cindy Green was pretty but not strikingly. She was beginning to show obvious signs of her condition. She fiddled nervously with the edge of the table as Nash went through the formalities for the tape. 'Before we begin the interview, Sergeant Mironova will formally caution you, but I should advise you that you're entitled to have a solicitor present during the interview, if you wish. Do you have one?'

She shook her head. Nash told her gently, 'I'm sorry, you have to answer out loud.'

'No,' Cindy replied, 'I don't have a solicitor.'

'One can be appointed for you. Just say the word, and we'll suspend the interview until a solicitor arrives.'

'No, let's get it over with,' the girl said wearily.

'If you change your mind, just say so and we'll fix it. Okay, I want to talk to you about what happened to Lizzie Barton. I have to tell you that we found some DNA traces on the knife that was used to stab her. Do you know what DNA is?'

'Yes,' Cindy replied, her expression haunted.

'And do you know that one person's DNA is different from everyone else's?'

'Yes.'

'We also have an eyewitness, who saw you close to where Lizzie was stabbed at about the time of the murder. And finally, we've received the result of some tests the pathologist carried out on the body.'

Nash paused, and let Cindy take in what he'd said. 'The findings point to what I think is the motive for her killing. They reveal that Ms Barton was HIV positive. We know your boyfriend Alec had been having an affair with Lizzie Barton. Did she infect him? And in turn did he infect you? Worst of all, did he infect your baby? Is that why you followed Lizzie Barton down that alley and into that yard? Is that why you stabbed her, Cindy?'

'Yes, I stabbed the slut,' the words tumbled from Cindy. The trickle became a stream, the stream a torrent. 'I killed her, and what's more I'd do it again and again. I killed her because she poisoned my baby. My little baby may never have a decent chance in life. I found out two weeks ago. When the specialist told me, I thought I was going to die. All weekend I thought about killing myself. Then, on Tuesday morning, I saw the slag walking past our house, bold as brass with her tribe of disgusting healthy children. Oh yes, her children are fine. Mine might never be well, and I can't even risk having another because of that whore. So I decided not to kill myself. I decided to kill her instead. Let her kids know a bit of pain. Let them know what life's really like. Let them sit through my trial and learn what a filthy whore their mother was.'

'Does Alec know any of this?'

'Him,' Cindy spat the word out. 'He's as bad as she is. If he hadn't kept going with her like a tom cat on the prowl, this wouldn't have happened. He doesn't know, because I've hardly spoken to him since I found out. I can't stand him near me. I can't bear to be in the same room.' Cindy fought back her tears. 'Well, you've got what you want. What happens now?'

'I'm very sorry, Cindy. I know that sounds like easy sympathy, but believe me this doesn't give us any satisfaction. We're human beings, despite what a lot of folk think. I just wish it could have been different. For you, and for your baby.'

Cindy nodded, unable to speak.

'Now, Sergeant Mironova, Clara her name is, will take your statement, and ask you to read and sign it. After that, she will charge you and I'm afraid you'll have to remain in custody until a preliminary court hearing. Do you understand?'

Cindy nodded again. 'Now, if there's anything you want, let the officers know. If they can't sort it for you, insist they ask for me or Clara, okay?'

Nash stepped into the corridor to find Pearce waiting. 'How did it go?'

'She admitted she killed Lizzie Barton. I hated every minute in there. I'm not condoning what she did, but I can understand why.'

'Jennings is waiting in the other interview room. What shall I tell him?'

'Tell him to....' Nash bit down on his anger. 'Tell him Cindy doesn't want to see him. Tell him why she's here. What she did, and why she did it. Tell him to go home and reflect on it. Don't mince your words either, tell him straight. Just don't let him near me, Viv. I might be tempted to say something I'd regret. Get rid of him. I'm going to my office.'

'Hang on, Mike, I've got something for you.' Nash stopped. 'I had a look through Bailey's file. He's only been at Rushton's eighteen months. He came from Lincolnshire, moved to Yorkshire in 1989. His first job there was with a firm of landscape gardeners. They contract out to local councils, maintaining sports fields, hospital grounds, and the like. I managed to get hold of the firm's boss. He remembers Bailey well. He said Bailey was in charge of the gang doing schools' playing fields in the area. He wasn't sure about the next bit, but he seems to think Bailey had lived in The Lake District, either there or Scotland, when he came back to England. He'd been working somewhere in America. He seems to remember Bailey saying he was moving from Lincolnshire because it was too flat and he missed the hills. It stuck in his memory because Bailey didn't strike him as the outdoor type.'

Nash frowned, something Pearce had just said made him think. 'That could be relevant.'

'Yes, but there's more. After he left there, Bailey got a job as a caretaker,' he paused and added, 'at Helmsdale Secondary School.' Pearce looked across at Nash. 'What is it, Mike?'

'The Lake District and Lincolnshire. Two places where Bailey and two of our victims lived. Now, is that coincidence? Or something far more sinister.'

After lunch, as Mironova negotiated their way through Helmsdale High Street traffic she asked, 'Where are we headed?'

'A place called Horton-in-Covermere. Just across the Cumbrian border, on the A66. Towards the northern edge of the Lake District National Park. Just keep heading west. Stop if you reach the Irish Sea. You'll have missed the turning.'

'Oh, very droll. What do we know about this victim?'

'Louise Harland, sometimes known as Lou, was twenty years old.' Nash referred to the file. 'She worked on the checkout at Good Buys Supermarket, Covermere branch. It was getting near Christmas, and everyone was doing extra shifts. After work, she went for a drink and a Chinese meal with some of her colleagues. She left to get a taxi home to Horton. That's where we're headed.'

'I don't know that area, do you? I mean, I know where it is on the map, but I've never been there.'

'I went a couple of times when I was younger. It's at the head of a dale, about the same size as Helmsdale. In fact, very similar to Helmsdale in a lot of ways. Some very expensive property.'

'Sounds nice.'

'The address certainly sounds rural, Keepers Cottage, Pheasant Rise. Anyway, Louise went for a taxi, or so she said. That was the last anyone saw of her. Her parents rang the supermarket first, then the hospital and finally rang the local police. That was next morning.'

Nash studied the file. 'It sounds as if Louise's parents are typical of the others we've met: father's an insurance broker, mother's a teaching assistant. The only difference is Louise had split up with her boyfriend a couple of months earlier. The boyfriend's definitely out of the frame. At the time she disappeared, he was in hospital with his leg in traction. Not the worst alibi I've ever heard.'

He read on. 'It says here, all the taxi firms in the town were contacted. None of them took a fare to Horton that night, male or female. None of them picked up a lone female around the time she disappeared. One took a group of three girls to the local nightclub from a pub in town. The driver's statement was they had to call a taxi as they were in no fit state to walk. That seems to rule Louise out.'

Nash fell silent. Mironova needed to concentrate on the road ahead and couldn't look at him for a while. When she risked a sideways glance she saw he was deep in thought. She waited in silence.

'I wonder how he managed it?' he asked eventually, to himself as much as to Mironova.

'Sorry, you're talking in riddles. Wonder how who managed what?'

'Accepting that he knew each of the girls, or he'd studied them carefully, how did he persuade Louise into his car? He must have done that. How else do you abduct a fully grown woman in a town centre, even late at night? Think about it, Clara. Even at midnight there are people about in Helmsdale. We have to assume Horton's similar. He'd be taking a hell of a chance, and one thing we do know about him is he's no gambler.'

'Perhaps his lust became too strong and overruled his caution?'

Nash shook his head. 'He doesn't work like that. He's much too clever to leave anything to chance. He keeps his feelings in check as he stalks them, watching the pattern of their movements for weeks, perhaps months in advance. He's prepared to wait. To be patient, plan each abduction to eliminate risk. Clara, this man is close to being a genius.'

'A genius? Mike, you must be joking. He's a crazy, sick, perverted bastard.'

'They reckon genius and madness are only a hair's breadth apart. Think of it this way, he's done it seven times that we know of. The only evidence we have is Sarah's handbag, which tells us nothing, and one surviving witness who can't tell us anything either.'

Clara was chilled by the phrase, 'seven times that we know of'. 'Dear God, how many more are there that we don't know about?'

'I dread to think.'

Nash fell silent again and let his mind wander. It was night time and the street lighting was augmented by festive decorations. Christmas was approaching. It was the season for office parties, works 'do's' and any other number of excuses to drink too much. The police would be on the lookout for drunk drivers. There would have been a campaign to persuade revellers to leave the car at home and use public transport. It would be a holiday time for most, a bonanza for one sector of the working population.

'Of course,' Nash breathed, 'how clever, how bloody clever. The cunning bastard.'

'What is it, Mike?'

'Picture the scene. It's less than a fortnight before Christmas, right. It's around midnight Friday, the pubs are closing. People are either on their way home, or going on to a nightclub. There's folk going here and there through the centre of the town. In addition, our lot are buzzing round, breaking up fights and looking for someone to breathalyze. If you've any sense you've left the car at home. So what vehicle's going to pass unnoticed, even if it's picking a young girl up?'

'A taxi?'

'Even if a dozen, two dozen people saw it, they'd think nothing of it. Probably wouldn't even remember. Let me ask you a silly question. You're a police officer; you've been trained to be observant. You're in and out of my office all the time. Tell me the subject of the painting behind my desk?'

Mironova thought about it. She knew there was one; she saw it every time she opened his door. She struggled and eventually guessed. 'Is it a castle? I think it is. I can't honestly remember.'

Nash grinned. 'The Archbishop might be annoyed. It's York Minster. The point is, you see it but you don't notice it, because you expect it to be there. However, if I took the painting down, or changed it for a Hockney or a Magritte you'd notice straight away. You'd probably comment on it. You'd certainly remember it, even if you couldn't be sure which way up a Magritte should be.'

'Okay, you've made your point. No need to rub it in. People wouldn't take notice of a taxi. I grant you it's a possibility, but what happens once she's inside the car. Surely she's going to kick up a fuss when she realizes he isn't taking her where she wants?'

Nash shrugged. 'It doesn't matter. He drives her out on the Horton road, which is what she'd expect, until it's safe to stop the car. He's already selected a quiet spot. That would be the first indication Louise had that she was in trouble. By then it'd have been way too late. He'd have prepared some way of overpowering her. Game, set and match.'

Mironova shuddered. 'It sounds horribly real. I don't want to believe your theory, but I can't think of an alternative.

Mike, this man's a sick monster. Once or twice I could almost understand. But seven times, seven different girls?'

'No, you're wrong,' Nash corrected her. 'He's done it on seven separate occasions, but not to seven different girls.'

'I don't follow you?'

'All the girls are blonde, blue-eyed and extremely pretty. Line them up and they could be sisters. Lower the lighting and they could all be the same girl.'

'Yes, I understand that. He has a perverted fetish for blue-eyed blondes.'

'I don't think it's as simple as that. I think our man has one particular girl in mind. From his own past maybe? A girl he perhaps loved; possibly one who rejected him? I think that they all became Melanie.'

'Melanie?' Clara asked in surprise. 'Who's Melanie?'

'Well, whatever his dream girl was called.'

'I still think he's a sick perverted bastard, who ought to be locked up and the key thrown away.'

'Of course he is, but I'm sure he doesn't think of himself that way. To him, everything he does is perfectly normal, absolutely rational.'

'Normal,' Mironova spluttered. 'What's either normal or rational about him?'

'Nothing, to you and me. Like I said, we know he's far from normal. I'm just stating it as he sees it.'

'Do you think Bailey's the man we're after?'

'He's the best suspect we've got. In fact, he's the only suspect we've got. What's more, every bit of information we uncover seems to point to him. But I haven't discounted anyone. I think that would be dangerous at this stage.'

Matthew and Linda Harland appeared rather more prosperous than the other parents they'd met. Keepers Cottage was a cottage in name only. The large double-fronted grey stone house was a solid, detached family residence with extensive gardens, standing on a hill at the northern edge of Horton.

Nash stared admiringly at the view. The front aspect overlooked Horton Village. Pretty stone cottages grouped round the village green. The patchwork quilt of countryside, arable fields and pastures stretched down the valley, framed by the backcloth of the moors on the horizon.

'What magnificent scenery,' he said. 'You've a lovely place here.'

'Yes,' Linda Harland agreed. 'We were ever so lucky to get this house. When we were trying to buy it, there were four other couples competing with us. It was only through Matthew's contacts that we beat them to it. Now I wish we'd lost out,' she ended pathetically, her face twisted with anguish.

'Now, now, Lin, don't go upsetting yourself,' her husband said quietly.

Linda Harland twisted a tiny handkerchief between her fingers. Nash guessed she'd been crying before they arrived. She didn't seem far from tears now.

'I'm sorry. I realize how distressing this must be. We wouldn't put you through such pain unless we thought it absolutely necessary. I believe my sergeant explained on the phone why we had to talk to you?'

Matthew Harland had his arm comfortingly round his wife's shoulders. 'She said something about another girl who'd gone missing. Is that correct?'

Nash explained the extent of their enquiry. The couple listened in increasing horror. They cooperated as best they could, but when Nash and Mironova left they were little wiser than when they'd arrived. Sadder certainly, but no wiser. Nash's abiding memory of the visit had nothing to do with the splendour of the view. It was of the torment in Linda Harland's eyes. Reflecting the agony of knowing her beloved daughter was probably dead. That she'd lost her child, without the chance to mourn her.

When they reached Helmsdale, Clara dropped Mike at the police station car park. 'Take tomorrow off, Clara. We don't have any families to see, and you need a break.'

'What about you? You're as knackered as I am.'

'I'll manage. Let's be fair, Clara. You've had to drive hundreds of miles these last few days. That's bound to catch up with you, particularly given the type of roads we've been on. Add that to the stress of running two murder investigations. No, you need the break far more than I do.'

'If you're sure. David's home, so it would be nice to see him.'

'Have fun with the army, and watch out for secret manoeuvres.'

It was the faintest of movements. So small, he wasn't sure if he'd imagined it. He watched for a repetition. It was several long agonizing minutes, minutes in which part of him hoped he'd been mistaken. When he'd persuaded himself he was wrong, there it was again.

It was no more than a fractional muscle spasm, not even a twitch, but it was enough. Enough to tell him it was about to happen. Each time he wondered if it would be different, but it never was. If he'd thought it over rationally he'd have realized the inevitability, but he was no longer capable of rational thought.

She would die soon. The muscle spasm was the first sign. There would be no escaping it. She would leave him, as she'd left him so often before. She would leave and he'd be alone again. That was the way it was. He was powerless to prevent it.

Already the spasm had become more noticeable. Soon the twitching would increase. Then the convulsions would start. She was beyond help, in a world of her own, a world he could not enter. The last stage would be the vomiting and the coma, the slow decline in her breathing as she sank towards death. It wouldn't be prolonged once she entered the comatose state between worlds. It would be a peaceful transition.

When she went away, she fulfilled the destiny that had been hers for more years than he could remember. She had to die. There was no alternative.

He walked from the nursery, through the kitchen to the room beyond. He unlocked the door and stepped inside the place he thought of as his workshop. Turning on the light, he looked round at the familiar surroundings. He was at home here, knew every inch, every detail of the contents. He began checking his equipment, the machines and specialist tools he'd need. Once everything was as he wanted, his final act was to test the extractor fans. They were in order, but he checked them twice, for that was his way, his obsession for scrupulous attention to detail and neatness. Returning to resume his vigil in the nursery, he took a rubber sheet from the chest of drawers and slid it beneath her. Only then was he content that the end would be perfect. Nothing less than perfection would be good enough for her.

He stared down at the girl lying so still, so peaceful, she might have been asleep. Only he knew she wasn't sleeping. 'Sassy,' his voice was a whisper, a caress. 'Sassy, you've left me. You've left me alone. Why does it always have to end this way?'

He asked, but he knew the answer. It would always end this way. If it didn't, it made what had happened to Sassy pointless. Her sacrifice would be devalued, and that he couldn't allow. He had recreated her glory; he had to repeat her sacrifice.

He was unaware of the passage of time as he stood watching the girl's motionless form. Eventually, when his emotions were under control, he carried her through to his workshop and gently laid her on the table. He began to remove her clothing. Once she was completely naked, he paused to admire every inch of her lovely figure. He reached out, and absent-mindedly caressed the smooth flesh at the curve of her breast. She was already beginning to cool down. He would have to begin soon.

He reached for the disinfectant spray, and using a succession of soft cloths, began to cleanse her skin, her eyes, her mouth, and every one of her body's orifices. He worked slowly, methodically, patiently. It was vitally important to be thorough.

When he was satisfied, he peeled off the pair of surgical gloves he'd been wearing, dropping them with the cloths into a bin. He pressed a switch on the wall, and the extractor fans began their gentle whirring sound. He put on a fresh pair of gloves to avoid contamination. He was scrupulous; had to be for her sake. He gently closed her eyes. Then he began to operate.

He worked patiently and painstakingly. He began with the needle injector gun. Then he took a scalpel and made a tiny incision under the right collar bone. He picked up the aneurysm hook and carefully separated the tissue, before probing for the artery. When he'd found and raised this, he'd be ready to insert the tube.

He checked it was securely in place, before lowering the other end into the container below the table. He waited, during which time he checked the machine settings before he flicked the power switch on. The faint humming sound told him it was beginning to work. He watched carefully to make sure this, the most critical stage of the procedure, ran absolutely smoothly. After an agonizing delay, the clear plastic tube turned darker.

When it was done, he connected the trocar to the hydro-aspirator. He made the abdominal incision with the sharp blades on the end of the trocar, and guided it towards the internal organs, piercing and draining, piercing and draining. Then he disconnected the hose from the aspirator, and screwed it on to the cap of the cavity fluid bottle.

He waited until the bottle was empty, then removed the trocar with painstaking care before screwing a trocar button into the hole in the abdomen. Connecting the shower adaptor to the taps in the adjacent sink, he began washing the body and hair. When he was satisfied all traces of extraneous matter had been removed, he dried every millimetre with scrupulous care. He stepped back to look at her. He felt his arousal grow once more. He took a glass from the nearby shelf and filled it from the tap on the container. He raised it, toasting her. 'Now we'll be one, forever.' He drained the warm, ruby-red liquid.

His final task was to dress her in the clothes he'd picked. He swung her from the table and cradled her in his arms. He whispered in her unhearing ear. 'Come along, dearest. I've some people I want you to meet.'

In his study he unlocked the cabinet and went unerringly to the file he wanted. Placing it on his desk, he opened the cover and gazed at the photograph. She would be next. She had been chosen. Reluctantly, he closed the file. The file containing the photograph of Monique Canvey.

CHAPTER FOURTEEN

Wednesday was calmer, a welcome respite after the traumas of the preceding days. Nash found it difficult to believe that it was nearly two weeks since Sarah Kelly disappeared, a week since the murder of Lizzie Barton.

He instructed Pearce to prepare the file on the Barton murder. 'We can't send it to CPS until we get Cindy Green's DNA analysis from forensics, but we should have it in a couple of days. Make sure everything else is ready, so there's no delay. I want the hearing as quickly as possible. I want the trial as quickly as possible. Cindy Green's got enough to contend with; the last thing she needs is a long spell on remand.'

'What about Bailey? I've phoned Rushton's again. He still hasn't turned in. Hasn't rung in sick either.'

'Nothing we can do, Viv.'

'But what about the schools thing? That connects him to the missing girls. Then he scarpered before we could question him. Isn't that enough?'

Nash smiled grimly. 'I'd advise you to run it past a decent defence lawyer and watch him sharpen his claws. He'd tear us to shreds if we pursued Bailey with nothing more than that. No, you'll have to be patient. Keep working through the files, compiling what evidence you can, until something breaks. It's about time we had some luck in this case. In fact, it's long overdue. Clara's not coming in and I'm hoping to be here all day.'

Nash dialled Netherdale. 'I agree with you,' Pratt told him. 'We can't do anything about Bailey without more to go on. Any ideas how to move things forward?'

'Not yet, at any rate. What I intend to do is review all we've found out and see if there's anything we've overlooked. Some clue to where we should look next. I can do that today unless a riot breaks out on the Westlea. I'm in the office so I should get a chance.'

'Don't say that even as a joke,' Pratt implored. 'Anyway, you're pushing it a bit, aren't you?'

'Not really. I've given Clara the day off, and I'll be giving Viv a hand tying up loose ends before he goes on his forensics course. He's away for two days from tomorrow.'

'Don't overdo it, Mike. I'm still trying to find cover for you to have a break. Now I've withdrawn the search parties I might be able to find someone.'

'I'll be okay, but while you're on, I need a favour. I've found a new flat and a reference request has been e-mailed in. Can you help speed it up?'

'Anything to do with HR could take forever. Tell you what; I'll write one and fax it through to you. That help?'

'Thanks, Tom. It certainly will.'

At lunchtime Nash went out for a sandwich. He took with him the fax he'd received from Tom. Monique was on the phone when he arrived at Charleston's. She waved at him across the office and mouthed the words 'two minutes'.

'Can I help you?'

Nash turned towards the speaker, a slim, erect figure in his early to mid fifties. He had a mane of blond hair, tinged with grey at the temples. 'I'm Peter Charleston. Excuse the dust,' he said as he brushed his hands together. 'I've just been helping our sign erector load his van.' He indicated his companion, a nondescript looking middle-aged man in a brown dustcoat. 'That's Les Franklin, our maestro of the "FOR SALE" boards.'

Nash shook Charleston's hand. 'Pleased to meet you; I'm Mike Nash. I'm going to be renting the Rutland Way property from you.'

'Ah yes, the policeman. Monique told me about you. Is everything all right?'

'Everything's fine, I've brought in a reference from my boss. I know how long these things can take through "channels".'

Charleston smiled. 'Oh, that's good of you. Well, I must get on. I'll leave you in Monique's capable hands. Nice to meet you.'

Charleston waved his hand in farewell and the two men walked through the door leading to his own office. Nash had a momentary glimpse of the tidy room before the door closed. He smelt a faint aroma. Was it after shave? He dismissed the idea. It was a chemical smell. Probably from the signs, or the paint they used. It seemed vaguely familiar.

Monique crossed the office. 'Hello, Mike.'

He explained the reason for his visit, and passed her the envelope.

'That was kind of you.'

'Your Mr Charleston said the same.'

'Oh, you've met Peter, have you? You're honoured, and lucky. He's hardly ever here. But that's his own fault. With the expansion of the company, everyone's workload has increased. He's just had a few days off in Scotland, now he's here today, then off visiting the other branches. Heaven knows when we'll see him again. Not that it matters too much. Everything runs well even when he's not here.' She coughed. 'That's down to the efficiency of the manager.'

'Who is the manager?'

'I am,' Monique laughed, 'why do you think I said it. The problem is, whenever he's been away, he always brings us a little present back. This time it was a young mountain of shortbread. And me on a diet.'

'Could have been worse. It might have been haggis.'

'No fear, not with Peter, he can't stand the sight of blood. I got a tiny paper cut on my finger once and asked him to put a plaster on it. I thought he was going to faint.' She looked around to see if she could be overheard. 'I thought you'd come about those questions you wanted to ask me.'

'Well, yes, but perhaps somewhere a little more private?'

'I'm busy all day, so it will have to be my place I'm afraid. Chicken dinner okay?' She was shocked at her boldness.

The afternoon was lacking in incident, at least as far as CID was concerned, so Nash had plenty of time to analyse the files received from other forces and study his findings.

He was unable to discover anything significant in either the original reports or from their meetings with the parents. Although there was nothing to show for his efforts, Nash was left feeling dissatisfied when he closed the cover of the last folder.

Something was niggling at the back of his mind. Something he'd seen or heard, or something someone had said or done? No matter how hard he tried, the memory eluded him. In the end he wearied of the effort and gave up, but the impression remained within his subconscious. At some point he was sure he'd been given a clue that would lead him to the killer.

Monique looked better, more like the photograph of Danielle. The strain in her face had gone. The tension behind her eyes was absent too. 'You look tired, Mike,' she said when he arrived that evening.

He felt it. 'I'd a lousy day yesterday. Today was just frustrating,' Nash told her.

'Are things going wrong?'

'Not really. We tied up the stabbing case, you remember, the woman who was stabbed in the pub yard? The result was very sad. I know all violent crime has a sad aspect to it, but this was very distressing.'

They were sitting at Monique's dining table. 'Are you allowed to tell me about it?'

Nash told her about Cindy Green's confession and the motive for the murder. 'How awful,' Monique exclaimed. 'What that poor girl must have gone through.'

'It was pretty harrowing,' Nash agreed. 'It's one of the few times I've empathized with a murderer. I'm not passing judgement on the victim either; her only fault was being betrayed by her own impulses and desires. Anyway, if that wasn't bad enough for one day, I had to interview more parents. Louise Harland went missing eight years ago. I find it impossible to talk to the families and hold back. The only problem is the inference they draw is blindingly obvious.'

'You tell them you're investigating the disappearance of all the girls like you told me?'

'What else can I do? If I didn't give some explanation, they'd either think I was off my head or start drawing their own conclusions. The truth's bad enough, without them indulging in wild speculation. It's only fair they should know. I'll tell you what's so distressing. These people make you so welcome. You sit down in their home and you tell them news that's going to shatter their last remnant of hope. Then you look into the eyes of the mother. It's as if someone's snuffed a candle out. The light disappears, and it's as if you're looking into the darkest place in the whole world. To be honest, the only time that didn't happen, was when I talked to you.'

Monique smiled. 'It didn't distress me as much because, as I told you, I'd already worked out that Danny was dead. I didn't know about the others, of course; that was a shock. I actually think your telling me about the others helped me, took away some of my guilt by providing an explanation for me being left whilst Danielle was taken.'

'That puzzled me too. Seeing that photo of the pair of you on the hall table started me thinking. I know you'd said you were identical, but until I took a peep at the photo I didn't realize how alike you were. I thought, why Danielle, why not you? At lunchtime I took a walk along the route you and Danielle, went before the assault. I wanted to see the place you were attacked. I have a theory which might explain why you survived.'

Nash paused and took a sip of water. 'I heard something once about twins often being right and left-handed, as if one side of the brain is predominant in either twin. Was that the case with you and Danielle?'

'Not entirely. I'm right-handed in most things, whereas Danielle was ambidextrous. What's that got to do with why I was attacked and Danielle abducted?'

'When you walked together, did one always walk on the right, the other on the left, or didn't it matter?'

Monique thought about it for a long time. 'I'd never given that a thought, but now you mention it Danny always walked on the left and I walked on the right. Is that important?'

'This is pure speculation, but when I walked along the footpath I noticed there's a bench set in an alcove, surrounded by a tall privet hedge. That would be the perfect place for someone to lie in wait. If I was planning to attack someone, I couldn't have designed a better spot. The point is you would have been on the side nearest the bench; nearest the attacker. If my theory's right, the reason you were attacked instead of Danielle is that you were walking on the right.'

'The more I think about it, whenever we walked together Danny automatically went to the left and I fell in alongside her. If that's the only reason, then I've been feeling guilty all these years for nothing.'

Monique reached across the table and laid her hand on his. 'Thank you, Mike. If it's any comfort to you, set that against all the unhappiness you've witnessed. You've put my mind at rest about something that's always troubled me. Now, if you've had enough to eat, I'll clear away.'

'Yes, thank you,' Nash responded, 'it was delicious.'

'By the way, I forgot to mention, I sent off e-mail requests for your bank references for the flat on Monday. I don't foresee any problems. With luck I'll have the replies soon.'

Over coffee, they talked about anything and everything apart from the case. Nash recounted one or two of the more amusing and less gory incidents from his career.

'What an exciting life you lead,' Monique commented. 'Do you enjoy your job?'

'Yes, I do. That might seem strange, considering what I've just told you, and some of the things we have to do, and the sights we have to see, but on the whole, yes, I do enjoy it. How about you? You made it fairly clear you enjoy yours. And that you're a super-efficient manager.'

Monique laughed. 'That was self-advertising at its worst. I enjoy it now, more than I used to before I was made manager. And I nearly didn't get the chance.'

'How do you mean?'

'Apparently, long before my time, the company was going to the wall. The lady who was manager before me told me the story. It was a much smaller firm, only three branches, and the owners drained all the profits, so that they were always fighting off bankruptcy. Then Mr Charleston bought them out and started to make things happen. He put a load of capital in, apparently, got the firm on a solid footing then started to expand. There are Charleston Branches covering most of the North. You'll no doubt be aware of the advertising slogan? "Charleston One Stop Home Sales". That was Peter's idea. He said when people move, it's stressful enough, without having to arrange everything themselves. So why don't we offer to do everything for them. From the survey, to the conveyancing, to arranging the mortgage, the lot. We even have a removals company in the group now, plus our own sign erector, who goes around putting up the FOR SALE signs where ever they're needed. He's constantly on the move. Because Helmsdale's technically the head office, I get to handle his expenses. The petrol bill alone is massive. He can be anywhere up to two-hundred miles away. Mind you, he adds to it by living out at Bishopton, which is another twenty miles on to every journey. But he's so efficient we let him use the firm's van, so he takes it home every night. When he's not staying away, that is.'

'I'm surprised his wife doesn't object. To all the travelling I mean.'

'Oh, he's not married.'

'I've met him. Isn't his name Franklin? He was with Mr Charleston when I dropped that stuff in. Either he or Charleston had an odd smell about them, I remember.'

Monique laughed. 'That'd be Les, I bet. Well, not Les, but the chemical he sprays the signs with. It helps protect them against the weather. Les is ideal for the job, really. A bit of a loner, but he does a good job. And it adds to the rounded service we can provide. The one stop idea's not exactly original, I know, but apart from us, it's only the big firms that have the backing to offer that sort of service.'

'Bright idea though, and it obviously works.'

Monique nodded. 'I get to see the accounts, and I can vouch for that.'

'Where did Charleston's money come from?'

'Stocks and shares, or so I was told. Then, when he thought that had peaked, he moved into property and made another fortune buying and selling land. He still has a huge property portfolio. He's one of those naturally acquisitive people who just can't seem to help making money, whatever they're doing.'

'I can tell you enjoy your work. It's about the most enthusiastic I've seen you.'

'I admit it. It's great fun and it's not really hard work. There's a great satisfaction in fixing people up with somewhere to live.'

'Like me, you mean?'

'Exactly. Don't get me wrong. We get some awkward customers now and again, but you were easy. I could sell to you all day.'

Nash glanced at the clock and realized he was in danger of outstaying his welcome.

Monique escorted him down the long hallway to the front door, where she handed him a bag containing a bottle of wine she'd secreted under the hall table. 'Here's a house warming present for you, along with my thanks.' She handed him the bag, leaned forward and kissed him lightly. She stepped back and smiled.

Nash opened the glass-paned front door. It was a bright, moonlit night. Monique hovered on the threshold. He held out his hand, and after a moment's hesitation she stepped outside. He continued to hold her hand as they looked up at the beauty of the night sky. They turned to one another and kissed once more. This time there was no avoiding the passion in their embrace.

'I'd better go,' Nash's words were muffled by her hair as he kissed her neck. 'If I don't, I won't be able to leave at all.'

'Yes, I think you should,' Monique agreed reluctantly. 'Otherwise I won't allow you to.'

He raised her hand to his lips and kissed it. 'Goodnight again, Monique.'

She stepped back into the doorway. 'At least you managed to get me out of the house,' she told him. 'Not far, I admit, but across the doorstep is a start.'

Monique watched him walk down the path. When he reached the gate she waved, then went inside and closed the door. She leaned against it for a while, her eyes filled with tears of frustration. Why hadn't she the courage to make him stay?

Fifty yards down the road, a figure sat in the darkness of an unlit vehicle, parked as far from the street lamps as possible. What faint light permeated the vehicle reflected the hot glitter of rage in the eyes of the shadowy occupant.

As Nash drove home, he was still trying to work out whether the present had been the wine or the kiss.

He opened the bottle and had a couple of glasses. The day had tired him and it was no later than 11 p.m. when he went to bed. He realized once he was in bed that he'd forgotten to take his tablets. He couldn't decide whether to get out of bed and go for them, but he knew he should. He'd left them in the kitchen again. The bed was warm and he was reluctant to move. He was still trying to make his mind up when he fell asleep.

During the early part of the night he slept well, but towards dawn he became restless. After waking and slipping back asleep several times, he sat up in bed. Something was plaguing him. That same distant memory, something that was ringing faint bells. The more he tried to grasp it, the more elusive it became.

CHAPTER FIFTEEN

'Morning, Clara, you look rested. Good day off?'

'Very good. I took David to meet my parents. He's going abroad again. I wanted them to meet him before he leaves.'

'Where's he going, do you know?'

Clara shook her head. 'They're not allowed to disclose anything.'

'Understandable, given his job.'

'Anything happen here?'

'Very quiet, for a change. While I see what we're faced with today, you write up your report on the Harland visit.'

Mironova had fielded a phone call from Tracey Forrest. 'You remember, her husband is a lorry driver on the Continent? His trip got cancelled, ferry strike or something. Mrs Forrest said if you want to see them, it'd have to be tonight. He's rescheduled to be away again tomorrow, and won't be back for ten days. Problem is, I've got a complimentary ticket to the re-opening of Netherdale cinema, so you'd have to go alone unless you really want—'

'I'm sure I'll cope.' Nash stopped suddenly.

'What is it,' Clara looked at him.

'Something you said just now.' Nash frowned with concentration, 'That's it. Something's been niggling away at me. You mentioned Megan Forrest's mother. Get Megan's file out for me, will you. I'm going to need it anyway. Look at the list of witnesses who were identified as being at the pub the night Megan was abducted.'

'Anyone in particular I should be looking for?'

'Yes, a man by the name of Franklin, Les Franklin. I'm sure that's where I saw his name before.' Nash explained his conversation with Monique. 'If he is on that list, he might be worth putting on our list of possibles.'

'We don't have a list of possibles other than Bailey.'

'Well, now we can start one. Although it may be nothing more than coincidence. After all, the man does live there, and it's not exactly a big place.'

'Okay, I'll check it out.'

With no chauffeur to take him to Bishopton, Nash read the file contents beforehand. Megan Forrest had gone out on New Year's Eve, two years previously. She'd left The Plough Inn on Bishopton Market Place at about 2.30 a.m. to walk home. She never arrived. Nash sighed, how many times had he read that phrase. He looked at the girl's description and the clothing she'd been wearing when she disappeared and blinked with astonishment.

A note further down the page provided an explanation, nevertheless the singularity of Megan's attire set Nash thinking. The Plough Inn had been holding a fancy dress competition. The event would have been well publicized. If Nash was right about the killer, he'd have known about it well in advance. It would have been easy to hire a costume. In a crowded town-centre pub, one more bizarre outfit would have passed unnoticed. Well, perhaps not unnoticed, but certainly not out of place.

Nash was certain that was what had happened. The killer would have his identity hidden behind the anonymity of his costume. Probably something requiring a mask; if he was known to Megan, he'd have to be masked. Perhaps a gorilla costume, or Darth Vader, maybe a cartoon character.

He could have loitered close to where Megan lived so he could see how she was dressed. He would watch her emerge from the house, note the clown's costume, then driven to The Plough. By the time Megan arrived, the killer would have been near the bar, drink in hand, hovering at the edge of a group perhaps, appearing to be part of it. All the time he'd be watching Megan from behind his mask, waiting for the moment she left.

The killer would have left before her, just one more reveller homeward bound. Once she was clear of the town, he'd have been able to carry out the abduction, safe in the knowledge that at that hour on New Year's Morning, no one would interrupt him. Nash shuddered at the cold-blooded simplicity of it.

He read on. Towards the bottom of the page a dismissive note had been added, presumably by someone from CID. 'No Facts' it stated, 'Nothing to work with.' 'I know just how you feel,' Nash muttered.

Mironova wandered in to tell him she was on her way home. 'Enjoy yourself,' Nash told her. 'Don't think of me slaving away, trying to solve a multiple murder case, will you?'

'I won't give it a thought,' Mironova replied with a grin. 'Is there anything you need before I go?'

'Just let me run this by you. See if you can spot any flaws.' Nash explained his theory about Megan's disappearance.

'Can't see anything wrong with that. I'm beginning to think you're right about this character. Maybe he is a perverted genius. Anything else?'

'I don't think so. No, hang on. Can you tell me where Deanery Close is in Bishopton?'

Mironova shook her head. 'Sorry, I don't know Bishopton well. I've just seen the Fire Officer heading into the building. He'll give you directions.'

'We might make a detective out of you yet.'

Mironova gave him a gesture which was unladylike, rude and certainly insubordinate. Nash grinned and returned to the report.

Megan had been eighteen when she vanished. She'd left school the previous summer and was unemployed. There was a note on the file, however, to the effect that in the run-up to Christmas she'd been working for a local chain of convenience stores, as a temporary seasonal staff. The report stated she'd been a bright but not exceptional pupil, and was well liked both at school and at the shop. So much so, that she'd have been first to be offered a permanent position when a vacancy arose.

Both parents had reported her missing. Steve Forrest had returned from the Continent late on New Year's Eve, having been delayed by storms in the Channel. He'd gone to bed as soon as he got home, and it was only when Megan's mother found her room empty, the bed not slept in, that the couple contacted the police.

Nash closed the file and left it on his desk. Douglas Curran, the Chief Fire Officer, was supervising a shift change, so Nash waited in the fire brigade canteen until he was free. 'Come through to my office.'

Nash was reminded of his visit to Rushton Engineering. Like their MD, Curran appeared to have a fetish for neatness. Nash thought of the organized chaos of his own desk and sighed wistfully.

'Now, Mike, what can I do for you? I thought you'd everything under control, you wrapped that murder case up so quickly.'

'Some of them are easier than others, Doug,' Nash said with a rueful smile. 'What I'm after is directions to a property in Bishopton. Do you cover that area from here?'

'We do, one of the so-called benefits of rationalization. I'm not sure how they thought the policy up. Fires don't burn slower because we've to travel further to tackle them. Why do you want to go to Bishopton? Is it another juicy murder, or can't you tell me?'

Nash smiled. 'To be honest, I've no hard evidence that a crime has been committed. Just a lot of supposition and guesswork. If I'm right, it's more than one murder.'

'How many?'

'At least seven.'

'Good God, tell me more!'

Nash outlined the disappearances, commenting on the ease with which the killer had picked up his victims.

'I understand that. We preach fire safety whenever we can, but time after time we get called out to fires because some idiot has failed to take the simplest of precautions. It doesn't make our job any easier, and they look at you as if you're mad when you bollock them for it. Deep down, you know you're talking to yourself. From what you said, all those girls were alone, at night, in the dark and for the most part in lonely places. If that's not inviting trouble, I don't know what is. I hope you catch the bastard. Now, tell me whereabouts you want to be.'

Nash climbed into the CID car and set out for his destination. He didn't have to go to Bishopton at all. Nash had been shown the location on a large map. The fire chief pointed out the best route. As Nash pulled out of the yard, he was unaware that Curran was watching him from his office window, a curious expression on his face.

Deanery Close was a terrace of mews cottages that had been renovated, within the last few years Nash guessed. Steve and Tracey Forrest owned the end house, the largest in the block. Steve Forrest, a thickset man in his late forties, answered Nash's knock and showed him through to the dining kitchen, where Tracey was seated at the table, nursing a mug of coffee. The room was light, airy, scrupulously clean and tidy. The overall effect was ultramodern, a kitchen for the space age, in contrast to the building's exterior.

Of the mothers he'd met, Tracey was the one most like her daughter. She too had a mane of lustrous blonde hair, and like Megan had the heart-shaped face and high cheekbones that promised a beauty that wouldn't fade.

They discussed Megan's disappearance for some time, then Tracey began telling Nash about their other children. Nash listened patiently as she told him about Steve junior, a fifteen-year-old with ambitions to become the next David Beckham. Of Rianne, now nineteen and studying law at Newcastle University, and of Shelley, rising twelve and torn between a desire to become a pop star and an ambition to win the Wimbledon Ladies title.

'You'll notice they're all aiming for better jobs than ours,' Steve commented ironically. 'They'll be able to care for us in our old age. There's not much money in road haulage these days, even less as a cook.'

'You don't seem to be doing badly,' Nash suggested. 'This house is lovely.'

Tracey said, 'It came on the market at the right time. We needed something bigger. It's too big for a lot of families and there's the disadvantage of it being so remote. Unless you've two cars, a family would be totally isolated out here. That's why it was for sale longer than the others. We were a bit cheeky with the bid. It surprised us when it was accepted.' Her face changed abruptly; her eyes filled with tears. 'At least we thought it was lucky at the time. I wish we'd never moved. If we'd stayed put maybe Megan would still be with us.'

Nash attempted to console her. 'I don't think you should look at it that way. If what we suspect is true, I don't think where you were living enters into it.'

'Can you explain that?' Forrest asked. He put a consoling arm around his wife's shoulder.

Once they'd assimilated the full horror of what he told them, Tracey Forrest was the first to react. 'Why has no one thought of this before? Why has it taken this monster to attack seven girls before anyone sits up and takes notice?'

'I can't answer that. Not satisfactorily, anyway. The other girls are mainly from out of our area and over a long period of time. I wasn't here when Megan went missing. I worked in London until two years ago. Perhaps it was a fresh pair of eyes, a different approach. Or maybe I'm more used to this sort of crime.'

Steve Forrest had been studying Nash intently. 'I thought your face looked familiar,' he exclaimed. 'You were in the papers back then. Weren't you the bloke who was responsible for catching Donald Marston?'

Nash was taken by surprise, he merely nodded.

'It was in all the tabloids,' Forrest explained. 'You read a lot in my job, waiting to be loaded and unloaded, queuing for ferries and the like, or when you're out of tachograph hours.' He turned to his wife. 'If anyone can find out what happened to Megan, Mr Nash is the man. I remember one paper said it was "a brilliant piece of detective work, close to genius". That's pretty strong stuff, even for the tabloids.'

The thought of Megan's fate proved too much for Tracey. She collapsed in tears and it was some time before her husband was able to pacify her. Nash realized he would do no good by staying. 'I'd best be on my way. Thank you for your time. I only hope we can resolve matters as soon as possible. You've suffered long enough.'

Tracey's look was heart-rending. 'Mr Nash, if you're right, we'll only be swapping one form of suffering for another.' Nash acknowledged the truth of this.

Forrest turned once again to his wife. 'But at least we'll know, love. I'll show you to the door, Inspector.' He paused in the hall, one hand on the doorknob, before letting Nash out. 'Do you really think Megan and the others might have finished up like Marston's victims?'

Nash caught the note of pleading; the need for reassurance behind the big man's words.

'That's impossible to answer. I don't want to cause mass hysteria but I'm not going to pretend it isn't a possibility.'

'At least that's honest,' Forrest conceded. 'Even if it does take away our last bit of hope.'

'Is it hope, or wishful thinking? I've met relatives of all the girls, as you know. Their families were closely knit like yours. None of the girls was the type to go swanning off without explanation. From the moment you knew Megan was missing, you must have guessed something like this had happened.'

Forrest nodded reluctant agreement. 'I suppose you're right,' he admitted. 'It's strange, isn't it? We didn't like to allow the possibility, even between ourselves, because we thought that might be letting Megan down. As if by thinking the worst, we'd make it happen. We should have realized it already had. One thing, though, Mr Nash. Try to get it over with as fast as you can. We need closure.'

Jimmy Johnson was a burglar. A careful burglar, cunning and keen witted. One of a brood of six, born to a single mother in Glasgow, Jimmy had overcome this handicap and now earned a comfortable living. During his career he'd suffered two set-backs, each providing him with a valuable lesson. The first: never work with a partner. Partners meant halving the profit, doubling the risk, and they could be less than trustworthy. Second: research your objective thoroughly. Both lessons had resulted in Johnson being a resident in one of Her Majesty's Prisons.

Few people would have guessed the occupation of the mild-mannered little man with the Glaswegian accent. A family man, whose wife worked at the local supermarket and with two young school aged boys. Neighbours assumed that he worked a night shift somewhere, which wasn't far from the truth.

His preferences were for jewellery and cash. He was particular in the jewellery he targeted. He avoided high value, readily identifiable objects, going instead for lesser value pieces, where the stones could easily be removed from the settings, rendering them anonymous.

His research led to him choosing Bishopton Hall as his next target. Jimmy was an avid reader of glossy magazines that specialized in printing photographs taken at social occasions attended by the region's major and minor celebrities.

It was in one of these that he'd seen photographs taken at a recent charity ball. Amongst those present were a couple captioned as 'Sir Ivor Quinn, millionaire industrialist and owner of the filly Cavatina'. Jimmy didn't spare Sir Ivor a second glance. His attention was drawn to Lady Helena, not for her looks, which, Jimmy thought, closely resembled those of Cavatina, but for the jewellery she was wearing. Hence Jimmy's recent observations of the daily routines of the owners at the Hall. And of the staff, who he'd established didn't live in.

An item on the local TV news had provided further valuable information. When Sir Ivor was interviewed about his filly's chances in her next race, he revealed his intention to take a short break immediately following the race meeting. Johnson watched the interview and made his plans. He checked the weather forecast. A dry evening was promised, ideal for the robbery. He'd use his scooter rather than the van. He preferred the scooter, whenever possible. It was manoeuvrable, could go where the van couldn't, and was easier to conceal. With only a small amount of jewellery and his tools to carry, a rucksack would be ample. Tuesday night would be the ideal time to hit Bishopton Hall.

Entering the building was easy. The house was silent, deserted, as he expected. He disabled the ancient excuse for a burglar alarm by disconnecting it at the alarm box. No matter how many beams he crossed, or wires he broke, they'd send their signals to the box in vain. It would remain mute. Jimmy replaced the ladder in the outhouse, and within minutes was heading for Sir Ivor's study.

The painting, of a disagreeable-looking female in Victorian costume, behind the desk, was hinged. Behind it was a wall safe, almost as old as the painting. It was one of the earliest combination models, the code consisting of three letters. 'Safe by name but not by nature,' Jimmy muttered as he set to work.

It took little more than a quarter of an hour to crack the combination. nation. The door swung open to his touch. 'I might have guessed.' To Jimmy's mild irritation there was no cash. He cursed the inventor of the credit card. No one carried cash these days, no matter how well-heeled they were.

He reached into the recesses of the safe and found what he was looking for; a large oblong jewel case. If Jimmy had been mildly irritated by his failure to unearth any cash, his feelings on examining the contents of the jewel case were unprintable. The first item he extracted told him the worst even before he examined it. The diamond pendant should have been heavy with the combined carats of the stones added to the ornate gold setting. It wasn't. 'I don't believe it,' Jimmy said in disgust. He hefted the pendant again to make doubly sure then peered at it carefully. 'Nothing but a set of bloody pebbles. Cheapskate! It's no wonder you've nothing more than an old tin box to keep your so-called valuables in.'

Jimmy checked the rest. The whole lot was costume jewellery. The combined value, Jimmy reflected bitterly, would scarcely cover the cost of his petrol. His irritation turned to contempt. He tipped the contents of the jewel case on to the desk and left the box alongside. He didn't bother closing the safe. As he left, he turned to secure the outer door then stopped. 'Ah, you've nothing worth stealing. Why lock the bugger at all.' He strode impatiently to the place he'd concealed his scooter, anger in every step.

Neither was paying attention. Neither was concentrating, their minds on other things. It would never have happened otherwise. Each of them blamed themselves, both were wrong. That apart, the outcome was a one-sided contest.

The first thing Nash knew was the impact. He heard the noise, steel on steel. Felt the shock of the collision run up the steering column, through the steering wheel and vibrate on his hands and arms. A split second later, he saw the man's body thrown sideways into the road.

It was fortunate neither was travelling fast. Nash leapt from the car, ashen faced and trembling. The car had dealt the scooter a glancing blow. The machine didn't appear badly damaged and the CID car's front wing had only been slightly dented by the collision. Nash hurried towards the rider, who was lying prone in the road where the impact had thrown him. The rider groaned, raised himself cautiously into a sitting position, and removed his crash-helmet.

Nash helped to ease the rucksack off his shoulders. As he set it down, something clattered on to the tarmac. Without thinking, Nash bent to pick up the small bundle that had fallen out and went to replace it. His hand stopped in mid air. He stared at the tools in the open canvas pouch. 'Well, well, well,' Nash murmured, 'what have we here?'

Jimmy Johnson groaned once more as the road swam in front of his eyes then returned to focus. 'What happened?'

'You've been in an accident. You were thrown off your scooter,' Nash told him abstractedly, as he rummaged within the rucksack. Apart from the tool kit it was empty. 'How do you feel?'

'As if I've been in an accident and got thrown off my scooter,' Johnson replied, then noticed Nash's activities. 'Hey, what d' you think you're doing?'

'Would you mind explaining these?' Nash held up the tools.

Johnson glared at him. 'That's my tool kit,' he said defensively.

'I know. Unfortunately, I also know what they're used for, and it has nothing to do with scooter maintenance. Before you start thinking of a plausible explanation, I should tell you I'm a police officer.'

'You're kidding,' Johnson looked at Nash's face. 'You're not kidding, are you? I should have stayed home tonight. It's been nothing short of a bloody disaster.'

'Never mind that. Are you hurt?'

Johnson shook his head.

'Can you get up if I help you?'

'I'll try.'

Nash supported Jimmy, as he got painfully to his feet. He stood for a moment, swaying as he waited for the road to refocus.

When the dizziness passed, Johnson let go of Nash's arm. 'It's okay, I'm all right now. I'll just be away home.'

'You're going nowhere. Not in your condition, and not on that scooter. What you're going to do is sit quietly in the passenger seat of the CID car whilst I wheel your machine off the road. I'll send someone to pick it up later. Then I'm going to drive you home. Unless you'd prefer to go to the hospital? On the way we can have a little chat about this interesting tool kit of yours.'

Johnson was emphatic, 'I don't need the hospital.'

The first part of the journey was conducted in silence, before Nash said, 'What's your name?'

'Jimmy,' Johnson replied cautiously.

'That's hardly original. What goes with it?'

'Johnson, Jimmy Johnson.'

'Now we're making progress. I'm Mike Nash; rank of Detective Inspector. Now, you know as much about me as I do about you. Let's see, your name's Jimmy Johnson, you're a professional burglar. Tonight you were in the process of burgling Bishopton Hall, but for some reason you left empty handed. Why might that be, I wonder? Were you disturbed, or was the security too tough for you? Do tell me, Jimmy. I'm really interested.'

For a few seconds, Nash was worried the bump on the head had made his passenger hysterical. Eventually, Jimmy's laughter died away. 'Security, what a bloody joke. They've no security. Why would that bunch of cheapskates need security?'

Nash was beginning to find the droll little Scotsman amusing. 'Don't tell me, they've nothing worth nicking?'

'Not a bloody thing. I spent more on bloody petrol than the stuff was worth. The night's been a bloody disaster. Apart from anything, I'll have to move on now, now I've bumped into you. It's a bloody shame. I was getting settled.'

'Tell me about it.'

Johnson eyed Nash suspiciously, muttered 'Oh what the Hell,' and began explaining about his speciality, and how it was becoming more difficult to earn a dishonest penny. Nash had no respect for violent criminals, but couldn't help liking the gentle Scot and listened with sympathy.

'Have you ever thought of quitting?'

'What would I do? I've a wife, in a job she likes, and two bairns. They need to be fed and clothed. What else do I know, apart from robbing?'

'You said yourself, things are changing. Fewer people keep cash about the house any more. The plastic revolution, I think they call it. And there's a lot less decent tackle for you to half-inch. It seems to me you're in a losing game, and it's bound to get worse. Why not look around, see if your specialist skills could be put to other uses. Go straight?'

'What?' Johnson spluttered in disbelief.

'You said you'd have to move on now that I've rumbled you. If your kids are at school and your wife's working, that's going to mean a real upheaval. It seems unnecessary. I reckon it'd be far better looking for a proper job and staying put.'

'I'd get less earache at home, that's for sure,' Jimmy admitted, 'but that's beside the point. You'll be charging me with "going equipped".'

Nash thought about it. He felt some responsibility for the accident that would cost Jimmy dearly, and didn't want that guilt. 'I take it you've got form?'

'Aye, I've done a three and a five.'

'And you really didn't take anything from the Hall?'

'I felt I ought to be taking something in. Not pinching it.'

'Is it such a joke?'

'Och aye, the alarm's been in fifty years or more. Belongs on the Antiques Roadshow, together with the tin box they call a safe. It took me twenty minutes to disable the alarm, get inside and open the safe. And that was twenty minutes wasted,' Johnson ended bitterly.

Nash studied for a while. They'd almost reached the outskirts of Helmsdale before he spoke again. 'Can I trust you, if you make me a promise?'

'I've never broken a promise since I was eight years old. I got a real skelping for it then. My mother told me I was never to give my word if I couldn't keep it.'

'Okay, I'll do a deal. You promise to find a job. One that doesn't involve breaking the law. Then I won't charge you over tonight's little escapade.'

Jimmy stared at Nash, his mouth agape with astonishment. 'Are you really a copper? Because you're like no other copper I've ever met.'

Nash smiled. 'Want to see my warrant card? Maybe I don't work like other coppers. Now what about it?'

Jimmy had little alternative. Above all else, he didn't want to face Maggie or his young sons with the news of another move. 'If you really mean it, Mr Nash, I promise.' He thought for a moment, 'Nash. I thought your name rang a bell. Last time I was inside, I was in Full Sutton. You're a hero there. You put Marston away.'

'That's right,' Nash was shocked that he'd been recognized twice within a few hours. 'Why does that make me a hero in the nick?'

'All the decent blokes inside hate perverts like that. They wanted to have a go at him for what he did to those wee laddies. What were you doing out there, Mr Nash, if you weren't after me?'

Despite his better judgement, Nash found himself telling Johnson brief details of the reason for his visit to Bishopton, about the missing girls. Johnson listened with growing revulsion. By the time Nash finished his tale, they were parked outside Johnson's house. 'It sounds like you've another sick bastard to catch, Mr Nash. I hope you do it before some other poor lassie gets hurt. I just wish I could help.'

'Thanks, Jimmy, you stay out of trouble. Keep your promise and I'll keep mine.'

CHAPTER SIXTEEN

Monique ate her solitary meal with scant pleasure. The food was tasty, but she missed Nash sitting across the table, watching his enjoyment. As she'd told him, cooking for one is a chore.

After clearing away, she glanced at the kitchen clock. It wasn't quite nine o'clock. She felt restless, unable to settle, but couldn't pinpoint the cause. She decided to start the book she'd taken from the library.

She walked through to the lounge, switched on the standard lamp and settled in her favourite armchair. It was a warm evening, and after a few minutes, her eyelids began to droop and she dozed off.

It was after eleven o'clock when she was awakened by a soft thud. She sprang to her feet in panic then realized the library book had slipped from her lap. She scoffed at her fear, but the incident unnerved her. She hurried across the room to draw the curtains. As she was closing the second one she saw, or thought she saw, a small movement in her peripheral vision.

Monique crossed to the chair in three swift strides, collected her book and switched off the lamp. Now in the hall, her heart was beating faster than normal. She checked the front door was safely locked and bolted, the chain in position, then raced through to the kitchen to make sure the back door was also secure. Taking the steps two at a time, she dashed upstairs to her darkened bedroom and walked swiftly to the window. As she was about to pull the curtains together, a car passed on its way to Helmsdale. The headlights picked out another vehicle, a large, silver-coloured saloon car, parked no more than thirty yards down the road. She was almost convinced someone was sitting in the driver's seat. While she continued watching, she moved instinctively behind the curtain. It was almost twenty minutes before another vehicle passed.

Forewarned by the approaching headlights, Monique focused on the point where she'd seen the parked car. This time there was no doubt. Someone was sitting in the stationary vehicle. It might have been a courting couple, but she'd sufficient time to see that the passenger seat was empty.

By now, she was in a frenzy of panic. She crossed to the bedside phone and dialled Helmsdale police station. A recorded announcement told her the call was being diverted. The wait seemed endless before a voice answered. After some effort, she persuaded the duty officer to send a message to Nash.

She sat on the edge of the bed. Not daring to move. Every sense strained for the slightest sound. The silent, motionless night seemed to mock her fear. When the phone rang, it startled her so much she almost dropped the receiver.

'Monique, are you alright? I got a message. The officer said you sounded upset. What is it?'

Monique stammered an explanation. 'There's someone sitting outside in a parked car, in total darkness. I think someone was hiding in the bushes near the gate earlier. I was closing the curtains, and I'm sure I saw a movement.'

'I'll get a patrol car to drive past, and I'll come along as well. Wait till you see both cars outside before you move or show yourself. Don't put any lights on, or give any indication you're not in bed.'

It seemed an age before Monique saw the welcome sight of car headlights reflected in the bedroom window. She sprang to her feet, and peered cautiously round the curtain. To her immense relief, she saw a pair of cars parked outside her drive. The first she recognized as the one Nash used, the other had distinctive yellow and blue panels, that Monique thought resembled the aftermath of an explosion in a paint factory. She blessed the designer who'd thought up the lurid colour scheme.

Both cars had their headlights on, and Monique saw Nash walk over to the police car and bend to talk to the driver. She switched the bedroom light on and returned to her vantage point. Nash waved and pointed towards her front door. Monique hurried downstairs to let him in.

She smiled nervously. 'Did you see anything?'

Nash shook his head. 'There was no parked car when we arrived. Did you see a car pull away while you were waiting for us?'

'No,' Monique replied instantly. 'I thought I'd heard the sound of an engine, but when I saw no headlights I thought I must have been mistaken.'

'I don't like the sound of that. Why would someone risk driving without lights if their actions were innocent? I've asked the guys in the patrol car to drive past every couple of hours. Is your sofa comfortable?'

'Very comfortable,' she echoed, mystified. 'Why do you ask?'

'If you can supply a blanket and pillow, I'll curl up on your sofa if it will make you feel any easier. It might help you get some sleep.'

'That's very kind, but you don't have to use the sofa. I'll make up the bed in Danny's room. I'll feel safer if you're close by. Whilst I'm doing that, let me pour you a nightcap.'

She handed him a well-filled whisky glass and went to make up the bed. Nash dug into his pocket and removed the pill box he kept for emergencies. He swallowed two tablets and washed them down with the whisky. He smiled at the thought that there are worse ways of taking medicine than with a single malt. When she'd prepared the room, Monique returned. 'If you fancy another drink I think I'll join you.' She fetched another glass and the decanter.

'It's not normally considered a woman's drink,' Nash commented.

'No, but I've already told you I'm not normal.' A stray memory crossed Monique's mind. Her face darkened with remembered anger. 'Certainly your colleague who did the initial investigation didn't think I was normal. Trying to make out Danny and I fought over me stealing one of her boyfriends. I tried telling him Danny had finished with the guy before I went out with him. But it didn't fit his theory, so he wasn't interested.'

'Why did she finish with him?'

'I'm not totally sure. She said he was a lousy lover. At the time I thought that was an excuse, because she'd found someone else.' Monique thought for a moment. 'However, I found out later he was useless in bed, so perhaps Danny was telling the truth.'

'Poor guy. What a dreadful reputation to live down. What happened to him?'

'He emigrated. I remember bumping into him just before he left and he was full of the excitement of it. You know, a new life, a new continent, etcetera, etcetera.'

'Whereabouts did he go?'

'America. He'd got a job offer in Seattle. I remember watching the film *Sleepless in Seattle* and hearing the statistic about it raining there nine months in every year, and thinking how appropriate.'

When they went upstairs, Nash looked round; everything about the room was feminine. Monique stood watching from the doorway. 'I hope you'll be comfortable.'

'I'm sure I will, thanks.'

She pointed to a door on the far side of the room. 'There's an en suite. I've put towels out, for if you want a shower in the morning.'

'That's kind. Let's hope for an undisturbed night.'

'Goodnight, Mike, and thanks again for staying.'

When he was alone Nash remembered the stray impression that was still niggling him. He needed something to jolt his memory. Another visit from Danielle perhaps? After all, where would she most likely be? This is nonsense; he tried to dismiss his thoughts. Fantasizing about the ghosts of dead girls really is madness, he was ridiculing himself as he fell asleep.

First he heard the sound as if from a great distance. As it persisted, the sound became clearer. He recognized the noise. It was the sound of someone moving, breathing. The footsteps were light, the breathing little more than a whisper, yet he knew it was inside the room. Had he heard the sounds? He couldn't have been mistaken, could he? 'Monique,' he called softly. 'Are you there, Monique?'

Another sound, a door opening. Nash glanced to his left. She was standing in the bathroom doorway. Her smile was enigmatic. 'Are you sure it's her you want? Wouldn't you rather have me?'

He stared speechlessly. She was wearing a close fitting coat that emphasised her superb figure. Then she spoke, 'This isn't a very good time. What do you want?'

He stared in astonishment. 'How do you mean, not a good time?'

'I still have feelings, you know. That's about all I do have. Feelings of sadness and happiness. Feelings of pain and pleasure. This is a very sad time. What do you want?'

'What do I want?' he echoed.

'You asked me to come here, so what's it about? Is it to do with finding out what's going on or is there another reason?'

As she spoke she moved slightly. He was transfixed by her loveliness. The movement caused the coat to part slightly and he could see she was wearing nothing underneath.

'I thought so,' she stood and faced him. 'Don't ask the question, it isn't permitted. I'll tell you instead. What you must do is work out the meaning of your dream.'

'What dream, this dream?'

'You'll know when you dream it. Do you understand?' He nodded, unable to speak. 'Then think about the message within it. Work the

rest out yourself. Now,' she moved across the room and sat on the edge of the bed. Her hand strayed to the belt of the coat, 'about the other reason you wanted me.'

His eyes devoured her. He was totally at a loss for words, for thoughts and for a moment for the power of action. Then with just the slightest movement she unleashed the belt, the coat fell further open. A small shrug of her shoulders and the coat dropped to the floor.

She seemed to melt into his arms and in an instant they were joined. He had no part in leading the encounter; he was merely a slave to her demands. Again and again she came for him. Again and again she took her toll of him until he was completely spent. She caressed his cheek. 'I have to go.'

He woke up. Was it seconds or hours later? He was alone. He turned over in bed. As he moved, the sheet felt damp under his hand. His mind was a whirl. Was it a dream, or had Danielle visited him? Was he going mad? Had it been Monique who had come for him? In which case, why had she left? It must be madness to dream of talking, or making love to or falling in love with a ghost.

He glanced at his watch. It was five o'clock. He fell back on the bed groaning with disappointment, and as if from a great distance he thought he heard, faint but distinct, the sound of laughter: her laughter.

It was a clear, bright morning. Monique woke refreshed and relaxed. She lay for a few moments in contented ease. She thought of Mike, so close, so strong and comforting. She smiled a little smugly and stretched. She rolled on her side and looked at the bedside clock. It was almost 7.30. She felt sure Mike would be hungry. She'd make breakfast for him. It was the least she could do.

She looked out, and was surprised to see Nash bending over the bushes by the front gate. He looked like a sleuth from a detective story. Monique stifled a giggle as she opened the window and called, 'Shouldn't you be wearing a deerstalker, smoking a pipe and peering through a magnifying glass?'

Nash straightened and looked back at the house. 'The deerstalker blew away in the wind, the Hound of the Baskervilles sat on the magnifying glass and the fire brigade confiscated the pipe as a fire hazard.'

'How about breakfast, Sherlock?'

'Sounds good. Detective work's hard on an empty stomach.'

'Did you find anything?'

They were in the kitchen. 'I'm sure you were right about your prowler,' he told her. 'That might be cold comfort, but at least our arrival scared him off. The lower branches of a couple of shrubs have been snapped. The earth below compressed, as if someone was standing there for a while. Unfortunately,' Nash concluded, 'the ground's too hard to get a footprint, but I suppose that would have been too much to hope for.'

'You were right when you said it wouldn't be a comfort. You're scaring me silly.'

'I understand that, but now we know about it, we can take precautions. I'll give some thought as to the best way of protecting you. Did you sleep alright, after your scare?'

Monique gave him a secretive smile. 'It was the best night I've had in ages,' she replied cryptically. 'Did you sleep? Nothing disturbed you?'

He glanced suspiciously at her, but her face was a mask of innocence.

Nash dropped Monique outside her office. 'I'll be in touch later this morning.' He watched her unlock the street door, then drove home to shave and change. On his way to the station he had an idea, one he cursed himself for not thinking of earlier. As soon as he reached his office he rang Netherdale and told Pratt what he wanted. He was on the computer when Clara strolled into his office. Nash signalled to her to stay.

'How did it go last night?' Mironova asked.

Nash told her the details of his meeting with Megan's parents, and of Monique's prowler, omitting to mention his encounter with Jimmy Johnson. 'So you stayed the night with her?' Clara's voice was expressionless, the inference pointed.

'I slept in Danielle's room,' Nash said defensively.

'And you didn't get any late-night prowlers?'

'What do you mean?' he asked sharply.

'I meant, did the mystery man reappear.'

'Oh, I see. No, nothing happened.'

'You mean you slept undisturbed?'

He was studying the screen, his reply came too late to be convincing. 'Yes, we did.

'Clara, look at this, we never checked. The DVLA shows Roland Bailey has a current valid driving licence. He's also the registered keeper of a Ford Mondeo five-door saloon car, listed as being Stardust Silver Metallic. This puts a whole different complexion on things. We need to put a trace out for the Mondeo. I've also an idea I'd like you to consider.'

Monique was on edge from the moment Nash left her. She was immeasurably relieved when the receptionist told her Mike was on the line, or, as she put it, 'That copper who fancies you wants a word. If it's a dirty weekend in Scarborough he's after, I'll go if you don't.'

The sound of Nash's voice was reassuring. 'Hello, Monique. I've been talking to Sergeant Mironova. You remember, you met her when I was viewing flats?'

'Yes, she was very kind.'

'In view of last night's events, Clara's agreed to stay with you. She'll meet you from work, drive you home, check the house over and stay. Next morning, she'll drive you to work. She'll continue until we've got things settled. How does that sound?'

'Oh, er, all right, I suppose,' Monique realized immediately how churlish that sounded. 'Yes, please,' she continued, 'tell her I'm really grateful, will you?'

Although Monique wouldn't admit it, her mild disappointment was due to it being Clara rather than Nash who would be staying with her.

'Clara, before we go off half-cocked, I'd like you to do one more thing. Give each of the parents a ring. Ask them if they can remember anyone connected with their school that showed a particular interest in their daughter. Not an unhealthy interest specifically. Keep your question open, vague almost. Don't mention Bailey by name whatever you do, don't even mention what his role was. Okay?'

Although none of the parents could recall immediately, Tracey Forrest phoned back a little later. Nash took the call. 'Something your sergeant said set me thinking. Megan did mention someone who worked at her school, who she thought might be a dirty old man. She said it was the way he looked at girls, when he thought no one was watching. It wasn't one of the teaching staff, I'm certain. I think he might have been a gardener. Is that any help?'

'Thank you, Mrs Forrest. It could be most helpful.'

He told Mironova the gist of Tracey Forrest's remarks. 'It's all starting to point towards Bailey. He lived close to Sarah Kelly, he works for the same company, and before that he'd worked at schools the girls attended, or where their mothers worked. Then there's his membership of that dodgy club in Netherdale. That shows he's the right type. His car fits the description of the one Monique's prowler used, and your friend Turner's statement also said the car he saw was silver. Then he vanished when we were about to question him about Sarah Kelly. That looks very much like the action of a guilty man. I didn't buy into it when Pearce suggested it but I admit it's beginning to look more of a possibility. I think we've enough now to request a search warrant for Bailey's house. Organize it, will you, we'll go in first thing tomorrow. I'll get Jack to sort out some uniforms to go with us. Despite everything, I'm still not convinced Bailey's the man we're after.'

'Why not?'

'It's more of a feeling than anything. All we've found out makes Bailey a prime suspect. I know we should assume the worst from the fact he bolted, but that doesn't fit with what we know about the killer. Everything so far has been carefully planned to avoid leaving the slightest clue.'

'You don't think Bailey fits that description?'

'Roland Bailey is high profile. The killer takes every precaution to ensure he remains low profile. I'm willing to bet that after each incident, he returns to what might be seen as a normal life. This man is like no other serial killer I've ever come across.'

'In what way?'

'Talk to prison officers and psychiatrists who come in contact with serial killers. They'll all tell you the same. After I caught Marston, I experienced it. They enjoy telling people exactly what they've done, revelling in the gory details. That's part of their desire for attention, part of the need to show how clever they are. Psychiatrists say serial killers actually want to get caught, so they can enjoy the limelight of their own notoriety. This one's different. This one doesn't want to get caught. He wants to remain hidden. He's secretive in the extreme. That's part of the reason none of his victims' bodies have ever been found.'

'Why do you think that is?'

'I'm not absolutely sure, but I'm beginning to get the idea. You've heard of people who commission high-value art thefts?'

Mironova nodded, bewildered by this change of tack.

'They do that, because they know that although they might gain possession of a Van Gogh or a Renoir, they'll never be able to share it with anyone. They don't want to share it. They don't want anyone else to see it. They put it into a private collection, for no one else to look at but themselves. I don't know the psychology behind that, but I reckon our killer's got a similar outlook. It's fairly common for serial killers to get in touch with the police or the press. Sometimes they send cryptic messages. Sometimes even souvenirs. They want to show how much cleverer they are than those trying to catch them. This one's not at all like that. He wants these girls as a work of art, a painting, a sculpture or a Ming vase, whatever. He wants them all to himself, a sort collection for no one else to see. That's what he is; a collector, a connoisseur.'

'But a body doesn't keep like an oil painting.'

'I know, maybe that's why he has to keep on getting a new subject for his adoration. What I can't understand is the long gap between abductions. All the textbooks say the perversion takes over to such an extent that the rate at which the killer commits the crimes increases, he becomes out of control.'

'I know, and I can't understand that either. Have you any ideas about what sort of man we're looking for?'

Nash considered the question. 'He lives alone. Possibly somewhere remote, certainly not overlooked. It's highly likely that's where he'll take the girls, although what he does with the bodies later I've no idea. He's middle-aged, meticulous to the point of obsession. Everything about his life will be ordered. He travels a lot, with a genuine reason for moving from place to place. His job involves him coming into contact with the public on a regular basis.

'Although he's comfortable amongst other people, by nature he's a solitary person, possibly self-employed. Certainly not in a regular nine to five, clocking on and off, sort of job. Not one where he has to report to someone else on a regular daily basis.'

'How are we going to spot him?'

'That's a tricky one. The reason I say that is this man has made being unobtrusive into a fine art. You could meet him at a party, pass him in the street, or sit next to him on a bus, and five minutes later you'd struggle to remember much about him. Give yourself another day and you wouldn't be able to describe him with any degree of accuracy. Another week and you wouldn't be sure if he'd been at that party, or if there'd been anyone walking down that street, or a passenger sitting in that seat.'

'That's going to make our job well nigh impossible.'

'On the face of it, yes. But it emphasises what I said earlier about the importance of establishing a link between the victims. If we can't find the man, we must find the link, and hope that the link will lead us to the man.'

'If you're right about the job and the man, I can understand your doubts about Bailey. So what next?'

'We have to trace Bailey. We still have to assume he's guilty and go after him full tilt. If we do that, we can at least eliminate him from our enquiries.'

Later, as Clara was leaving, Nash promised to phone her that evening. 'What happened last night was serious. Monique was certainly spooked by it.'

'You don't think she might have imagined it, or exaggerated it? Or even made it up for your benefit?'

Nash stared at her. 'What do you mean?'

'Put it this way, Mike. You've had one or two "romantic" dinners together. I don't want to pry, but did you really sleep in Danielle's bed last night, or was it Monique's? The way you looked this morning, I'd be more inclined to believe you were screwing Monique all night.'

'Of course I slept in Danielle's room. You've got a very dirty mind, Sergeant.'

'Maybe. I just wondered if Monique wanted more from you than just a dinner companion.'

'I don't think you're being very fair. When I got there, Monique was close to breakdown. Put yourself in her place. The assault left her with a phobia against leaving the house after dark. She suffers dreadful nightmares, migraine attacks and has a severe lack of confidence. Despite all that, she lives alone in that house, with only the memory of Danielle and her parents for company. You mustn't forget, it was there that Monique's mother committed suicide.'

'Sorry.' Clara held up a hand in surrender. 'I was out of order. I'd better be off. I'll go collect my things and act as guardian cum nursemaid. You don't want me to put in a good word for you, then?' She added wickedly.

'Get out of here.'

He'd been lucky last night. Now, as he recalled the narrowness of his escape from being discovered he trembled with fear. There'd been no sign of life from within Monique Canvey's house for so long, he'd assumed she'd gone to bed and decided to give up his observation.

He'd driven to the end of the road without lights. At the junction he'd switched them on and driven no more than fifty yards when a police car had passed him going in the opposite direction. There'd been no sirens, no flashing red and blue lights, but the high speed suggested urgency, possibly emergency.

He'd watched in horror through his rear view mirror as the police car turned into Monique Canvey's road. He'd no reason to suppose the car was there because of him, but the police would have been highly suspicious of a man sitting alone in a darkened car at that time of night.

It'd been a narrow escape. One he couldn't risk happening again. He'd had the chance of this girl once, but had taken her sister instead. Now the urge demanded this one.

His plans were almost laid. There must be no margin for error. He needed a safe vantage point. He remembered something he'd seen a few days earlier. He wouldn't need long; then the girl would be added to his collection. She'd become his prize specimen. The very thought of it was unbearably exciting.

Rochester Way was a cul-de-sac of detached houses. Almost all the occupants, in keeping with their perceived status and the need for privacy, had planted *Leylandii* along their boundaries. Over the years, the shrubs had matured into dense hedges that achieved the required effect admirably.

Number six had been unoccupied for two months. None of the residents saw the silver-grey saloon car glide to a halt in front of the garage. Although it was virtually dusk when the car came to a stop, it displayed neither headlights nor sidelights. When the door opened a few minutes later, the courtesy light did not come on. The door closed with a barely audible click.

The driver stood silent and motionless for several minutes. Once satisfied his arrival had gone unnoticed, he walked slowly round the garage and down the lawn.

There was yet more protection to the rear of the gardens. A variety of shrubs provided screens that would have defied any Peeping Tom. He stepped carefully over the flower bed and wriggled his way through the shrubs until he reached the boundary fence. From there he had an uninterrupted view to the house in the next street. He could see all the rear of the building opposite, in particular the kitchen and dining room.

His fingers trembled with anticipation as he lifted his binoculars. He was immediately rewarded. Monique Canvey was standing in front of what he guessed to be the cooker. She appeared to be talking to someone outside of his field of vision. Was this the man she'd been kissing? A jealous rage made his gut churn, but then the second occupant of the room came into view.

He caught a glimpse of her, before she moved beyond his line of sight. Enough for him to see her face, enough time for him to recognize her. It wasn't possible! It couldn't have been her. He'd convinced himself he was mistaken, when she moved back into view. This time there was no doubt. It was her. But how? How could she be there? Why should she be in Monique Canvey's house? What he was seeing was impossible. Yet it was happening. There she was, alive and well, drinking red wine. Behaving like a perfectly normal house guest. Suddenly, as if sensing his presence, she turned and stared out of the window towards him. It really was her. No one else looked quite like that, no trick of the light could have hidden her identity. Not from him. The moment passed. She turned away, leaving the watcher with a sense of loss. His excitement became an arousal almost too painful to bear, at the thought of what he'd seen. At the possibilities it raised. He'd need to rethink his plans. He blundered his way back through the shrubbery; joy and excitement mingled with shock and disbelief.

CHAPTER SEVENTEEN

Nash rang Monique shortly after 10 p.m. He spoke to both her and Clara, who assured him all was well. There'd been no sign of a prowler, no strange vehicles in the street, but they'd enjoyed a superb dinner, one or two glasses of red wine, and were getting on famously. Mironova told him, 'If I'm getting overtime for this, I can continue as long as you want.'

Nash still felt slightly uneasy. He'd no reason, but the doubt remained. He finished his own wine, took his tablets and went to bed. Sleep didn't come easily. Although he didn't realize it, a part of him was longing for a repeat of the previous night's encounter.

He switched the bedside light off at 10.30, but an hour later he was still awake. When eventually he fell asleep, he was immediately plunged into a strange and terrible dream that rapidly became a nightmare.

Nash was lying on Mexican Pete's dissection table. The pathologist was preparing to cut him open and conduct a post-mortem, apparently deaf to Nash's protestations that he wasn't dead, merely sleeping.

The scene changed, and Nash was packing prior to moving home. The house was like no other Nash had ever seen, let alone lived in.

When he was working in the front part of the house everything seemed absolutely normal. Nevertheless, he felt a terrible sense of unease. The house held an unidentifiable but unmistakeable aura of menace.

The rear of the property was like a large warehouse, cavernous and poorly lit. He could see little of his surroundings, or the shadowy companion who was helping him pack the seemingly endless stacks of belongings.

The feeling of unease intensified. Something evil was about to happen; something beyond his power to prevent. He worked on and on, but this unknown terror was growing.

Some agency, stronger than he, was in control now. He looked across the strange building, seeing for the first time the steel support pillars, the dusty grey concrete floor. Reluctantly, although everything within him cried out in protest, he looked upwards. In the farthest, darkest corner, a flight of steps led to a mezzanine floor.

He could just discern a line of figures pacing, with slow, measured strides along the mezzanine and back. Each of them clad from head to toe in black, hooded and cloaked.

He counted the figures. There were nine. He cried out in alarm. He knew this to be wrong; there should only be seven. 'It's too many,' he shouted. 'There are too many.'

Louder and louder he shouted, until the figures ceased pacing and turned towards him. This caused his panic to rise to alarming heights. The fear became dread. The dread turned to horror and Nash began to scream, 'Go away; get out of here.'

Slowly, one by one, the figures began to descend the flight of steps, towards where Nash was standing transfixed. 'Go away, leave us alone. Get away from us. No, no, you can't do this,' but they paid him no heed. Desperation and fear overcame him, and he began to weep, a loud keening wail of utter misery.

Slowly, the line of figures passed him and Nash was able to see their faces. His horror mounted, as he saw their identical eyes, identical hair, identical features. They were one and the same. They were all Sarah Kelly, but then again they weren't. Five of them had passed, and Nash knew the seventh was Sarah. Sarah was flanked by two more, the two that didn't belong. They turned towards him and Nash felt a crescendo of terror. They were faceless.

'No, no, please, no,' Nash shouted again, but was silenced by a touch on his arm. An unseen hand gently persuaded him to turn, but Nash was too afraid to look. The hand was placed under his chin, gently forcing his head up. 'It's all right, Mike.'

It was Danielle. 'It's not you. They don't want you.'

'Please, don't let them do this,' he begged her.

'I can't stop them, Mike,' she told him sadly. 'No one can.'

*

Nash woke up. He grabbed for the light and looked round. The room was empty. He was sweating profusely, yet he was cold. He tried to dismiss the nightmare from his thoughts. He needed to rest, but was afraid to go to sleep. The clock radio on the bedside cabinet showed it was 2 a.m. Morning seemed an eternity away.

Later in the night, he found himself once more in the nightmare.

Again he was in that strange building. Again the figures patrolled slowly past him in accusing silence.

Although they did not speak, he knew the message they were conveying, the accusation in their dead eyes made it obvious. It was he who was to blame. His failure was their distress. As the final two approached, Nash saw with mounting horror that they were no longer faceless. He tried not to look. They turned when they reached him, turned and looked him straight in the eyes. Now he knew. He screamed in horror as he recognized them. Then, they were gone.

'Now you know the worst.' The voice came to him out of the darkness. Was it the darkness of his anguish? He knew the voice, it was unmistakeable. That amused, half-mocking tone could only belong to Danielle. 'It's what you feared. There's still time for them, time for you. But that time is running out. Everything has changed, you must not see me. You would no longer want me, if you saw me now. I will tell you this, then my time with you is over. You already know the answer. Goodbye, Michael.'

He wanted to cry out, to ask her, beg her to stay just a moment longer, if only to explain, tell him what it was he knew. But it was already too late. He could hear the mocking notes of her laughter fading into the far distance.

He sat up in bed, shivering and sweating at the same time. He rolled to one side and glanced at the clock on his bedside cabinet. The two hands were in almost identical positions, 3.15 a.m.

Nash woke feeling tired and stale. He'd slept very little, terrified the horrors would return. He headed for a shower, then wandered into the kitchen and brewed a mug of coffee. The caffeine would do more good than harm in his stressed condition.

He turned to sit at the breakfast bar. He felt some vague thought stirring, as he tried to recall the elusive memory he'd wrestled with for days. He gave up and left for work.

'How did it go last night? No problems, I take it?' he asked Clara.

Mironova smiled. 'We'd a very pleasant evening. I looked out a few times, but there was nothing to see. I slept in the room next to Monique. Just to be on the safe side, we left our bedroom doors open, but there was nothing. In fact,' Mironova paused, 'the only thing worth mentioning was a weird experience I had.'

'What was that?'

'I had this odd sensation at one point. As if someone was in the room. I actually sat up in bed, switched on the light and looked round.'

'I take it you didn't see anything?'

'Absolutely nothing,' she laughed. 'Except the clock! 3.15 a.m. and wide awake.' Mironova saw the colour drain from his face. 'What's wrong?'

Nash told her a little uncomfortably about the nightmare. 'When I looked at my clock the time was exactly 3.15.'

'That's strange.'

Nash hadn't told her everything. Hadn't told her he'd seen the faces of the two hooded and cloaked figures. Dared not say hers was one of them.

Pearce walked in with news. 'Mexican Pete was one of the lecturers on my course. Told me he's hoping to bring you the reports on the Lizzie Barton killing tomorrow. Apparently there are a couple of details he wants to explain.'

Jack Binns appeared at the door, waving the search warrant triumphantly. 'Are we all ready?'

'Come with us, Viv, we're going to visit a friend of yours.'

There was no car on the drive, and the house appeared quiet. Protocol demanded they rang the doorbell, before smashing their way in. There being no response, a member of the squad attacked the door with a door-enforcer. They charged inside, checking every room for the suspect. They found Bailey cowering in a built-in wardrobe in the master bedroom.

Nash stared at the wall in the study. Every inch was covered by photographs, all of Sarah Kelly. All obviously taken without her knowledge. Some were intimate, revealing shots. Skill and patience had resulted in a highly sensual effect. But then, Bailey was an ordered and meticulous man.

During the search, two more items of interest were found. The first, a blue boiler suit covered in dark brown stains, neatly folded, along with a balaclava. It was inside a carrier bag hidden beneath a pile of clothes in a drawer. Later, a baseball bat was recovered from under a pile of timber at the rear of the garage. It too was badly stained.

'Blood?' Pearce asked.

'Looks like it.'

'Sarah Kelly's?' Pearce was becoming animated.

'Get these to the lab. See if we get a match.'

Bailey was bundled into the car and taken to Helmsdale where Nash explained the interview procedure to the man fidgeting nervously before him. Then he began, 'Why were you hiding?'

'I was scared, didn't know who you were. Bursting into my house like that.'

'Come off it, Mr Bailey, you knew perfectly well who we were. Why did you leave the police station on Monday?'

'I got tired of waiting, had things to do.'

'Did these "things" involve Sarah Kelly?'

Bailey stared at the floor.

'When I spoke to you before, you denied ever noticing her. That was a lie. Of course you've noticed her. You admire her. So much so, you've taken enough photographs to start your own gallery. Now, we know you watch out for her. Every time she goes out or comes home, she has to pass your house. You must watch for her, otherwise you wouldn't have that huge collection of photographs. Did you think perhaps because she'd had a drink, she'd come into your house, might let you take some more? You watch Sarah sunbathing, so you must think she's very attractive, isn't that so, Mr Bailey?'

'I suppose so.'

'She got you excited, is that it? You saw her, and got aroused? Did you get fed up with just her photos? Did you get her into your house? Did she resist you? You couldn't stand that, could you? The rejection would be too much. Are those her bloodstains on your boiler suit? Did you get angry? She wouldn't play, is that it? Is that why you beat her with your baseball bat?'

'You made that up.' For the first time there was a degree of emotion in Bailey's voice. Was it anger, or fear?

'But you obviously fancy her, Mr Bailey. And you did watch out for her?'

'What if I did, it's not a crime is it?' Bailey raised his voice in a pathetic attempt at defiance.

'You work at the same place, live two doors away, take candid photographs of her and yet claim never to speak to her. I find that very strange. Can you explain it?'

Again he remained silent.

'And then, of course, there's your car. Where were you on Thursday night?'

'At home.'

'No, you weren't, Mr Bailey. We know that, because we've been looking for you. Where were you?' Nash paused as there was a knock at the door.

'For the benefit of the tape, Sergeant Binns has entered the room.' Jack looked Nash directly in the eye as he handed him a slip of paper. Nash read it and sighed heavily.

'Okay, that's everything for now. Detective Constable Pearce will take your statement and arrange bail. Then you can go.' Rising to leave, Nash leant forward towards Bailey, menace in every word. 'But believe me; I'm not finished with you yet.'

Nash left the room, anger in every step.

Binns was waiting in the corridor. 'Sorry, Mike, I thought you'd want to know at once.'

'Not your fault, Jack. We weren't to know it wasn't Sarah's blood.'

'No, but it begs the question, whose is it?'

'I want us all here at eight sharp tomorrow. We've wasted a day, so the earlier we get moving the better.' He turned to Mironova. 'It'll mean leaving Monique early, but this takes priority.'

Nash arrived at the CID office by 7.45. Pearce was already in the office, but there was no sign of Mironova. Eight o'clock came and went, without any sign of her. By 8.15, Nash was becoming annoyed. 'Where the hell's Clara got to? Ring her mobile. Try her radio as well. She knows we've got an early start.'

Pearce came back a few minutes later. 'She's not answering; either her mobile or radio.'

'Keep trying. I'll phone Monique Canvey's house, see if she's set off.' Nash dialled, there was no answer. He let it ring for five minutes, then disconnected. He glanced at his watch, it was almost 8.30. Pearce came back into the room and shook his head. 'The estate agency doesn't open until eleven on Sundays. So there's no point trying there.'

Nash looked up and Pearce saw the anxiety in his eyes. 'I don't like this at all. Go round to Monique's house and see what's going on.'

Nash rang Tom Pratt at home. 'Mironova's not turned up for work. I can't get any reply from the house, nor can we raise Clara on her radio or mobile. I've sent Pearce to the house. I'm beginning to get a bad feeling.'

'I'll be right there,' Tom assured him.

Nash had barely replaced the receiver when the phone rang. It was Pearce, his voice tight and urgent with stress. 'Mike, I think you should get here, pronto. The front door was closed but unlocked. There was no sign of either of them. The CID car's in the drive. Clara's radio and mobile are on the kitchen table, along with the car keys. I went upstairs and checked all the rooms. None of the beds has been slept in. I checked the sheets for warmth. The bath, the shower, the washbasin and the towels are all bone dry, and so is the soap.'

Nash tried to calm Pearce. Although he felt far from calm himself. 'I'm on my way, Viv. Tom's setting off from Netherdale. I'll redirect him and come straight out. Just to be on the safe side, I'll order SOCO.'

Nash stared round Monique's kitchen. It looked as neat as always. He looked longest at the draining board, taking in the washing-up, neatly stacked to drain. Apart from the pans and cooking utensils, there were two dinner plates, two side plates and two sets of cutlery. It was obvious they'd eaten their meal last night. Everything looked normal. Nash was about to turn away when something caused him to look again.

He stared at the objects, as Pratt walked in. 'What is it, Mike? Found something?'

'It may be nothing. The dinner pots are all neatly washed up, two sets of everything. That tells us the two girls ate dinner, okay?'

Pratt nodded.

'So why are there three coffee mugs?'

'It might mean one of the girls was thirstier than the other.'

'I know,' Nash agreed wearily. 'I'm probably clutching at straws.'

As he moved away, Pearce opened the front door to admit The SOCO team. The slight draught conveyed a faint aroma to Nash. He paused and sniffed. There was a hint of some familiar chemical smell, one he'd smelt quite recently. But he couldn't place it.

Pearce showed his warrant card to the neighbour. 'Zak, shut up, you noisy bugger,' the man said with mild irritation. 'Sorry,' he turned to Pearce. 'I just can't keep the little sod quiet. It goes with the breed, I'm afraid.'

Pearce glanced down at the pair of beady eyes glaring venomously round the edge of the door. 'I'm glad he's only a Jack Russell.'

'Don't tell him that,' Zak's owner grinned, 'he thinks he's a Rottweiler. What can I do for you?'

'We're anxious to find out if you saw or heard anything suspicious last night or this morning. In particular, we're concentrating on Ms Canvey's house, number 3.'

'Is she all right? Has something happened?'

'I can't tell you at the moment. We're not sure ourselves. But we do need to know if you've seen or heard anything, and we're treating it as urgent.'

Zak's owner thought for a moment. 'I did see something. Last night, when I was walking Mr Noisy, there was a car parked outside number 3. Zak pissed on one of the tyres,' he added inconsequentially.

'Did you notice what make or model it was?'

'That was dead easy. I've got one myself.' He pointed to the car on his drive.

Pearce fought to control his excitement. 'Can you remember the colour?'

'Silver, of course. Aren't they all?'

'What time was this?'

'I can't be precise. Somewhere between 9.30 and 9.45. I know that because when we got back the programme I wanted to watch was starting.'

Pearce thanked him and started to walk down the drive, to the accompaniment of Zak's farewell fusillade of barking. The Jack Russell's owner noticed he was already on his mobile before he reached the gate.

News that a car similar to Bailey's had been seen outside Monique Canvey's house caused a stir. Tom Pratt was becoming tense. 'What next?'

'Just because we couldn't match the blood to Sarah Kelly, doesn't mean he's not involved. Will you sort out an arrest warrant? Let's have him in again.'

'Get something that'll make it stick this time.'

The discussion was broken up by Nash's mobile, it was the duty officer. 'I've Professor Ramirez waiting. He's very insistent.'

'He would be,' Nash said. 'Show him to my office. I'll be back in ten minutes.'

Ramirez was seated by Nash's desk, talking on his phone. He waved a greeting. As Nash passed behind the pathologist, he noticed an aroma. He stopped dead and sniffed. It was similar to the scent he'd smelt in Monique's kitchen, far stronger but definitely similar.

As they shook hands, Nash said, 'Please don't take this personally Professor, but what's that smell?'

Ramirez smiled. 'One of the drawbacks to my profession; it takes days to get rid of. It clings to everything, clothes, hands, hair. It gets on me every time I'm doing practical anatomy demonstrations. It's formaldehyde. We use it for preserving specimens.'

'Of course, I should have recognized it.' Nash's mind was racing. Had he smelt it in Monique's kitchen? 'Was DC Pearce present when you were doing the anatomy demonstrations?'

Ramirez shook his head. 'No, Pearce wasn't even in the same building. Today was the first anatomy class I've taken for a couple of weeks. Pearce only attended the DNA profiling lecture I gave.'

If Pearce hadn't been the source of the smell in Monique's kitchen, where had it come from? Somewhere, he'd caught a whiff of that aroma before, but where? He needed time to think, time on his own. He ran through the report findings with Ramirez, and thanked him for bringing it. He watched him leave and turned to go back into the CID room.

'I'm going back to Monique Canvey's house. I take it the door's still unlocked?'

'Yes, we've got a uniformed man standing guard and SOCO will still be on site,' Pearce told him.

'Viv, I want you to stay here as a point of contact. Tom,' Nash turned to the Superintendent. 'You'll be on call if I need you?'

'Of course.'

Incident tape had been stretched across Monique's drive and front path. Nash nodded to the officer standing in the porch.

He walked slowly from room to room. He wasn't sure what he was looking for, but hoped being in the house might help his thought processes. He spent longest in the kitchen, but still no inspiration came to him. He climbed the stairs and went into each of the bedrooms in turn. He sat on Danielle's bed, then on Monique's but was still no nearer a solution when he returned downstairs. The house is too big for one person, he thought. It must be difficult for Monique, living here alone with those bitter memories, and the ghosts of her family for company. He remembered her words. 'Sometimes, I wish we'd never moved here'.

Realization came like a physical blow. He sat down, as the implication of Monique's remark came to him. Then he remembered. He'd heard it said by someone else. Then he knew where he'd smelt that chemical odour before. His and Monique's words came back to him in a series of flashbacks.

"I've met him. His name's Franklin, isn't it? I met him with Mr Charleston. One or other of them smelt funny.

"That'd be Les. Well, not Les, but the chemical he uses on the signs.

"He travels all over the north. Lincolnshire, Northumberland, the Lake District.

"Doesn't his wife object?

"He isn't married. A bit of a loner. Lives out Bishopton way. Been with the company ever since Mr Charleston took over."

Nash gasped at the significance. Bishopton, where Megan Forrest lived. He'd been in the pub. Bishopton, where she'd been abducted. And at least three of the missing girls' relatives had told him they'd moved house. What if Charleston's had handled all the transactions and used their one stop service. Including erecting FOR SALE boards?

He rang Pearce. 'Viv, I'm on my way back. I want you to do something.'

He looked round the kitchen again. He visualized Monique and Clara, their evening meal over, sitting drinking coffee. Their companion smiling, and chatting, as he waited for the drug in their drinks to take effect. He pictured him: watching them fall into unconsciousness, and carrying them out to his car. It must have been so simple.

He was in a fever of impatience when he reached the CID office. 'Well?' he demanded as he burst through the door.

Pearce nodded. 'I've spoken to five of them. They all confirm exactly what you asked. How did you know?'

'Something Monique said. Allied with a statement Tracey Forrest made when I went to see her. They both told me they wished they'd never moved house.'

'But what about Bailey's car being seen outside Monique Canvey's house last night?' Pearce objected.

'Correction, Viv. A silver Ford Mondeo was seen outside Monique's house. Remember the old joke? What's the difference between a father and a Mondeo?' Pearce shook his head. 'Every bastard's got a Mondeo. You told me the neighbour said, "aren't they all silver these days".'

'What about the bloodstains at Bailey's house?'

'I'm sure they'll prove he's committed a crime. Just not the crime we thought. I think we'll get a match to Lee Machin's blood. Bailey gave a false alibi for the night Sarah vanished. I reckon it's because he was meeting some of his mates from the Gaiety. I bet he was paid to administer a beating to Machin. That's why he ran. He thought we were about to charge him with assault or attempted murder.'

'But now we've only got a suspicion based on what the parents said and your sense of smell. We've no proof,' Pearce pointed out.

'I know, but suppose I'm right. Do a DVLA check and go through the Sex Offenders Register again. I want the details of any silver Ford Mondeo registered in the Bishopton area. And see if any of the addresses tally with someone on the SOR. Whilst you're waiting, ring Charleston's. I want the name and address of their sign erector, plus any other members of their staff who live in the Bishopton area. Whilst you're on with them, give them the list of towns where the victims lived. Ask if they've branches in those towns.'

Nash paced the floor whilst he waited.

Viv came back, almost at a run. 'You were right, Mike. They've got branches at each of those towns. I got a hit from the DVLA too. There's only one silver Mondeo registered in the Bishopton area.'

'Let me guess, the registered keeper is Les Franklin.'

Pearce stared at him. 'No, here, look.' He thrust a piece of paper into Nash's hand.

'Good God!'

'Now what do we do?'

'The only thing we can do. Get round there, and quick.'

'We won't get a warrant on this alone,' Pearce objected.

'We can't wait. And I daren't go through official channels. It'd take too long.'

'You're not going to involve Superintendent Pratt?' Viv was aghast.

'He'd want things doing properly and we don't have time. We can't afford a delay. Anything could happen. We may be too late already.'

'All through this you've said how careful this man is. How everything he does is planned to avoid detection. How are you going to get proof, without tipping him off? He'll probably be up to his armpits in security. If he's got alarms, CCTV, etcetera, how will you get past them? By the time you get to the girls he'd be long gone. He'd sacrifice Clara and

Monique. You haven't a hope. You'd never be able to bypass that sort of security.'

Nash stared at him for a moment. 'You're right, but I know a man who can. All I've got to do is persuade him to break a promise. Are you with me or not?'

CHAPTER EIGHTEEN

Maggie Johnson answered the phone, then held out the receiver for Jimmy. 'It's for you. He says it's extremely urgent.'

Jimmy listened for a while. 'Okay. How long? Oh, I'll be right out. You got my tools?'

He turned to Maggie. 'I'll likely be late home so don't wait up for me, hen.' He picked up his torch from the hall table.

'Here, you'll need these.' Maggie passed over a set of door keys. 'I'm not having you locking yourself out. Not that you need them.' It didn't really matter that they were her set. He grinned, gave her a quick peck on the cheek and was gone.

The car was waiting. Jimmy climbed in the back and sat forward as the car moved off, listening to Nash's attempts to dissuade Pearce from joining in the venture.

Nash had calmed down slightly. The risks were now becoming apparent. 'There's no reason for you to be part of this, Viv. What we're going to do is totally illegal. We've no evidence, just guesswork. If we're caught, it'd mean the end of your career.'

'What about your career? You've more to lose than I have.'

'That doesn't matter. I've gone as far as I want to in the job. I came back to Yorkshire for a quiet life. If I've to leave the force, it wouldn't worry me, but you've a great future in the police. Why risk it?'

'I can't stand aside and do nothing.'

'You can stay with the car and act as back-up.'

'If I do nothing, I'd never be able to look Clara in the eye again.'

Mike gave up flogging a horse that was obviously dead.

'I need to know what sort of customer we're dealing with,' Johnson said. 'It's useful to know what sort of precautions he'd take.'

'He's a very clever planner, ultra cautious. He leaves no trace, no evidence.'

'How long's he been at it?'

'Eighteen years to our knowledge.'

Johnson whistled. 'How did he pick the lassies, what made him choose them?'

'They look alike, Jimmy. All extremely pretty, with blonde hair and blue eyes.'

'Like dollies, then?'

'Bloody hell,' Nash exclaimed. 'That's it. Why didn't I think of that?'

'What?' Pearce asked.

'Don't you see? What Jimmy said, it all makes sense. They're not dead; at least not to him. He thinks of them as dolls, to keep and play with.'

'But he couldn't, not for long anyway. I mean, well, to be blunt they'd start to smell after a while wouldn't they?'

'Think about it. When Mexican Pete came to see me, he stank of formaldehyde. I smelt it earlier too, only I couldn't recall what it was, thought it was some chemical they use on the FOR SALE signs. When I smelt it in Monique's kitchen I thought that's what it was. But I was wrong. Formaldehyde clings to you for days, and to everyone round you. It takes some shifting, no matter how often you wash or change your clothing.'

'What is it, this formaldehyde?' Jimmy asked.

'It's a very strong chemical. Scientists use it to preserve anatomical specimens. It's also the main ingredient in the embalming process. That's how our man would be able to keep his victims. He embalms them. That explains the length of time between the abductions. He didn't need a new victim to gratify his lust.'

'Jesus, what sort of maniac is he?' Jimmy muttered.

'They call it necrophilia, Jimmy, having intercourse with the dead.'

Jimmy shuddered. 'How did he find these lassies?'

'He didn't, they found him; or rather their parents did. They'd all bought houses via Charleston's Estate Agents, and the purchase of each of those houses was handled personally by Peter Charleston. That's highly significant, because Charleston doesn't have time to handle individual sales. So why did he get involved in those deals? The answer is because he was lining up another victim.'

As Nash was talking, they swung off the main road, following the signpost marked 'Bishop's Cross; Village Only'. The road narrowed, and just before they reached the outskirts, a pair of large stone gate posts was set at right angles to the lane. On one of these was the inscription 'Quarry House'.

Pearce swung the car into the opening, confronting the wrought iron gates, now brightly lit by the headlights. Johnson scanned the scene, his voice urgent. 'Either reverse the car, or start kissing each other. Do it now.' Johnson had assumed command.

'I'll move the car,' Pearce muttered, engaging reverse gear and continuing along the lane.

'What's wrong?'

'Sorry, Mike; not in my job description.'

'No, I mean what's up, Jimmy?'

'Bloody great CCTV cameras, on top of the gate post. Now, just drive slowly,' he instructed Pearce.

'What was it about kissing?'

'There'd be only two innocent reasons to stop at the gate, well three. Either a courting couple, someone taking a piss or somebody lost. To take a piss'd mean getting out and chance being recognized, so it had to be one of the others. Slow down. You're supposed to be lost, remember.'

Nash grinned in the darkness. 'I still think you should have kissed me.'

'There's a limit to what I'll do, even for Clara,' Pearce replied.

Jimmy exclaimed in disgust. 'You'll not go far in the police,' he told Pearce. 'Mind you, it's the other end you have to kiss, as a rule.'

The grounds of Quarry House were protected by a high stone wall. Johnson scanned the wall and the area round it. After a few hundred yards he grunted, 'He may be a cunning and perverted killer, but he's also as big a con man as any estate agent.'

'How do you mean?'

'So far, I've counted fourteen CCTV cameras, all very obvious, mounted on posts over the wall. The reason they're easy to spot is because they're only for show. Unless he's got a team of security guards watching monitors, they'd be no use. Nobody could watch that many screens at once. They're like the speed cameras you lot put inside bright yellow boxes by the roadside. You know, the ones with no film in? Just there to slow people down, or in this case to frighten them off.'

'You mean this boundary isn't protected?'

'I wouldn't say that,' Johnson disagreed. 'My guess is the camera at the gates works, and the gates probably have a photo-electric cell across them. The wall should be no problem, once I find the best place to climb it.'

They'd travelled another two hundred yards, when Jimmy commanded, 'Stop the car. This looks okay.'

'Shall I get the big torch from the boot?' Pearce asked.

'No need,' Jimmy told him.

The topmost three courses of stone were missing, reducing the height of the wall to less than five feet. They got out of the car, closing the doors as quietly as possible. The night was cloudy, and without the headlights they were in total darkness, until a strong torch beam lit up the wall in front of them. 'Nobody should leave home at night without a Maglite,' Johnson explained.

Climbing the wall was easy. The next part presented a far sterner challenge. The torch picked out a tangle of bracken, shrubs, briars and brambles.

'Keep to the wall side; it's not as dense there. Walk along till we find a better place to get through.'

After a few minutes, they found a less overgrown patch. They forced their way through and emerged, at the cost of no more than a few scratches. They were standing on the edge of a large lawn. It sloped gently up towards the house, which they could just make out against the night sky.

'This is where it gets trickier,' Johnson told them. 'Follow me, and don't wander about. Walk exactly where I do.'

They moved slowly across the grass in single file, the detectives relying on Johnson's instinct. 'I can't use the torch. We're too exposed,' he whispered.

It seemed an age before they reached the front of the building. 'What now?' Nash's whisper sounded like a shout.

'Round the back, it's never as well protected,' Johnson instructed them, his voice barely carrying.

When they reached the corner of the building, Johnson flicked his torch on. 'Concrete,' Johnson muttered with a trace of contempt. 'An amateur, just as I told you. If he'd been serious he'd have put gravel down. You can't walk quietly on gravel.'

They rounded the next corner, and the torch was lit again. The beam played over the back door, up the back wall and across the flagged patio area. After a quick glance round, Johnson directed the beam up the wall to an alarm box. He chuckled quietly, then redirected the light back on to the patio, illuminating the heavy mahogany table and chairs. 'Bring that table over here and set it down against the wall, then bring two chairs. Put one of them alongside it, the other on top.'

He took a small, slim canister from his tool kit, turning to Pearce. 'You're the tallest. Get on the table and brace yourself against the wall and steady me. Mr Nash, I want you to keep watch.'

Seconds later, he was balanced precariously on the chair. The detectives heard a hissing sound. 'Okay, help me down. Now we've to wait five minutes.'

Pearce asked, 'What did you do?'

'It's a kind of foam. I sprayed it through the louvers on the front of the box. It expands and sets like concrete. If we trigger the alarm, it sends a signal to the box and the bell will sound. Only it won't 'cos I've muffled it.'

Five minutes later Johnson tackled the door. Less than a minute later, he turned the handle and opened it. 'Said he was an amateur. He should have bolted the door.'

'It's like watching a magician,' Pearce muttered.

'Would bolts have been a showstopper?' Nash asked.

'No, it'd have just taken longer.'

The house was as dark and silent inside as it had appeared from the outside. They entered through the kitchen, and moved into the dining room, then out via a solid-looking door to the hall. Apart from the brief flashes of illumination provided by Johnson's torch, there wasn't a glimmer of light to be seen. Not a breath of air moved. Nash shivered. The place felt like a grave, dark, cold and airless. 'I don't like this place,' Johnson whispered. 'It reeks o' death.'

Nash sniffed. 'You're right, Jimmy. What you can smell is formaldehyde. Charleston may not be here now, but he's not long gone, either that or he stores the stuff here.'

Fear was contagious. 'Let's get on with it, Mike,' Pearce said in an urgent whisper.

The sitting room yielded nothing of interest, but the door in the far corner led to a study. Johnson's torch swept round and settled on the desk. Nash strode across and looked at the open file resting on the blotter. 'Look at this.'

Pearce and Johnson looked at the papers. 'Who's Monique Canvey?' Jimmy asked.

'One of the two abducted last night. Charleston abducted her twin sister a few years ago.'

'Mike, look there,' Pearce pointed across the room.

The wall behind the desk contained three photographs of the same subject, a young teenage girl.

'It's Clara,' Pearce breathed incredulously.

Nash crossed to the wall. 'Bring the torch closer, Jimmy. No, it isn't Clara. But it's a damned good likeness. Look at the clothing, it's years out of date. When Clara was this age it would have all been nineties fashion. This is more like they wore in the sixties and seventies.'

'If it isn't Clara, who is it?'

Nash pointed to the top photo. 'Shine your torch here. There's an inscription in the corner. It's faded a bit, but it says To Charlie, With All My Heart, Sassy.'

'Wow, that's a bit steamy for a kid to write,' Pearce suggested. 'But who was Sassy, and for that matter who's Charlie?'

'There's a filing cabinet in the corner,' Johnson pointed out. 'That might give you some clues.'

Nash tried the handle. It was locked. 'Jimmy?'

'Ten seconds, Mr Nash.'

Inside the cabinet, they found files relating to each of Charleston's victims. Another set of folders, they guessed might be potential targets. The horror these files revealed paled, when Nash discovered another in the bottom drawer. As he read the contents, Nash realized who Sassy was, and Charleston's true identity. Then he discovered the reason for Charleston's fixation. The final piece of information Nash read, revealed the full extent of Charleston's depraved insanity. He handed them a newspaper cutting.

CARLISLE NEWS & STAR

Thursday 21 August 1975
LONG AWAITED HEARING OPENS AT LAST

The inquest opened today of Carlisle teenager Samantha Peterson, the fifteen-year-old schoolgirl who died five months ago. The inquest heard from the senior Cumbrian pathologist that Samantha had taken a massive cocktail of sleeping tablets and antidepressants. He also revealed that the dead girl was two months pregnant.

The *News & Star* has learned that an extensive series of blood tests has been conducted to determine the paternity of the dead girl's unborn child. Samantha's family has suffered further heart-break following the mysterious disappearance of her brother. Charlie, who discovered the body of his sister and is three years older than Samantha, was last seen a week after his sister's death. He was reported to have been 'traumatised beyond belief' by the death of his sister, to whom he was devoted. 'Charlie and Sassy were very close', a family friend told the *News & Star*, 'they were more like twins than brother and sister'.

Police commented that they were baffled by Charlie's disappearance; and highly concerned over his whereabouts and well-being. 'We are more than anxious for his safety', a police spokesman revealed, 'especially with the shock his sister's death will have caused him'. The inquest resumes tomorrow.

Nash turned to the last item, a sheet of writing paper. 'This is a letter from the dead girl to her lover, the father of her child. He vanished a few days after she died. Charleston was her lover, the father of the child she was carrying. Only he wasn't called Charleston then. His real name is Charles Peterson. Samantha, the mother of his child, was his sister.'

'Did he rape his own sister?' Pearce asked in horror.

'I don't think so,' Nash held up a bundle of letters. 'These are letters written to him by Sassy. She sounds completely besotted with him, more than happy to consent to the incest.'

'And the girls he's abducted since then?'

'Don't you see? They're replacements. Each one, a new Sassy; that's why they had to die. They had to die, because Sassy died. It was history repeating itself. Charleston couldn't let a replacement live when Sassy had died. I bet he believes he wasn't responsible for Sassy's death. If he thought that, it would destroy him. So, he rejects it.'

Nash stopped abruptly. He pictured another room. A group of young women, their faces staring impassively, sitting in eternal silence. Complete and immaculate, their beauty preserved for all time. They were close. They had to be. Charleston would want them near him.

'We're no nearer to finding them,' Pearce's voice contained a hint of desperation. It broke Nash's spell.

'I know, but they must be close. He'd need his collection of dolls nearby, so he could play with them whenever he wanted.'

'In the hall, Mr Nash, I spotted a big aerial photo of the house and grounds.'

They examined the image, huddled closely together. Pearce pointed towards a large building near the edge of the photo. 'What do you think that is? It looks like a barn or cattle shed.'

Nash felt a cold shiver run through him. 'It's not a barn. At least I don't think so. Remember the name of the house.' He pointed to an outline in the photo, where the land formed a depression. 'I think that's the quarry. That could be the old quarry office.'

'You think that's where the girls are?'

'I do, and that's where Charleston will be.'

'I'll call for back-up.'

'Not yet. If we delay and that costs lives, we'd never forgive ourselves. We're on our own. We've got to reach that place as fast as possible.'

'What if we're too late?'

The tone of Nash's reply made Pearce shiver. 'I've broken enough laws tonight; one more won't make a difference. If he's killed them, I'll save the nation the cost of a trial.'

Johnson secured the back door behind them. They felt relief being outside again. 'There must be a track. The quarry's on this side of the house, so the path should start somewhere round here.' Nash headed across the drive.

'Mr Nash, the garage and the rest of the gardens are on the other side. If you remember from the photo, all there is on this side is more shrubbery.'

'What's your point, Jimmy?'

'What's that for, then?' Johnson's torch beam picked out a gate, halfway along the interwoven fencing.

'Jimmy, I don't know where we'd be without you.'

'Probably in one of your own nicks, on a burglary charge.'

The gate opened easily. Pearce spotted a narrow gap in the bushes, far to their left. It was the beginning of a path.

The darkness was intensified by the woodland. Their route grew steeper with almost every stride. It was clear they were descending into the quarry. Nash glanced back; the trees and shrubs they'd passed seemed higher, more threatening. He turned hastily to concentrate on the track.

After ten minutes, the path levelled out. Nash guessed they'd reached the quarry floor. 'We can't be far away,' he whispered.

Johnson's torch picked up the outline of a pitched roof, against the cliff face. The track took a serpentine course across the old workings, but eventually led them to the front of the building. They examined it by the light of the torch. The office was much larger than they expected, built of stone and looked well nigh impregnable. The windows had been secured with solid steel shutters. No casual trespasser would have been able to get inside. There was a door at one end of the facade.

'What do you think, Jimmy?' Nash whispered.

'It's not going to be easy.'

Pearce interrupted, 'Shine your torch over there a minute, beyond the end of the building.'

The torch beam picked out the distinctive outline of a silver Ford Mondeo, parked close to the end of what Nash guessed was the old quarry road. 'Charleston must be inside. This is where we'll find the girls. Let's get on with it.'

Johnson inspected the door closely. 'This is a bit different. See those locks, Mr Nash? They're going to be tough. The two Yales need to be turned together, after the mortise lock's been opened. That's easy enough with keys, almost impossible with picks, not without making a hell of a din. I'm going to need your help, so we don't attract attention. We call it aiding and abetting,' he added.

'What do you want us to do?'

'I want you to hold the picks in the top and bottom locks in the engaged position 'til I'm ready to unlock the third. Then I want us to turn all three together.'

Five minutes later, Nash and Pearce held the slender picks in position, their fingers trembling slightly with the effort. 'I'm going to count to three. As soon as I do, turn the picks. Ready. One, two three….'

CHAPTER NINETEEN

'My dearest, this is the most pleasant surprise. I never dreamed I'd see you again, let alone be near you. Be with you; together again. It's nothing short of a miracle.'

She was trying to remember what had happened. Where was she? What was going on? She listened, heard the gently caressing tones with complete bewilderment. She could make little sense of what he was saying. Who was he? Who did he think she was? She didn't recognize the voice, couldn't place the accent. It didn't help that her head was muzzy. She realized there was some sort of hood over her head. She attempted to move, but could feel the restraints, knew she was tied to a chair.

The voice came again. 'Be patient, my dear, for a while. I have things to do before we can be together. My dear, my darling, Sassy, returned to me. You and I, together again as we were always intended to be. In the meantime, you must relax. I have something that will help you.'

She realized she'd been given an injection. Was this going to be the end? She opened her mouth to scream, but it was too late, consciousness deserted her before she could utter her desperate appeal for help.

He was both excited and confused. Confused by what had happened. So excited the need overpowered him, caused him to ignore the sacred ritual. He'd wanted this for so long. Now he was overwhelmed by the prospect. He wanted Sassy, and he wanted her now. His excitement grew, and wouldn't be denied any longer. His desire was almost out of control.

His hands trembled, as he measured the liquid into a glass of water. After stirring it, he placed it on the draining board then hurried back to the room behind the kitchen. He went to one of the bound, hooded figures. As he untied the ropes, he removed the hood and carried her through to the nursery, laid her on the bed and undressed her. When she was naked, he savoured every curve, stood looking at her until the ache in his loins grew unbearable.

He brought the glass, raised her and supported her as she sipped at the drugged liquid. Then he gently lowered her back on to the bed and walked softly from the room. The glass remained unwashed on the sink, as he hurriedly cleaned his teeth, and returned to the nursery. He stood, drinking in her beauty, the beauty that in a few minutes would be his. Then he began to unbutton his shirt, slowly at first, but with increasing haste as excitement threatened to engulf him.

Something distracted him; it was no more than the faintest whisper of sound, but enough to make him pause. Listening, one hand on the last of his shirt buttons, he heard it again, a soft, scraping sound. He tiptoed back into the kitchen, quietly closing the door behind him.

Once inside, he heard it again, much louder this time. His desire turned to rage. Someone was trying to break in. At any second the intruder would be inside. His fury was as strong as his frustrated desire. Anger and panic combined. They fuelled his movement, as he raced to the door of his workshop and flung it open.

'Jimmy, get yourself into hiding. Viv, follow me.'

'Ready, Mike.'

Nash waited until Jimmy had hidden in the bushes; then opened the door slightly; blinking in the sudden brightness. He thrust the door wide and stepped through into a kitchen.

There were three doors leading from it. He selected the one at the far end of the room and walked as quietly as he could, then gently turned the handle. It was a child's nursery. As the door widened, he saw Clara lying on the bed. Her clothing had been removed. Nash thought they were too late. Then he saw the rise and fall of her breasts. She wasn't dead. Relief flooded through his whole body. He heard a sound behind him, and turned slowly.

For a split second, the two men faced one another. Hunter and prey, but which was which? Nash saw Charleston's face distorted by rage. Saw the gun in his hand. Saw the barrel lift and, almost in slow motion, saw the whitening of Charleston's finger as he squeezed the trigger. He flung himself to one side, as the gun bucked and reared in Charleston's untutored hand. Shot after shot rang out. One, two, three, four, five, Nash counted the shots. He felt a searing agony in his chest.

Pearce tore through the outer door, in time to see his boss slump to the floor, blood staining his shirt. Charleston spun round and raised the gun. A click, then silence. The chamber was empty. He flung the weapon aside. Pearce was nearly on him when Charleston raised a lump hammer, and brought it crashing down on Pearce's skull. He collapsed over Nash's body.

Charleston walked forward, unrecognizable from the mild-mannered estate agent. His expression a raging, maniacal fury, as he raised the hammer to finish off the interfering fools.

He froze. It began as a wailing moan: a sound like no other. It grew in volume. The screaming howl of a thousand demented souls, a banshee wail. Whatever the awful thing was, it was coming closer. His rage was gone, replaced by fear, then panic as the sound grew more dreadful with every decibel.

His nerve broke, he ran from the building. Still, the sound pursued him. Ever louder, ever closer. He dived for the car, and flung himself into the driving seat, desperate to escape that awful thing. It was gaining on him with every second. He fumbled with the ignition key and careered wildly up the quarry road, in his panic to escape.

Jimmy stepped over the threshold and stared at the two bodies. Hearing a groan he gently eased Pearce to one side. Kneeling, he checked the DC's pulse and for a moment got no response; then he felt a feeble flicker.

He turned his attention to Nash. He was in a bad way. A large patch of blood was staining his shirt and the floor alongside him. 'Mr Nash,' Johnson wailed. 'Mr Nash, are ye alive?'

'Jimmy?' The sound was a mere whisper. 'Where's … Charleston?'

'Driven off, like a bat out of hell.'

'The … girls?' Nash coughed, and flecks of blood appeared at the corner of his mouth.

Johnson scrambled to his feet and crossed to the nearest open door. A naked girl lay on a bed. Johnson saw her chest move. Without thinking, he gently placed the duvet over her. He opened another door and noticed the cloying, powerful stench of formaldehyde. Inside the room the sight was appalling. He felt his stomach churn with nausea; hot bile raced upward to his throat.

The room had eight occupants. All but one stared at him with dead eyes, in impassive silence. It seemed a lifetime before Jimmy recovered enough to move. He began to walk slowly forward, with the reverence of someone inside a church. He glanced fearfully about him as he approached a hooded figure lashed to a chair.

He removed her hood, untied the ropes at her wrists and ankles and gently laid her on the floor. She was breathing, but Jimmy was unable to rouse her. He hurried back to Nash, glancing fearfully over his shoulder as he went.

The detective's face was distorted by pain.

'I've found them,' Jimmy gulped. His voice trembled as he continued, 'All of them. Two alive, but I can't wake them. I think they've been drugged. The others,' Johnson paused, 'they're all dead. All dead, Mr Nash,' he repeated, his voice tinged with hysteria. 'But they're sitting round a big table like guests at a bloody dollies' tea party.'

'Viv? What … about—?'

Jimmy looked back at Pearce. 'I think he's dead. He was hit on the head.'

Nash's voice strengthened with anger and grief. 'No, no!' The fearsome pain in Nash's chest was worsening. He winced as he spoke, a fresh wave of pain threatening to engulf him. 'Mobile … pocket. Super …' he gasped and fought to continue, '… Pratt … tell him … get … Mexican … he'll know—'

'You lie still. Whatever you do, don't try to move or speak anymore. Leave it to me. Call it part of my promise.'

He retrieved Nash's mobile phone and keyed in 999. There was no response, no tone. He checked the screen, 'no network coverage'. He looked round for a telephone, there was none.

Jimmy swore under his breath. 'I'm going to have to leave you. I can't get a signal. I'll have to get out of this quarry.'

'Careful,' Nash warned; his voice noticeably weaker.

Johnson stumbled from the building, his torch illuminating the narrow track as he dashed back in the direction of the house. He barely noticed the branches that whipped against his face, his arms, his legs as he ran. He paused to try to phone again. The same error message came up. Jimmy realized Bishop's Cross was outside the range of the nearest cell. He'd no alternative. To get help, he'd have to go back into the house and use the landline.

His fear increased sharply, the instant he opened the gate. The house that had been in darkness when they left was now ablaze with light. At the far side of the building, Jimmy could see Charleston's silver Mondeo next to the double garage. Johnson was no coward, but there was no way he was going to enter that building with an armed maniac inside. He'd already witnessed what Charleston was capable of. Yet he had to reach that phone. A thought struck him. 'Why not?' he muttered.

Jimmy watched Charleston dive into his car and reverse at breakneck speed towards the front of the house. He swung the car round and went hurtling down the drive. Jimmy waited for it to slow down, he's travelling too fast, Jimmy thought. But as the car approached the gates they began to open. Charleston obviously had a remote control.

The headlight beam shot first skyward then traversed an arc back towards the ground. Totally out of control, the vehicle plunged across the road, first on one side, then its roof, then the other side. There was a loud crash; then a few seconds silence before an enormous bang was followed by a leaping, dancing sheet of flame that engulfed the car instantly.

Jimmy ran to the house. The back door was wide open. He summoned the ambulance, then spoke to an incredulous Superintendent Pratt. As soon as he rang off, Jimmy raced back to the quarry.

Nash was barely conscious. 'Let me try to help you, Mr Nash. I'm going to try to stop you bleeding so much. Here, I'll use this clean towel. You'll feel a mite pressure on your chest. The ambulance is on its way and I've spoken to your boss.' Jimmy rambled on, trying to stop Nash lapsing into unconsciousness, beginning to feel the effects of the shock. 'I think Charleston's dead. He panicked, drove out of control. The car caught fire after it crashed. Unless he got out of the car, he'll be barbecued.'

'That … awful … noise?' Nash struggled to speak.

'Spooky, wasn't it? I set it off. Maggie gave me her house keys by mistake. It's her personal attack alarm. When I heard the shots, I pulled the pin. Worked a treat. Charleston bolted as if the hounds of hell were after him.'

Jimmy watched, as Mike's eyes began to flicker then closed. 'Mr Nash, Mr Nash.'

CHAPTER TWENTY

The strange building had changed. The figures within it had also changed. Before, the building had been dark. That had puzzled him, for if it was dark how had he seen the figures inside when they'd all been clad in black?

Now, the room was white. A pure, arctic white. The figures inside were no longer dressed in black, hooded, sinister cloaks. They were all in white now. Were they angels? Was he dead? Was he in some other place, beyond life? He couldn't make out their faces.

Occasionally, one figure appeared whose face was visible. He should recognize her. He knew this, knew he ought to say her name, but by the time he remembered, she'd gone. She'd been troubled by something. What was it? Now, she was smiling. He liked that. He loved her smile, that same secret smile that had attracted him.

Was this a dream? Did she exist? He was sure she did. There was something he had to tell her, something important, something he couldn't quite recall. The effort was tiring. He always seemed tired. Why was that? He'd go back to sleep until he could remember.

Every visiting time, the staff nurse had looked with mild envy at their blonde, blue-eyed good looks. The girls looked alike enough to be sisters, close relatives surely. 'Excuse me,' she said. 'Is one of you called Stella?'

'No,' the older one replied. 'Why do you ask?'

'The patient you're visiting, it's Mr Nash, isn't it?'

'Yes,' it was the older one again. 'But I'm called Monique and her name's Clara.'

'Then who's Stella? Mr Nash keeps asking for someone called Stella.'

The younger woman spoke for the first time. 'Stella was a girlfriend of Mr Nash.'

Monique glanced at Clara, a puzzled expression on her face.

The nurse continued, 'I think you should ask her to visit Mr Nash, if it's possible. He seems to have something very important to say to her. I'm sure it will do him good.'

Clara's lip trembled; she was on the verge of tears. 'That won't be possible,' she told the nurse quietly. 'I'm afraid Stella's dead.'

'Oh dear, I am sorry,' the nurse was flummoxed by her gaffe.

Monique put her arm around Clara. 'Can you tell us how Mr Nash is, before we go in?' She asked, both of them dreading the answer. For over three weeks, Mike Nash's life had hung in the balance and it seemed the balance was tipping the wrong way. The shock of the bullet wound had almost killed him. The post-operative shock had almost succeeded where Charleston had failed.

The staff nurse was more forthcoming than usual. 'He seems a little stronger today. The specialist saw him this morning. After the operation, he rated Mr Nash's chances as no better than 80/20 against. Now he puts them at 60/40 in favour.'

Nash's third visitor joined them. 'What's the news today?'

'We may have to cancel the wreath,' Clara remarked as her composure returned.

They moved into the ICU and ranged themselves alongside the bed, Monique taking the side nearest the bank of monitoring equipment. The other two stood on the opposite side. Monique and Clara gently took hold of Mike's hands.

Mike looked old, old and frail, Clara thought sadly. For the first time in all their visits, his eyes flickered, flickered then opened. He looked at Monique. He smiled, no more than a slight twist of the lips, 'Hello,' he said in a pitifully weak whisper. 'You okay?'

She nodded, close to tears. 'Yes, Mike, thanks to you. How are you?'

'Bloody awful,' he whispered. 'What do you mean, "thanks to me"?'

'You saved our lives, mine and Clara's. You were only just in time.'

'Clara, she's okay?'

Monique laughed. 'Who do you think's holding your other hand? See for yourself. She's at the other side of the bed.'

Nash's memory returned slowly. He didn't move his head but stared at Monique. His face contorted with grief, 'Viv,' he said, in a whisper so quiet they nearly missed it.

Nash's third visitor laughed. 'I'm here too. I'm just not holding your hand.'

Nash turned his head slightly. He smiled as he saw Pearce standing at the foot of the bed.

'I've got a hard head. And Charleston's arm wasn't quite strong enough.'

Nash's smile became mischievous. 'I remember; you wouldn't kiss me. Now you won't hold my hand. I don't think you care.'

'Right, that'll have to do, I'm afraid.' They looked round. The staff nurse pointed firmly to the door. 'Five minutes is all you're allowed.'

'We'll be back tomorrow, Mike,' Monique promised.

Nash smiled his thanks then turned his head for the first time and looked at Clara. She squeezed his hand encouragingly. 'Bye for now, Mike.'

For several days after their first visit Nash was lucid and seemed well on the road to recovery. On the Wednesday of the following week Monique went to visit Nash alone. It was the day the inquests into Charleston's victims opened and Mironova and Pearce were required in court. When the Coroner had adjourned, Clara switched her mobile on. She listened to the voice mail message. 'Monique wants to speak to me,' she told Pearce. 'She sounds upset.' She dialled Monique's number. Pearce couldn't make out what Monique was saying, but the agitated tone of her voice was enough to start alarm bells ringing. 'Right, we'll be straight over,' Clara told her.

'What is it? What's wrong?' Pearce demanded.

'When Monique went to the hospital, they wouldn't let her see Mike. They told her there's infection in the wound and he's developed a high fever and pneumonia. Viv, she thinks he's dying. She said even the doctors don't hold out much hope.'

*

It was a long battle. Clara lost count of the nights she spent in the armchair alongside Nash's bed. For over two weeks she wasn't sure whether he was even aware of her presence. When Nash was well enough to sit up and talk, she sat on the edge of his bed and held his hand.

'This is devotion above and beyond the call of duty,' he told her weakly. It was a poor attempt to tease her, but it was the first sign of Nash's sense of humour returning.

'You saved my life,' she answered defiantly. 'It's the least I can do to try and help you recover. But I want to ask you something.'

He looked at her questioningly. 'When you found us in that quarry,' Clara paused. She was watching him carefully and saw his expression take on a guarded look. 'I know you may not want to be reminded of it, but do you remember seeing me before Charleston shot you?'

Nash pictured Clara lying on the bed, her glorious blonde hair tumbling about her shoulders, the honeyed sheen of her skin, her rose-tipped nipples topping her proud breasts, her long straight legs. He looked her straight in the eyes. 'I walked into the building. There was a kitchen. I walked across the room. I started to open the door. There was a sound behind me. I turned round and he shot me.'

Clara's worried frown disappeared. She smiled at him. 'Little Jimmy, the burglar man, put a duvet over me before anyone else arrived. Peterson undressed me after he drugged me, you see. We think he was about to rape me when you arrived.' She squeezed his hand. 'So you see, Mike, I owe you more than just my life. In the circumstances, it would have seemed extremely churlish to be upset if you'd seen me without any clothes on, but I'm glad it didn't happen.'

Nash smiled at her. 'Spoilsport.' He was pleased she was so relieved. He wondered if she'd ever realize, he hadn't actually answered her question.

Shortly before he was released from hospital Nash received a visit from the head of the medical team. 'I'm glad to see you appear to be mending well, but I have a few questions. It must seem strange for you to be on the receiving end for once.' He tried a reassuring smile. 'I need to ask about the medication you've been taking. I got the information from your GP. I rang him and he filled me in with the reason the tablets were prescribed for you. It so happens I've a bit of experience of this drug. I wondered if you'd help me with a study I've been doing.'

Nash nodded his agreement.

'Do you ever have any side effects: suffer from hallucinations or hot sweats? Either when you're awake or asleep?

You might regard them as nightmares or severe bad dreams. They'd leave you feeling drained the next day.'

'I've had some vivid nightmares. I also visualize crimes being committed. But then I've always done that.'

'I'm not talking about those incidents. I imagine most good detectives do it. The nightmares are a different matter. Tell me, do you ever take the tablets when you've had a drink?'

'Occasionally I do,' Nash admitted.

'And would you say your nightmares are worse on those occasions?'

Nash looked bewildered. 'Are you saying that's what's caused my nightmares over the past couple of years? Those tablets?'

'Not necessarily the tablets on their own, although in severe cases they might work alone. Obviously, you take more of them when your stress level is highest. But when they're combined with alcohol it drastically increases the chances of the side effects. I'm not saying do without them if you really need them. Any more than I'm suggesting you sign the pledge. Just don't take the two together.'

Tom Pratt came to see him several times. On his last visit Pratt talked about the case for the first time. Charleston, he told Mike, had been dead before the car caught fire. The impact had driven the steering column through his body, puncturing several organs. At Mexican Pete's insistence a urine sample had been taken from Clara. 'Apparently the date rape drug he used was gamma hydroxy butyrate, do you know it?'

Nash nodded. 'GBH,' he said softly.

'Forensics found a stock of it in that bloody dolls house. The professor's report made very interesting reading. He reckons the embalming work is the finest he's ever seen. Apparently, Charleston kept them sedated with a normal sedative until he was ready to rape them, then fed them with GBH repeatedly. But that had its inevitable result of convulsions, fits, coma, and ultimately death.

'We put Charleston's details on to the computer and sent them worldwide. We got a report back from the FBI. His fingerprints match those of a mortician working in Forest Lawns Funeral Parlor in Seattle during the early eighties, a man they knew as Peter Charles. He was wanted in connection with the deaths of three girls who'd gone missing in the Seattle area. Those girls were also blue-eyed blondes. Their bodies were found after Charles vanished. They'd all been embalmed.'

When Nash was well enough to leave hospital Clara picked him up. She drove to his new Rutland Way flat. 'Why are we here? I haven't moved in yet.'

'Oh yes you have. We decided you'd be better here, without steps to climb while you're still fragile. David was home on leave and everyone pitched in. Your key, sir.' She passed him a set of door keys. 'Do you need a hand?' Nash insisted he could cope on his own. Clara smiled secretively. 'In that case I'll leave you to it.'

Nash was far from fully recovered, but he was glad to be out of hospital. He unlocked the door. The flat must have been closed up for some time. He expected that musty smell associated with a building starved of fresh air. Instead he was greeted with a wonderfully fresh mixture of aromas, a combination of fresh flowers and furniture polish. The flat was sparkling as if an army of charwomen had just marched through. All his furniture arranged more or less as he would have set it himself. There were flowers everywhere he looked. Almost every available surface had some adorning it. He was still peering around in surprise, when a voice behind him said, 'If any more flowers arrive, I'll have to buy more vases.'

Monique stood in the hall entrance, a carrier bag in either hand. 'What have you got there?' Nash asked.

'Food,' she told him. 'I've been appointed to ensure you get a good healthy diet.'

'Who by and what's all—?'

'By the people who sent these flowers. They're from parents, mainly. Parents who are at last able to mourn their daughters and to bury them with dignity. Also the parents of the girls who were on Charleston's shopping list. They know what a narrow escape they had. They know their daughters are alive, thanks to you.'

She made dinner for them, which they ate in companionable silence for the most part. Towards the end of the meal, he remembered Monique's fear of the dark. 'How are you going to get home? I'd forgotten you don't go out at night.'

She smiled. 'We'll sort something out.'

The 'something', she explained, as she was doing the washing up, involved her staying at the flat. 'I made up the bed in your spare room,' she told him. 'I hope you don't mind. You need someone to look after you until you're strong enough to fend for yourself, and in any case I don't like that house anymore.'

It was a week later when things changed. They'd eaten another of Monique's superb dinners, washed down with a bottle of red wine. Nash walked with Monique as she went to the spare room. Outside the door he took her hand and kissed it. 'That's to say thank you for looking after me.'

The touch was like a tiny electric pulse between them. She turned to face him and they kissed. The spare bed remained unused. Theirs was a fierce mutual hunger that would not be easily satisfied.

Two days later Monique sat opposite him over breakfast. 'Mike,' she began a little hesitantly, 'I've made a decision.'

'About us, do you mean?'

'Partly; I'm going to live in France. I can't stay here any longer. Helmsdale has too many unhappy memories. My one regret is leaving you.' Her mouth twisted with pain. 'That was tearing me apart. But something made me realize it was better for me to leave.'

'What was it?'

'You made love to me last night, and it was wonderful. But you called me Danny. You didn't even realize you'd done it.'

Nash wanted to protest.

'No, Mike, my mind's made up. I'm leaving as soon as I can make the arrangements. Maybe it could be different sometime. But there are too many ghosts here. For both of us.'

About eight months later, as Daniel Michael Canvey was being born, Nash's phone in Helmsdale CID rang. Apart from a spate of shoplifting and a minor act of vandalism there was nothing criminal going on.

Nash eyed the phone for a moment before picking up. Something told him his peace was about to be shattered.

'Mike, Tom Pratt here. How busy are you?'

'Not rushed off my feet, Tom, even the Westlea's quiet at the minute, although I reckon that won't last.'

'Actually it's to do with the Westlea that I was ringing. Can you come over to Netherdale tomorrow morning? Something's come up that we need to deal with.'

Nash didn't regret answering the phone at the time. That came later.

THE END

The D.I. Mike Nash Series

Book 1: WHAT LIES BENEATH
Book 2: VANISH WITHOUT TRACE
Book 3: PLAYING WITH FIRE

Please join our mailing list for updates on D. I. Mike Nash, free Kindle crime thriller, detective, mystery books and new releases.

www.joffebooks.com

FREE KINDLE BOOKS

Please join our mailing list for free Kindle books and new releases, including crime thrillers, mysteries, romance and more, as well as news on the next book by Bill Kitson! www.joffebooks.com

Thank you for reading this book. If you enjoyed it please leave feedback on Amazon or Goodreads, and if there is anything we missed or you have a question about then please get in touch. The author and publishing team appreciate your feedback and time reading this book.

We're very grateful to eagle-eyed readers who take the time to contact us. Please send any errors you find to corrections@joffebooks.com

Printed in Poland
by Amazon Fulfillment
Poland Sp. z o.o., Wrocław

55870135R00146